THE MARRIAGE PLEDGE

A MARRIAGE PACT ROMANCE

JEAN ORAM

The Marriage Pledge: A Marriage Pact Romance
(Veils and Vows book 5)
By Jean Oram

© 2018 Jean Oram
All rights reserved
Large Print First Edition

Printed in the United States of America unless otherwise stated on the last page of this book. Published by Oram Productions Alberta, Canada.

COMPLETE LIBRARY OF CONGRESS CATALOGING-IN-PUBLICATION DATA AVAILABLE ONLINE

Oram, Jean.

The Marriage Pledge / Jean Oram.—1st. ed.

Large Print ISBN: 978-1-989359-64-8, 978-1-989359-65-5

Paperback ISBN: 978-1-928198-84-0, 978-1-928198-45-1

Ebook ISBN: 978-1-928198-37-6

First Oram Productions Edition: November 2021

Cover design by Jean Oram

A NOTE FROM THE AUTHOR

Every book is different. Some are easy and fast to write. And some keep my puzzled for months and months at a time.

Amy and Moe's story was a real puzzler which is something I hadn't expected seeing as I've known Moe for quite some time—since I first put pen to page with Rum and Raindrops (the second manuscript I ever wrote). He's been there throughout the stories as the jovial, helpful friend and bartender in Blueberry Springs. But I never really knew him as a man with those hopes and dreams he kept close to his chest. All I knew was that he was in love with his best friend.

And sometimes that's where the best stories start.

But then who was his best friend Amy—really

and truly? Why did their romantic relationship always fail whenever these two best friends came together?

So I did what most writers would do and I fed them straight through the wringer—and at one point sent them clear across the continent to one of my favorite fictional places (Indigo Bay).

It was a journey for them and one for me as well as they found their way past their worries and fears, sorting out how to claim the love they so rightly deserve—and without fear. While they took their journey I took one as a writer as well, moving past some of my own fears and blocks including ones I didn't even know I had.

But in the end, this is their story, not mine, and I hope you love it as much as I do.

～

Happy reading,
Jean Oram
Alberta, Canada 2018

ACKNOWLEDGMENTS

~

With a gracious heart I thank the following people for being a part of this book's journey.

To my family, for understanding that this summer I didn't get to play quite as much as usual while I puzzled out this book. The picnics out on the boat (thanks Dad!), and the leisurely swims were excellent writing breaks during the heat wave —heat wave? What heat wave?

To Julie F. for helping me with the blurb way back when this story was still just an idea I wanted to explore.

To my beta sisters who helped me iron out the kinks where I thought one thing, typed another, and messed up something else... Thank you for each and every comment you made on the drafts I uploaded. Your feedback helps me not only write a tighter book, but also helps me become a better writer. To Margaret Cambridge, Connie Williams Mechling, Lucy Jones, Sharon Sanders, Sarah Albertson, Erika H., and Donna Wolz.

To my editor Margaret C. for loving the book and telling me so. I nearly peed my pants when you emailed me a few weeks after receiving the book, saying we needed to talk on the phone. You've never called me before and I, of course, assumed the worst about the book's potential. Turns out you'd emailed the wrong Jean. Thanks for the edits. And for not needing to phone me.

To Emily and Erin for proofreading and catching all those spots where my eyes skipped over the errors I made while changing things around.

Thank you.

The Marriage Pledge

PROLOGUE

Three years ago

"Tonight's the night," Amy said to her friend Hillary.

"Really?" The other nurse's eyes lit up and she clasped her hands together as she did a little dance.

"I think so," Amy Carrick replied, smoothing her skull-and-crossbones pirate-themed scrubs over her curves. "Dexter's been talking about settling down and he called, asking me to meet up with him so we can have The Talk tonight. Well, a talk."

"Are you nervous? You look nervous."

"Why would I be nervous? Just because we're

talking about forever." She rubbed the spot on her chest where her ribs met, trying to get the tightness there to ease off a little.

"You're totally nervous," Hillary stated with a knowledgeable nod.

"I've met his son and we hit it off. We've been dating for a while and this is the next logical step," Amy replied, straightening the patient clipboards lined up at their nursing station. "My parents will be delighted."

"I hope you will, too," her colleague said pointedly.

Just because she didn't walk around clutching a scrapbook of dream homes and curtain patterns like the hospital's recreational therapist Beth Reiter had all those years ago before she'd married Oz, it was as if the town expected her to drop the man in her life if something more exciting came up.

Sure, she thrived on adventure, but it didn't mean she didn't want that happy, cozy feeling of forever with that special someone in her life. She'd been making a point of trying to show Dexter that she was ready for a commitment and all that came with it. Children included.

"I'm ready for this, Hillary. I'm ready for the long haul."

She was going to get married because she wanted it, not because her parents were still waiting with bated breath for her to settle down. To finally develop into someone more like her older sister had been.

For Amy, marriage was about no longer having to babysit for friends so she could revel in the feeling of quiet contentment that settled over her as she held their sleeping infants. As she secretly fantasized about what would happen if her friends never came home and she was left to care for the sweet little beings. Marriage was about creating that for herself. She could be herself *and* be a mom. Someone who was fun and carefree as well as full of adventure. She'd let her kids be whoever they decided to be and it would be wonderful. Absolutely wonderful.

Dexter, the father of a free-spirited son, was the man she'd been waiting for. The two of them were different, but not so different that their love couldn't bridge any gaps.

Hillary held up Amy's left hand, gazing at her bare ring finger. "I hope he picks something delicate. I don't think you could pull off something big and pretentious. It wouldn't go with your tattoo," she added wryly, tapping the rose above Amy's wrist. It was small enough to cover with the face of a watch—should she ever choose to do that. "Does this mean you won't be going to Belize?"

"No." She'd still go on the trip. She massaged the skin where the ring would soon be. "Why?"

"Because you're going to be saving up for a wedding."

Amy snorted at the idea, hefting a carton of supplies. "I'm still going. I paid for my scuba lessons in advance. The wedding can sort itself out."

The nurse laughed. "You are *so* not a details person."

"Hey, I succeed at this job, don't I?"

"You do know that husbands typically aren't nuts about their wives switching careers—just dropping nursing whenever it suits them so they can mix it up or take a trip, right?"

"I've barely changed jobs in the past few years."

"How many times have you quit nursing now?" Hillary chided with a grin.

Amy wrinkled her nose. "It's weird to pick something and stick with it forever."

"You feel ready to settle down? For real?"

Amy sighed. Hillary was starting to sound like her parents. "The man I'm meant to be with loves me for who I am, and that means he understands that while I love adventure, I'm also ready for marriage. Dexter is that man."

AMY WALKED DOWN THE STREETS OF BLUEBERRY Springs, noting that the surrounding mountains looked extra massive in the late summer sunshine.

She wasn't worried about Dexter. He understood her love of life and adventure. He *got* her. All of her—just like her best friend, Moe Harper, did. Because when you loved someone, that's what you did. You saw the whole picture and accepted each other for who you were. You didn't just see random pieces, like some of her exes had.

Seeing as she had some time before she was due to meet up with Dexter, she turned down a tree-lined street and crossed the gravel parking lot of the brew pub where she used to work with Moe.

He was, as usual, behind the long bar in Brew Babies, pouring a draft for one of the locals as happy hour drew near. The pub was still relatively quiet, the night ahead soon to build in its predictable, easy pattern, leaving Amy with a pang of nostalgia for her old job as Moe's right-hand barkeep.

She took the stool across from where he was working, earning a warm smile that made the tanned skin around his kind eyes crinkle. It was an open smile that he seemed to reserve only for her, and it made her feel special each and every time he turned it her way.

As he slid the beer to the customer, she

scanned the length of the bar, finding memories slipping through her mind like a slide show. Some of them were of customers, but many were about working side by side with Moe. They'd always seemed to find a rhythm where everything just flowed, and together they could serve more people than any other team in the pub, helping draw in even more customers than the owner's brand-new sister pub, Brew, Too, in the city.

"Have you quit nursing to return to me yet?" Moe asked.

"Nah, Dexter would have a fit." He was a good guy, but every boyfriend had his limits and, as a serious single dad, Dexter might object if she took up bartending again.

Moe placed his palms on the counter and leaned forward as he took her in. "Looking hot, my friend."

She batted her lashes at him. "As always."

"Need a drink to fortify yourself for the upcoming ring-on-the-finger moment?"

She narrowed her eyes in reply. "You know I'm fearless."

"Unless it's gummy bears."

"I'm not afraid of them," she said quietly, so nobody would overhear mention of her odd phobia. "They're just weird. All squishy, but not gooey. Sort of rubbery and..." She gave a small shudder, her throat feeling oddly thick.

"Says the nurse who can oversee an operation with great enthusiasm."

"That's different." She pulled a menu toward her. "Hey, are you going to create that onion ring double burger I keep telling you would rock the socks off your customers?"

Moe made a face that aptly expressed what he thought of the combo. "I will if you come back and work here again."

"Can't get by without me?"

He shrugged. "It was fun working alongside my bestie." He scooped a green olive out of the jar in front of him, mocked a throwing motion, then tossed it her way when she tipped her chin up to say she was ready to play.

She leaned left, catching the olive in her mouth, and talked around it as she said, "I just upgraded my nursing degree to nurse anesthetist." Thanks to her parents' insistence, as well as financing.

He tossed her another olive. She ate it, too.

"I can see why you might not want to come back to the pub," he said. "Again. Even if I'm here."

The thought was tempting. Moe was Mr. Straight and Narrow and All Planned Out, but together they had this weird synergy that just worked. She missed how even when they'd have a busy, difficult night, it still had a casual, fun feel to it when she was elbow-to-elbow with Moe.

"With tips I made pretty much the same money."

"I see you considering," he said in a singsong voice. Without being asked, he poured a glass of ice water with a wedge of lemon and handed it to her.

"Thanks," she said, taking a sip.

"So?" He jerked his chin her way. "You going to say yes to Dexter tonight?"

She nodded, the earlier strange thickness returning to her throat. Had she been thinking about gummy bears again?

"And if he doesn't pop the question?" Moe asked.

"Then I will." She downed half the glass of water.

"Take the bull by the horns."

"Have you ever known me to sit around and wait for life to happen?"

He chuckled. "It's one of the things I love most about you."

Amy leaned across the bar to place a kiss on his cheek, enjoying the warmth of knowing that Moe would always be there, understanding and steady.

"What's that for?" he asked. "My charm and good looks?"

"You're the best friend a gal could ever ask for."

"Too bad you and I didn't work out, huh? Imagine the cute kids we would have made."

"Adorable." Amy slid off her stool onto her feet. "Intelligent little pranksters, too. I'll catch you later."

"Speaking of pranks, are we still putting Frankie's precious Mustang up on blocks to celebrate his birthday tomorrow night?"

Amy nodded and flashed him a thumbs-up.

She headed back out into the sunshine to meet Dexter in the square downtown. He was standing under the large tree that a local feline, Fluffy, liked to yowl from. Today the tree was quiet, and Amy went up onto her tiptoes to give Dexter a kiss. He turned his face so her kiss landed on his cheek, something he did when others were around. She peeked over her shoulder. They had the square to themselves.

"Was I supposed to bring the picnic?" she asked. His large hands were empty, and no signs of a picnic were been laid out in the late August sunshine. "Wait, you didn't say picnic, did you?"

Man, she was nervous. Why had she imagined he'd have a picnic? Because they went with proposals. And instead of doing something romantic, he was just standing there, shifting from foot to foot and not making eye contact. It made her spine tingle as if her body was preparing for a sudden sprint—out of his life.

"There's something I want to talk to you about." Dexter took her hand.

Amy's shoulders lowered and she let out a sigh of relief. He'd taken her hand. It was all going to be okay. She'd been overreacting, misreading his cues.

Dexter led her farther into the square and sat her down on a bench beside a pretty flower garden.

This felt right. It would be just like in a scene from the movies.

Although he'd said he wanted to "talk."

But proposals were talking, right?

Still… She hadn't heard any rumors floating around town about him shopping for a ring. Maybe he'd bought it elsewhere? Or maybe he wanted her to choose her own? That would be okay. She did have to wear it for the rest of her life, and her tastes were a bit particular.

It could also be a breakup talk, warned an annoying know-it-all voice in the back of her mind. Almost all her breakups had started with something along the lines of "Let's talk."

Except for with Moe. They'd tried dating twice, and neither time had there been an official "talk," because both times they'd slipped back into the friend zone as though their temporary friends-with-benefits trial offer had expired. Their breakup conversations had been more along the lines of "Are we still dating?"

"It doesn't seem like it…"

"Weird."

"Yeah."

"Are we okay being friends again?"

"Of course. We always will be."

Then they'd laugh, and just like that, they'd be nothing more than buddies again.

Easy. Painless.

Amy didn't foresee a conversation with Dexter going that way.

What was she thinking? This wasn't going to be a breakup. This was the beginning of forever. No more breakups. Ever.

There was no reason to panic.

Still, she felt like she should panic.

In a burst of spontaneity, she blurted out, "Do you want to come to Belize and learn to scuba dive with me? We could go while Evan's with his mom. It'll be fun. We can rent a scooter and see the area and eat from little food stands along the beach. Maybe tent in the dunes. What do you say?"

Dexter inhaled, but didn't reply, as though unsure what part of her little speech to address first.

"It doesn't have to cost much," she continued. "When was the last time you put yourself first? You know, treated yourself to something fun?"

Finally, Dexter spoke slowly and carefully. "You know I love your energy."

She braced herself for the incoming barrage that would surely start with "but…" Moe was the only person she knew who didn't use the word *energy* like a polite insult. Instead, he said it with a touch of awe and approval. Good ol' Moe.

"But I've been thinking," Dexter said. "We've been dating for ten months now."

Amy held her breath and nodded to show she was listening, was patient. Good qualities in both a wife and a mother.

"And I fear that the potential problems in our relationship aren't about me or you, but are about us not being a good fit."

Amy blinked, feeling numb. "I don't understand."

He remained silent, simply waited while his words sank in, hurt her, ended her.

"I'm breaking up with you," he said, when she finally opened her mouth to speak. "It's not me, it's you. You're attractive and I'm completely dazzled by your whimsy and how you just run off after things." He smiled and swung his arms through the air. Then went quiet, taking her hands in his. "But long-term I'm not going to be exciting enough for you."

"You want me to settle down? Because I *want* to settle down."

"I don't have any interest in learning how to dive in Belize." He said it as though his refusal of her earlier invitation was some kind of wholesale relationship deal breaker, some huge illustration of why they couldn't be together.

"We can be interested in different things," she said, forcing the words to come out evenly. Surely she could make him see sense. "Being dissimilar is more sustainable than being the same." There was a sharpness to her tone and he released her hands, then crossed his arms as well as his ankles. "In fact, I think that would make our connection stronger. It's healthy to have interests outside of a relationship. I thought you liked that I was so independent."

She stood, angry for letting herself believe that he was different from her exes. That their relationship was going to be different. She had fooled herself, so desperate for his love and that feeling of belonging that she'd overlooked one big thing: he was never going to be the one she came home to.

"Amy." Dexter pronounced her name so carefully she felt like a six-year-old with her hand caught in the cookie jar after she'd already been told no. "I need someone who isn't going to run off on adventures. I have a son to think about."

She spun, facing him, satisfied that he was still sitting so she could tower over him. "You don't ask the person you love to change who they are. That's not true love. You want to make me into someone I'm not. And that's *not* what I'm looking for. I want a man who makes me a better person, not a man who squelches my personality to fit into some stifling mold just so he can feel safe and secure."

"I have my son to think about," Dexter snapped, like an alligator defending its territory.

"And he's a fun-loving ball of energy. Are you going to stifle him, too? Snuff out his spark?"

Dexter stood, briskly brushing the wrinkles from his pants with one harsh stroke. "It's been fun dating you, and I love that your parents tell you that you can do and be anything, but that's not the father I will be for my son. There are limits to everything, Amy. And you and I are adults. It's time to grow up. It's time to settle down."

Amy sat as though her legs had been knocked out from under her.

"I'm sorry," he said immediately, his fight already gone. "I'm sorry if I was harsh. I love who you are." He scratched the back of his neck. "I just... We're too different. I'm sorry." He turned and walked away, leaving her wondering how he hadn't seen that he had everything she wanted, and that she would have been more than happy to fit herself into his life, his world.

AMY RETURNED TO BREW BABIES IN SHOCK. HAD that really just happened? Why had she been so certain she was about to get engaged? How had she convinced herself that Dexter was the real deal, and that he understood her and saw her for who she really was?

He hadn't even tried to let their love bridge everything.

Her love hadn't been enough; it hadn't mattered to him.

Maybe it hadn't even been love.

"So?" Moe asked, as he spotted her moving toward him across the pub. He started forward, a bounce to his step, but after one swift glance he slowed. Instead of meeting her with the bar between them, he came around the end and eased onto the stool beside her.

She glumly plunked her chin in her hands, elbows on the counter. Moe slipped an arm across her shoulders, pulling her into a half hug.

"I'm sorry, Amy." His voice was full of comfort, like bread pudding made with real cream, fresh out of the oven on a freezing winter's day.

"I can't believe I let myself get suckered into a fake dream again." She heaved a sigh so deep it could have shook the town. "He broke up with me."

Moe gave her shoulder a squeeze.

"Why can't I find someone to love me for who I really am?" She looked at him, unafraid to show him the pain she knew was evident in her eyes.

"I love you for who you are."

"Not like that."

"All nutty and adventurous?"

She felt glumness descend over her like a storm cloud settling in over the mountains surrounding Blueberry Springs. "What's wrong with us?"

Moe's chest expanded and he stared at the bottles lined up on the wall behind the bar. He finally let out the breath. "It beats me. I'm a catch. You're a catch. I have this fabulous shaggy hair all the women go for, and you have an amazing figure. And on the inside I'm pure steady, reliable husband material. Meanwhile, you're fun and adventurous. I think the world must be full of stupid people."

He hunched over the bar, forehead furrowed, then tipped his head her way, a lock of that shaggy hair falling over one eye. It gave him a playful, mischievous, cavalier look.

He flicked his hair back. "Don't you think?" he asked.

Amy reached over and grasped his face, tipping

his head down so she could place a kiss on his forehead.

"What was that for?"

"For being the best friend a woman could ever want when love sucks." She let her shoulder bump his.

He stood, looking slightly bashful at the heart-felt compliment. "Can I get you a drink?"

"Only if you join me."

Moe glanced down the bar. It was still just him and the regulars keeping the lights on in the place until happy hour began in earnest and drew in more customers.

He gave a shrug. He typically didn't drink while on the job, but occasionally made exceptions during celebrations. Or for her.

He went around the bar and began mixing them each a whiskey sour—their traditional someone-got-dumped drink.

He passed her one and she lifted it, clinking the glass against his. "To a world full of stupid people."

"To stupid people."

They each took a sip.

"So? Now what?" Moe asked, setting his glass down.

Amy shook her head. "How could Dexter not see that I wanted what he has—a family, content-ment? He...he didn't even try to love me for who

I am. How can something like that be called love?"

Moe's frown deepened, once again furrowing his normally smooth forehead.

"A few hours ago I thought this was it. Now there's another guy I'll never see again."

"You could remain friends, you know."

Amy sent him a dark look. "Please. People don't stay friends with their exes."

"I do."

She wrapped her hand over his, giving it a squeeze. "Yeah, but you're different."

"I'm the only ex you've stayed friends with, aren't I?" For all their late-night talks, they rarely shared their romantic histories.

He was watching her, with something in his gaze suggesting that he was coming up with a new conclusion about her. If it had been anyone else, she would have tried to interrupt the thought. But it was Moe, and she knew he'd never think anything but good things about her and the way she led her crazy life.

Amy let go of his hand and grumbled, "I feel like I'm running out of time."

"To have a family?"

"Yeah."

He gave a grunt of acknowledgment and

swirled his almost-empty glass, watching the ice slide and spin.

"Do you want a family?" she asked.

"Someday."

She finished her drink, then muttered into her glass, "You're lucky. You're a guy. You can have babies when you're eighty." She felt let down, and a bit heartbroken now that the shock was wearing off.

"I think I'd like to start sooner than that."

"Me, too."

"What about a sperm donor?" Moe had bent over so he could lean against the bar, contemplating her.

She scrunched up her nose. Going it alone felt difficult, as though she'd always be floundering and running around like crazy. She didn't envision that warm content feeling she had when she held other people's babies. "I want the nuclear-family option."

"Million dollar family."

"Million dollars?"

"One boy, one girl. Nuclear family. Amazing and perfect. I think the million means that it'll take a million to raise the kids, but I'm not sure." He called down to a regular, Cole, a young cowboy from Texas who'd come to climb some mountains years ago and forgotten to return home. "Hey, why's it called a million dollar family?"

"The father is the Million Dollar Man," chortled the man in reply, readjusting his cowboy hat.

"Helpful smart aleck," Moe muttered.

"What if I'm still single when I'm thirty?" Amy moaned.

"You have a few years yet."

"If I want to have a couple of kids I need to be married by then. Expectant mothers are considered to be old by the age of thirty-six, as the risk of health issues increases. If I'm married by thirty, I could have the first baby by thirty-one or -two. Give us a year or so, then have the other one by thirty-four. It could work, but unfortunately, I don't feel very confident that I'm going to meet and marry someone by then." She gave a sad sigh. "My luck sucks. I was supposed to be married by now. Dexter wanted me to be different—men *always* want me to be different. Why can't I find someone to love me just for who I am? Is that so impossible?"

Moe scooped up her empty glass, tipping it her direction as he often did when he was about to present an idea. "Tell you what."

"What?" Amy asked, feeling impatient. Moe didn't often try and perk her up, but rather listened and sympathized. The perfect bartender and best friend. So if he was going to come up with some grand plan about how she could immediately find her Mr. Right, she was out. She had energy, but not that kind of energy.

"If neither of us is married by the time you turn thirty, we marry each other and start a family."

"A marriage pledge? Are we seriously that pathetic?" She dropped her head in her hands.

"Yup."

"I thought you said I was hot and wonderful."

"You are."

"But I have to depend on my best friend to have sex with me so we can have a baby?"

"I didn't say anything about sex."

She looked up at him, finding the room slightly blurry after pressing the heels of her hands against her eyes. "It's kind of how babies are made."

"Nah, we get in vitro. Keep it platonic and without complications."

Amy thought about it. As a nurse, she probably should've thought of that. "Okay."

"So, a marriage pledge?" Moe asked, eyebrows lifted as if in surprise.

"What? You weren't serious?" She couldn't take having her hopes dashed one more time today.

"I am if you are."

"I am." They studied each other for a moment. He was serious. Her kind, fun friend was serious. The corners of her lips twitched, despite her mood. "It's brilliant, actually."

Moe buffed his fingernails on his shirt as if he had aced her problems, giving her a pleased look that made her giggle.

"You're ridiculous," she said.

"We'll have brilliant babies."

"This could work, actually."

"You may refer to exhibit A—my brilliance."

She ignored his chatter, focusing more fully on the idea, her excitement over it building. "You like me for who I am. Love doesn't have to be involved. It'll never be a part of this, which makes it beautifully simple." Even Moe hadn't been able to love her in that romantic capacity when they'd dated, and he was her best friend, the man who knew every tiny thing about her. Therefore, it was easy to see that she was never going to find love, so she might as well have the next best thing—a man who understood her. She sat a little taller. "We're awesome friends, and when we used to work the bar together we could tag-team like nobody's business. We would be fantastic parents!" She leaned over the bar to give him a high five.

His hand smacking hers echoed through the air.

The plan *was* indeed perfect. "What you're good at I suck at, and vice versa."

"What do I suck at?" Moe asked, with a rather wounded-looking frown.

"Being spontaneous and living for adventure."

22

"You suck at details," he countered.

"Making us a perfectly balanced, nutty match."

Moe's smile was more goofy leer than genuine as he made an hourglass shape in the air with his hands. "Plus you're hot and we'd make cute babies."

"You're not bad yourself," she teased, giving him a long, slow look filled with a simmering heat she didn't have to fake. He was appealing, definitely good-looking, and yet not conceited. He also had a sweet, carefree, yet solidly reliable personality to go with all that appeal. He knew her likes and dislikes, and she could act like she was into him without worry that he'd go all weird or think she wanted to hit the sack ASAP as a result. Quite simply, he was the best kind of man there was and would be the perfect fake husband.

Should she ever need to cash in on the pledge as her backup plan.

"You do a pretty good job of keeping your hands off of me," he pointed out.

"You just said I'm hot and yet..." She ran her hands down her sides, recreating the hourglass shape he'd sketched in the air. "...I don't see *you* mauling *me*."

He leaned over the bar, and for a second she thought he was going to kiss her. Instead he whispered, "Because I'm a gentleman. You don't usually date those, and have forgotten how they behave."

She patted her mouth, giving a fake yawn. "Bor-ring."

He chuckled and began fixing a refill for Cole, who was still seated at the end of the bar. "You didn't seem to find our forays into the bedroom boring."

Amy let out a bark of laughter at the unexpected comment. "True." Her face was heating from the scorching memories suddenly flooding through her mind. Their relationships had been good in the friends-with-benefits department, but they'd never really been able to make that into something more, something that lasted beyond a few weeks. "Screw love," she announced, slapping a palm on the bar. "We've got a marriage pledge." She snagged Moe's hand as he put down the bottle of whiskey, and gave it a shake. "If neither of us are married by the time I hit thirty, we marry each other and have babies."

He pumped her hand once. "Deal."

Amy grinned, feeling as though the pressure she'd felt for the past six months had suddenly lifted. Marrying Moe was the perfect fail-safe plan.

She stood on the crossbar of her stool and tipped herself over the barrier between them to place yet another kiss on Moe's forehead. "Thank you, my shaggy-haired friend."

"If we get married you're going to have to start

landing those lips on mine again, you know." He tapped his mouth as though she'd forgotten where his lips were located.

She gave him a teasing smile. "You couldn't handle the heat."

"My prediction is that you're going to sabotage every relationship from now until your thirtieth birthday just so you can have babies with me—the old-fashioned way." He lowered his voice to a low, seductive drawl. "Just you wait and see, Amy Carrick. Just you wait and see."

CHAPTER 1

T hree years later

WERE ALL BRIDES THIS NERVOUS? AMY DIDN'T THINK so. Then again, they probably weren't as nervous because it was unlikely that they were about to marry their best friend. A friend who wasn't marrying her for love, but because he felt bad about her inability to land and keep a man.

Moe's well-meaning marriage pledge had seemed like a brilliant idea up until this very moment. Now Amy felt plagued by selfishness and doubt. What if she was locking Moe into something that would prevent him from running off into the sunset when his Mrs. Right came along?

Amy sighed, gazing at her reflection in the tall mirror propped against a wall of the tent. Moe. Sweet Moe knew all her hopes and dreams, and was now setting his own life aside in order to help her achieve them. He deserved so much more. He was a completely lovable, total catch of a man that any woman would be lucky to have.

And right now he was outside the little tent, waiting for her at the edge of Blueberry Lake so they could commit themselves to each other for the rest of their lives. She could envision him in his charcoal suit, his tie matching the ribbons in her bouquet because that's what she'd wanted—a real wedding. He was ready to say *"I do."* Ready to help her find that settled, confident place inside her that nobody could take away. She was going to marry a man who didn't love her as anything more than a friend, but he at least understood who she was and didn't demand that she change.

After her thirtieth birthday, they'd moved fast, from fulfilling the pledge to buying a house to having a wedding, but Moe would have backed out if he didn't want this. He wouldn't have bought a suit and cut his well-known and beloved shaggy locks. He'd said yes to the pledge because he wanted kids, too, and had proved himself to be as hilariously hopeless at love as she was. They were a good fit.

"Are you ready?" Amy's mother asked as she entered the tent. Faith Carrick came to a halt, her eyes filling with tears, her shoulders rounding as though the sudden emotional hit of seeing her daughter dressed as a bride was too much to bear. "Your father and I have waited for this day for so long. If only your sister..." Her mother tipped her head up and sniffed, shaking off the emotion.

Amy steeled herself against the comment that was sure to come, a comparison to her late sister, Jillian. The daughter who'd been taken too young, and who surely would have lived her life the right way. Sticking with one career that changed lives, instead of going back to waitressing at the pub once again. Settling down with Mr. Perfect. Marrying for love... The list went on.

Her mother made her way across the grassy floor of the tent, hands outstretched to no doubt try and strap the ditched corsage over the rose tattoo on Amy's wrist. Amy's gaze cut to the small table at her side, wishing she had disposed of the corsage earlier. She already had her favorite flower on her wrist—embedded into her skin with red ink.

"You and Rodney will be so happy together." Faith plucked the corsage from its plastic case and held it up, poised and ready.

Amy sighed and slid her hand through the

stretched band of elastic. "Nobody calls him Rodney." He'd always gone by his nickname, Moe, which stood for Middle of Everything. Nobody except her mom and medical personnel ever used "Rodney."

"There, isn't that better?" Faith asked, admiring the flowers strapped to Amy's wrist.

"I don't like it." She quietly slid the band off as her mother moved behind her to fuss with her hair, which she'd left down.

Faith didn't meet her eyes in the mirror as she said, "Don't be afraid of what this could truly be."

"Mom, it's not that kind of marriage."

"He's a good man."

"I know."

Her mom continued to fuss, her cool fingers subtly adjusting the straps of Amy's long, fitted, eyelet sundress. She kept opening her mouth as though she wanted to say something.

"All good marriages are based on friendship," she finally murmured.

Amy relaxed. That was as close to approval as she'd get from her mother.

"I just wish…"

And there it was.

"It's my life, Mom."

"You keep telling me that." There was a sharpness to her mother's voice. "You also keep changing your mind about what you want in it, too." Her tone shifted. "And because I love you, it causes me to worry that you're too impatient, and that you will lose out on the good things that take time."

Amy turned to face her. "I keep changing my mind because everyone keeps telling me what I want, and sometimes I just want my own thing. I want something different."

"Like your tattoo?"

Amy instinctively clasped a hand over her forearm to cover the object of so many fights. "I *like* the tattoo."

"Good."

"What, Mom?"

"I'm glad." She gave a small, quick shrug.

"Just say it."

"Marriage isn't like nursing," she said in a burst. "You can't just spend all this money on it and then discard it when you get bored."

Amy blinked. Faith had never spoken up about all of her career changes. Ever. Not even after paying for her nursing degree and then the upgrade.

"I'm sorry," Faith said. "I love you. I only want what's best for you."

"If it's about money, I'll repay you for the wedding."

She knew her mother would say no. When

Amy had said she was paying for it all, her parents had gone on about wedding traditions, and had insisted they cover the cost as the parents of the bride. She'd managed to hold out until they'd gotten teary-eyed and brought out the big guns—dancing around the fact that there'd never be a wedding day for Jillian—and how they just wanted to be involved in Amy's special day. Of course she'd caved. And once she had they'd had their list of stipulations such as the itchy wrist corsage.

Her mother inhaled slowly, then smiled serenely on the exhale, no doubt trying to lull Amy into a false sense of security so she'd think she was done with the topic. But Amy knew that when she was feeling the least prepared, there would be an ambush. Probably some critical comment about marriage and love, and why on earth couldn't she just figure it out and fall in love with Moe already?

Her mother placed her hands on Amy's cheeks. "Okay," she said.

"Okay?" Amy's stomach clenched. Where was all of that insistence on wedding tradition now that she needed it? Amy had just bought a house with Moe that they'd yet to move into. She didn't have money for a wedding. Even one this small.

"Maybe it's time you stood on your own two feet and faced the consequences of your decisions."

"This isn't a mistake." Moe wouldn't have agreed if it was—not even for her. She trusted him.

"I didn't say it was."

This was a good thing. It had to be.

Amy met her own gaze in the mirror before quickly looking away.

Moe's breath caught as Amy walked through the wild grasses growing along the shore of the crystalline mountain lake, the breeze messing with her brown, wavy hair. He hadn't seen her dress beforehand, and for some reason he hadn't expected something so delicately feminine from a woman who tended to balk at conformity as well as tradition. He noted the way the fabric hugged her curves, highlighting her strength as well as her whimsy. It was perfect.

She returned his smile with what looked like relief, and when she reached him at the water's edge, took his offered hand, giving it a squeeze.

Mary Alice Bernfield, a local who was certified to perform wedding ceremonies, began speaking.

Amy's chest expanded as she pulled in a breath, her eyelids fluttering. Moe couldn't recall his friend ever looking so nervous. Her hand was damp and something was off—even more so than when she'd told her parents that she was leaving nursing for good. They hadn't exactly been thrilled that she was going to "throw it all away" and work in the pub with Moe once again.

Personally, he'd been thrilled at the announcement, having missed working alongside her. And she'd seemed more confident than ever, even though she'd have to face the firing squad.

But today? She looked uncertain.

"Hey," he murmured. "You okay?"

She gave a quick nod, looking away as though distracted by the birds circling above the lake.

Nope. She definitely wasn't all right.

Did she need him to call this off and send everyone home?

He gave a light tug on her hand and she returned her gaze to him. He lifted his eyebrows.

"Are you—" Amy broke off, not finishing her whispered question when Mary Alice paused in her speech.

"Do you need me to stop?" the woman asked.

Amy leaned forward, murmuring quickly in Moe's ear, "Are you sure you're okay with this?"

His head snapped back in surprise. He searched her eyes for clues. "Yes."

There was nobody else in his life he'd rather do this with. It was easy and fun being with Amy, and they'd create a great family together even if they weren't in love. They had more than most couples had. History, respect, friendship and trust. There wouldn't be endless nights of fighting where their kids hid under their pillows, in an attempt to block out the sound.

The definitiveness of his answer must have silenced her doubts, because after a long moment of simply watching him, Amy gave a nod. She turned to Mary Alice, giving her a nod, as well.

"Okay then..." Mary Alice said, before launching in once again, her voice loud and clear.

Moe kept his gaze on Amy, watching for signs that she wanted out and was simply afraid to say so. If worse came to worst, they could get an annulment in the morning and break their pledge.

Amy quirked her head at him, looking thoughtful.

"What?" he mouthed.

She stuck out her tongue, making him chuckle in surprise.

Amy was going to be all right. He could relax. She had simply been looking out for him, like the good friend she was.

She was warm and kind, with a refreshing unpredictability. He didn't have it in him to let go and change his life on a dime the way she did, discarding careers she'd worked hard to get into if they got in the way of following her heart. It was a trait he admired and one he hoped would be passed down to their kids.

Kids.

Man, they were going to be amazing parents. They were fantastic lifelong friends, who could laugh off spilled beer and always hated the same movies. They didn't argue and they would make some pretty darn cute kids, with Amy's wavy brown hair and his own dark eyes. They were the best kind of partners and, quite simply, this marriage was going to rock.

"Did you have vows prepared?" Mary Alice asked.

"Oh, right." Moe probably should have been listening and not staring at Amy's long lashes while he ran through contingency plans and visions of the future.

He reached into his suit pocket, pulling out the two short paragraphs he'd prepared as a way to keep the ceremony's focus on their friendship rather than the typical stuff about devotion and undying love.

"Do I go first?" he asked, brushing a hand through his foreign, short hair.

Mary Alice nodded. She was being uncharacteristically quiet, and he wondered what the diehard gossip was thinking.

He cleared his throat, looking up to make eye

contact with Amy. Her dark mascara made her amber eyes seem even larger.

"Amy, you are my best friend."

That sounded really lame.

He studied her for a long moment. She was gorgeous, funny and as sharp as a tack, and his written words failed to express that. He folded the paper in half, noting that her doubts seemed to rise, the longer he took to find the right words for the moment.

"Amy, all I want is for you to be happy."

There. Her shoulders had gone down a notch.

He continued, "When you feel lost, just look to me and I will be your compass."

Well, that was a bit cheesy and cliché, but it seemed to be working. Her eyes were smiling now. Probably due to the high cheese factor present in his words. Later, she'd undoubtedly make a crack about how he was the proud owner of a cheese factory, and that he'd made her lactose intolerance act up thanks to the high levels of dairy in his little speech.

He held back his own mirth and added, "When you feel unsettled and awash with rogue waves, look to me and I will be your anchor, your calm seas. When you want to fly, look to me and I will be the air that lifts your wings." His amusement faded as his words, corny as they were, spoke an element of truth. "When you need someone to hold you, my arms are yours. You make my days brighter, and I love how full of life you are. I love that I never know what you're going to say or do, or even who you will be in the next moment, the next month or next year. You keep me on my toes and remind me to live my life to the fullest, and not settle into a routine just because it's easy and what I always do. We bring out the best in each other, both as colleagues and as friends. And as your husband, I want you to know that I will continue to be as devoted to your plans as you are. Know that I will always be here for you, and we will always be friends."

Amy's eyes had grown wet as he spoke, and now the tears spilled over. She gave a little hop when he finished and threw herself into his arms, squeezing him tightly. Moe rubbed her back until she slipped from his embrace and faced Mary Alice.

Amy cleared her throat, and her voice was higher than normal as she asked, "My turn?"

"When you're ready," the woman said, dabbing at her own eyes.

"Moe," Amy said, not bothering to dry her wet cheeks as she read from a Brew Babies cocktail napkin, "I don't know what I did to deserve such a wonderful, kind, loving and supportive best friend, but I'm grateful." She looked up. "Even when you're super cheesy." A glint of humor twinkled in her eyes.

He chuckled. "Way to work that into your vows."

She flashed him a wink and drew in a shaky breath, the note in her hands trembling ever so slightly. "Any woman would be honored to have a man like you in her corner, and even more honored to have him step up as her husband. I hope…" Her voice suddenly wobbled dangerously. "I hope—"

Moe edged into her personal space, cupping her bent elbows in case she needed support. She rested her vows against his chest and looked up briefly before bending her head to read from the napkin again.

"I hope I don't fail you," she whispered. "I hope that I'm able to give you at least half of what you give me, because it's so much. My life is better for having you in it, and every sacrifice you have ever made for me has not gone unnoticed."

Moe's mouth quirked as he tried to comprehend where she was coming from. He hadn't made any sacrifices. Amy was a dedicated friend, and everything he did was for *them*. That's how their friendship worked, and always had.

And when it came to their marriage, he couldn't

imagine either of them living with anyone else. All the men in her life had come and gone, just like the women in his. Their pledge was perfect. Their friendship was perfect.

"It will only be a sacrifice if you start making me watch horror movies," he said.

Amy giggled, her body relaxing as it bounced against his. He drew her into another hug. There was a lightness inside her when she was happy that made everything feel easy.

Mary Alice went through a few more lines of legalities, binding them together as husband and wife.

They were married.

Moe grinned at Amy.

"You may kiss the bride," Mary Alice said with a hint of mischief in her voice.

Amy's mouth dropped open ever so slightly, and Moe leaned back.

Oh.

Right.

Of course they were going to have to kiss. That was kind of a staple activity in weddings, even between two friends.

Moe studied the woman in his arms, a warm feeling of calm coming over him. She was looking at him expectantly, her grip on him tightening.

They'd kissed before. No big deal, right?

Although maybe they could skip that part of the ceremony, since it felt a bit too...*real* right now.

Amy was watching him, and despite this being a marriage of convenience, he knew that the appearance of a somewhat traditional marriage was important to her. She wanted to have this for their kids, to make them feel as though they were part of something genuine, something real. One kiss wouldn't change a thing between them, right?

And everyone knew they had a friendship-based marriage pledge, so likely didn't expect anything more than a quick peck, even though the two of them had tried dating a few times.

"Shall we?" he asked.

Amy nodded, her cheeks an endearing pink, her amber eyes a sunny golden color as she watched him move closer.

They could keep things platonic. He could give her a closemouthed kiss that looked convincingly appropriate in terms of levels of passion.

But as he lowered his mouth to hers he wondered how exactly one was to pull off a kiss like that with the alluring woman who was now his wife.

MOE WAS KISSING HER—KISSING HER LIKE THERE WAS something between them. Something that had never shown up the two times they'd forayed into the territory of lovers.

There was a depth and meaning to their kiss that didn't make sense to her. They hadn't married for love. They were only friends.

Was the wedding ceremony getting to them? Was it because their sweet vows had felt like heartfelt confessions? Was it the white dress? The "I do" and "you may kiss the bride"?

It had to be.

And yet this felt like something that went way beyond any of that.

Amy stroked the unfamiliar short hair at the nape of Moe's neck as they continued to kiss, his strong arms secure around her waist and back as they embraced. The kiss grew more intimate and she wrapped her arms around Moe's broad shoulders to steady herself. His strength was natural and came from carrying kegs of beer into the brew pub where they both worked. She'd found herself distracted from tallying inventory more than a time or two thanks to the fluid way he moved, chucking cases of alcohol and soda with such ease she wished she was a filmmaker so she could capture his movements. Graceful, yet powerfully masculine, in control and yet so carelessly casual, too.

She froze midkiss, her fingers woven into his soft hair, realizing that her best friend was lighting a fire within her that hadn't burned in a very long time.

But before she could stop herself and break free, she found herself drifting back into the kiss, trying to let go of the nagging feeling that this boundary-blurring body contact could quite easily complicate their simple, platonic pledge.

She'd married him because he was the husband type who could give her what she wanted, not because she thought he was the thrilling type who might get her interested in an intimate relationship. There was no room in this marriage for anything that might upset their perfect friendship. They were planning on bringing children into the equation.

She pulled back.

Children. Marriage.

Her mother's not-so-secret belief was that this was a mistake, and that Amy would hurt Moe.

She didn't want to hurt him for anything in the world, and kisses like these were equivalent to taking the express route to hurt city.

Moe was still holding her in his arms, and blinking at her as though she'd stunned him with unexpected life-altering news.

"Wow." He was breathless, his gaze so focused

43

on her that she wanted to clutch his face and lay another one on him.

Obviously realizing they had an audience, Moe slowly released her. He took a step back and rubbed the nape of his neck. She missed the feel of him pressed up against her already.

Amy took a small step forward, whispering, "I'm sorry."

His hands caught her waist in a move so natural she knew her mother would soon be harping on about Moe, true love and all that she'd never have.

"You always surprise me," Moe whispered, just before her parents joined them to offer their congratulations. Amy shivered as a breeze came off the lake, but knew it wasn't from the cool air washing over her, but rather from Moe's words and the low rumble of longing filtering into his voice.

He turned away from her to give her father a hearty handshake before accepting a hug from her mother.

"It's about time the two of you got back together and made it official-like," Mary Alice said, dusting her hands as if she'd accomplished bringing them together romantically rather than simply making their unorthodox arrangement legal.

"You know it's not like that," Amy said quietly.

"Just wait and see, dear." She lifted her chin smugly and went to chat with a few of the guests.

"That was some kiss," Amy's mother said. She was studying her, head tipped to the side, lips pulled into a smile.

Moe and her father were laughing about something, looking at the lake and gesturing. Faith hooked her arm through Amy's and murmured, "I heard Moe's heartfelt vows."

"Mom," she warned. "It's not like that."

"I heard yours, too." She lifted one eyebrow, arching it like it was a bow, silently challenging Amy to shrug things off.

"We're really good friends. That's all."

Moe's vows had been amazing. Romantic. The way he'd said them with that tender look in his eyes, as if he'd protect her from anything and everything, had made her entire being want to melt. It had made her want, just for a moment, for all this to be real.

But it wasn't. And because it wasn't, it would last. That's what mattered. Not that flicker of gooeyness that felt like it could be something akin to love.

"So I hear you two are planning on kids right away," Amy's father said, bringing Amy and her mother into the conversation he'd been having with Moe.

"They'll be very cute and smart," Moe said, winking at Amy. "Just like your daughter."

Well, that idea left a warm feeling deep in her gut.

"Just do a better job than we did with helping your kids find a career they'll love," Amy's mother said, her smile not quite as free as a happy one, her eyes damp. "Make sure what they find makes them content." She clung to Amy's hands, giving them a squeeze.

Amy had to clear the emotion from her own throat and look away.

"If they turn out anything like your daughter, we'll all be very blessed," Moe declared.

"Yes, we sure will," Faith said unsteadily. She took her husband's arm and headed toward Mary Alice and the champagne laid out on tables along the water's edge.

Moe said to Amy, "That will be fun."

She let out a long breath, shaking off the emotion. "What will?"

He nudged her with his shoulder. "Helping you make some babies, then raising them."

"I'm sure all men dream of in vitro."

"I like in vitro. It ensures separate bedrooms, which means no wife stealing my blankets in the middle of the night."

"You're a pillow hog," she murmured in reply,

mulling over the warm feeling that had washed over her when he'd referred to her as his wife. She liked the sound of that word.

He let his arm rub against hers as they walked. "And you like to put your cold feet on my thighs," he grumbled.

"You're always warm."

"Are you having your first fight?" his sister, Lily, asked, coming over to hug them and offer congratulations.

"Yes, and it won't be our last," Moe announced.

"What else are we going to fight about?" Amy asked.

"Money, politics, religion?"

"Speaking of money…" Amy turned to him "My mom and I kind of had a thing earlier. I'll be repaying them for all of the wedding costs."

Moe was watching her, waiting for the punch line. Finally, he simply said, "Oh. Okay."

"That wasn't much of a fight," Lily said, looking from bride to groom, then back again. "I was hoping for some fireworks. Speaking of which, you didn't invite Mom or Dad?"

Moe, who had been watching Amy, and in true Moe fashion was likely putting together pieces she wasn't sure were actually there, turned his attention to his sister, an immediate tension washing over him, settling into his muscles.

"You know I haven't seen Mom since we were kids, and Dad hates planes," he said, his words clipped.

"Have you talked to them?" Lily asked.

"Dad hasn't picked up the phone since we signed our lives away on that little house for him back in May."

Amy automatically gave Moe's arm a supportive squeeze, knowing that he'd always worried about his father's financial security, sending money for rent, groceries and medical bills. He'd even partnered with Lily recently, dipping into his personal savings, to ensure the man had a roof over his head out in South Carolina. Moe had bought one-half of two houses—for his dad and for them—in the past few months. The bank must be loving him about now.

"He's been busy getting into gardening," Lily said, idly rubbing her right arm with her left hand, giving Amy the impression she had something to hide.

"He's avoiding me. I've wounded his pride. And why would I talk to Mom?"

"No reason." Lily shifted, eyes darting to the side.

"Wait," Moe said, slowly. "You've talked to Dad."

"It was barely even a conversation."

"We could fight about…" Amy racked her brain,

sensing that if they kept talking about their absent parents a real fight might break out. She couldn't imagine what it would be like not having her mom and dad in her life, meddling and helping all the time. All those opinions and judgments, that unconditional love and support. Amy knew that, even though it was a pain in the tush, it was something Moe longed for. Something he'd been denied when Lily and his father had moved across the continent shortly after Moe's high school graduation, creating more emotional distance between him and his father, and even less between their father and Lily. He wanted to be close to his family and had tried to convince his father to move back West when Lily had over a year ago.

"We could fight about who'll take the late-night feedings," she suggested, her voice rising hopefully.

"The baby will sleep in your room," Moe said decisively. He'd crossed his arms, his brow pinched as he stared at his sister.

"That's too gender specific." Amy waved a hand. "The baby can sleep in your room. You can be the poster child for a modern-day dad."

Moe snorted, his posture loosening.

"It would be easier to fight it out if you were sleeping in the same bed, you know," said Lily's husband as he joined them. Ethan shook Moe's hand before hugging Amy.

"These two are in denial about their marriage," Lily told him. She hadn't broken eye contact with Moe yet and Amy was curious which sibling would back down first.

"Denial?" Amy asked.

Lily made a heart shape with her hands, causing Moe to snort again and Amy to laugh. Just like that the spell between brother and sister was broken.

"By the time the babies start coming they'll be sharing a bed." Lily spoke with an authority that made Amy inexplicably nervous, because after that kiss, anything felt possible when it came to their marriage.

"So?" LILY DEMANDED.

Moe cringed as they uncovered the picnic wedding feast his little sister had prepared. He knew she was curious about the truth of his marriage, thanks to the way he'd poured out his heart and then kissed Amy like they had something going on. If all kisses between "friends" were that good he should have tried kissing more friends.

Indicating the food spread out in front of them, he said, "Your cooking skills sure have come a long way since we were kids."

"You're avoiding the question."

"That wasn't a question. That was a trap."

Shortly after Lily was born, their mother had left them, pretty much ignoring the fact that she had a family, other than sending the odd birthday card. Moe wasn't sure if his mother had remarried, but his father hadn't. He likely hadn't had the time, as he'd spent most of his waking hours working low-level jobs to put food on the table. That, and complaining about The Man crushing the uneducated little guy—him.

With their father pulling twelve-hour shifts in the now-closed local coal mines, he'd missed more suppers than he'd been present for. As a result, Moe and Lily had taught themselves to cook, but after high school, Lily had taken it up a notch by attending a prestigious cooking school. She now owned a restaurant in Blueberry Springs that had belonged to her one-time childhood protector, Ethan Mattson. Through some strange business deal Moe still didn't completely understand, the two had gotten married. They hadn't planned to stay together after the restaurant and catering business switched hands, but they were, and seemed happy. Heck, these days Moe didn't even recognize his old friend Ethan half the time, due to the way he was always smiling.

The only black cloud in the romance had been an incident between Lily and an ex that had almost cost her her life. Moe knew his sister was seeing a therapist as a result, and still had the odd nightmare.

"How are you?" he asked, turning to Lily, arms crossed. He knew she'd understand from his tone what he was really asking.

"Today isn't about me." She put her hands on her hips and tipped her head to the side, her hair pinned loosely in a high bun. "It's about you and your little marriage pledge and how you're going to have children—" she formed air quotes with her fingers "—*platonically*." She gave him a sly smile normally reserved for when she was doing something like slipping hot chili peppers in his cocoa— which turned out to be pretty tasty, actually.

"For the record," she continued, in a bossy, know-it-all tone, "platonic never lasts when you're married. Especially if there's history."

"We're not you and Ethan. You two had it bad for each other for a long time. Amy and I tried that dating thing. Failed. We're over it. This marriage of convenience isn't going to lead to romance."

"Sure, sure," she said, waving off his argument before going back in for another attack, as only a sister would. "How many times have you two gotten back together?"

He pretended to think. "About half a dozen."

Lily rolled her eyes at the exaggeration. "You

guys know artificial insemination is expensive, right?"

"I'm sure Amy has it all figured out." Moe slid his gaze toward the woman in the white dress. His best friend. His wife. The mother of their future babies.

Thinking of her that way made him feel protective, and a wave of warmth settled in his bones.

But *had* she planned for the cost of in vitro? Amy wasn't exactly a details person, especially when it came to money. It seemed her parents were often bailing her out here and there—although apparently they had closed the Bank of Mom and Dad if she was springing for the wedding on her own. Well, he would split the cost like they had with the house, of course, even though he would have been happy with a quick little appointment at the courthouse instead of an actual wedding.

The problem was that their existing medical insurance plans likely didn't cover something that was surely deemed a nonessential procedure. But Amy was a registered nurse. Surely she knew the ins and outs of medical plans, and had something up her sleeve.

"Maybe you'll have to take that offer from Cesar's estate and buy the pub, so you'll have lots of money."

"Don't think owning a business is like having a money tree."

Moe had worked in the pub for years, helping the owner, Cesar Phipps, care for it, while mainly tending the bar. Since Cesar's sudden passing last month Moe had found himself thrust into a managerial role as well. For three months—from late June to late September—he was running Brew Babies single-handedly. At the end of that trial period, if he maintained profits, he could purchase the pub for approximately half its market value, the other portion being bequeathed to him. If he failed, the business would be liquidated, all proceeds going to Cesar's children, Kimi and Spencer.

The problem was Moe was suddenly working two jobs—his old one, plus everything Cesar had done behind the scenes from the city and on his biweekly visits. So far it wasn't nearly as much fun as mixing drinks behind the bar, but Moe felt taking on the challenge was the right way to go. Cesar had been like a father and was trying to share his legacy with Moe. He had to respect that even though the man hadn't trained him well enough to take over. Not on his own. Not yet. But as a man with a mortgage, depleted savings and kids soon to be on the way, he needed to figure it out.

In his shock over Cesar's death, the latest crisis

with his dad and the flurry of his and Amy's marriage, not to mention the house hunting, he hadn't planned for the almost two hundred thousand dollars he'd need to purchase Brew Babies. Honestly, the pub deal still didn't feel real. He kept waiting for the other shoe to drop, revealing that he didn't simply have to run the place profitably, cough up some cash and it would be his. Moe kept dealing with the most urgent matters first—getting a roof over his father's head, after his latest eviction for not paying his rent, then fulfilling his promise to Amy—all the while hoping that something would work out regarding the extra money he needed. Such as Wini at the bank saying that being bequeathed half the pub's value would do fine in lieu of an actual down payment on his loan.

In other words, he'd pulled an Amy and closed his eyes, hoping everything would work out.

It wasn't a good plan.

And yet he had faith that he'd figure something out. It worked for Amy, right?

"Still, to be an owner and in control of your destiny... Why wouldn't you want that?" Lily pressed.

"I'm not sure," he said, not bothering to list all the reasons he wasn't certain about how things would turn out.

"If you don't buy the place and start banking

profits each month, you might only be able to afford to have kids the old-fashioned way," she whispered, sending a whole new flurry of distracting thoughts through Moe's head. Especially if fulfilling the biggest clause in their marriage pledge came down to a mission between the sheets.

CHAPTER 2

Surrounded by boxes, Amy sat on the floor of her little apartment overlooking Main Street in Blueberry Springs. She'd been living in the homey space since Mandy Mattson had given it up when she'd married Frankie Smith. Amy hadn't been there all that long, but it felt like home, and she knew she'd miss it. Watching all the action on the street below was better than television most days. Especially when "Gramps," aka Ethan, Mandy and Devon's grandfather, decided to give everyone in town an eyeful and went for a stroll in his boxer shorts.

As Amy rearranged dishes in the box she'd just packed, her gaze caught on the simple wedding band on her left hand, the feeling of it still unfamiliar. They'd taken possession of their new home three days ago and Moe had moved in immediately. How was he always so organized? It seemed every time Amy turned around there was something to distract her from finishing packing.

Their wedding, only six days ago, already felt like a dream, a dress-up party similar to ones she used to have during recess in elementary school, where she would "marry" various boys from her class.

But that kiss. It had felt real, and had made their marriage feel real, too, made it feel fraught with potential. Potential for heartbreak.

What if she failed at being a wife? What if she hurt Moe? What if her mother was right and marrying him would turn out to be a mistake? A fun idea that, on a whim, she'd followed through on, without taking the time to fully think about the possible consequences.

She shoved the box away and got to her feet. Things between her and Moe already felt different. In the pub there was an awkward hiccup whenever they talked, with both of them waiting for the other to speak, then stumbling when their words came out too fast.

Amy glanced up at the ceiling and let out a groan. That kiss had really gotten under her skin, messing with everything.

She sighed and tossed a magazine into a new

box, then pulled it back out. It was an issue where one of her sister's articles had been printed. Jillian had been only sixteen at the time, but already starting to make a name for herself as a writer.

Her sister had beamed when the issue had arrived in the mail, her eyes so full of excitement that despite her envy, Amy had been happy for her.

"Look what Jillian's done!" their mother had said, holding the magazine up like a trophy for all to behold. "See, Amy? All you have to do is *focus*, and you can achieve whatever your heart desires."

"Fine, I'll finish cleaning my room." Amy had rolled her eyes and glanced at her sister, uncertain about the comparison. Jillian was older by seven years. She'd been a smart, high-achieving, mature and organized, all-around-amazing big sister, and everything nine-year-old Amy felt she would never be. Jillian had known what she wanted and gone after it, selling lemonade in front of the house at age four, homemade cookies at seven, her own newspaper at nine.

Amy stroked the old magazine, then carefully tucked it inside the box so it wouldn't get damaged in the move.

Jillian had had so much potential. She wouldn't have agreed to a marriage pledge and a wedding she couldn't afford. She wouldn't have had to, because everything would have fallen into place, since she would have already done whatever was needed to keep her life from disintegrating into one big mess.

That day of the magazine article had been one of the last truly happy ones. Their family had driven to the city that night, dining at a fancy restaurant where the waiter had a silver crumb sweeper to clear the tablecloth when they were done eating their bread. Her mom hadn't even tsked at the amount of crumbs in front of Amy, as she'd been too busy pointing out the article to everyone who passed their table.

The polite but genuine admiration of strangers for Jillian's skills had been heady, leading Amy to pipe up that she was Jillian's sister. And that, yes, she was proud of her and wanted to be just like her when she was older.

But over the next few years the pressure to be more like Jillian and find her passion, as well as to be more organized, had increased, the comparisons never-ending. The expectations had become binding, confining Amy like a mighty python, despite the way her sister stood up for her and changed the subject whenever possible, trying to shield her.

When Jillian died four years later, Amy had thought her parents' grief might somehow distract them, finally allowing her to breathe and be her normal messy self. Instead, the feeling that she now had two lives to live had settled over her. Her mom and dad were shells of themselves and she found herself striving to be more like Jillian in an attempt to make things feel right and normal again. She'd tried everything to make her parents light up even a fraction of the way they had when Jillian was alive. But Amy had had to struggle to keep it up. She'd do things like keep her room clean for an entire month and then snap one day, painting the whole space lime-green, without permission.

Nursing had been a career they could all settle on, but Amy's need to bolt had reared up more than once, sending her flying into a new adventure, a new job.

One day. One day she'd get it all right. And hopefully soon, with a family.

Amy chucked a pair of flip-flops into a box of kitchen gadgets and sealed it shut, feeling sweat forming along her brow. She needed to get away from Blueberry Springs and just *breathe* again. Not for long. Just a weekend, or a few weeks or something. Maybe go scuba diving once more.

There was a knock at her door and she leaped to answer it, welcoming the distraction.

The door opened and Moe's head peeked in.

"I didn't recognize you with your haircut." Her teasing tone lacked conviction. His shorter hair gave his jaw a more defined look, but seemed to strip him of his devil-may-care image. She'd liked how it had contradicted the fact that, despite his easygoing manner, he was as solid as a few hundred feet of bedrock. Now he looked like the man he was.

And she'd noted that more than a few female customers in the pub had noticed, too.

Moe took in the stacks of boxes with a sweep of his brown eyes. "Ready?" he asked.

Was she?

What if Moe expected her to be as neat and tidy as he was? What if he didn't like the way she enjoyed really long hot showers? They should have talked about this before the wedding. She should have thought it all through, point by point. She couldn't lose him. He was the only one who didn't hold up a picture of a perfect life, then look at her and shake his head with disappointment.

"Come on, Amy," he prompted. "You need to decide."

"On what?"

"An annulment."

The firmness in his voice made her head snap up. *Annulment?* The thought left her cold inside.

"Are we moving in together and setting this plan in motion or not?" he asked in a no-nonsense tone he usually reserved for unruly patrons in the pub. "I'm ready to do this, but you're dragging your feet."

The idea of Moe giving up spurred her into action. She picked up the closest box and pushed it into his arms. "I'm not dragging my feet. I'm just disorganized."

She met his eyes, struck by how warm they were despite the firmness of his words. His gaze was like chocolate fudge. His kisses made her forget why she was fighting the world.

"Hi," she said softly, remembering their old times together, how easy and free they'd been. How good he felt at her side, those strong arms wrapped around her, her head against his chest.

"Quit undressing me with those eyes, woman. Separate bedrooms, remember?"

She let out a choked laugh.

"Seriously," he said, his voice loaded with fake disgust. "This is the last time I ever cut my hair. I'm not a piece of meat. I have feelings, you know. Dreams. Aspirations."

Amy giggled. Leave it to Moe to take her worries and wash them away in a matter of moments.

"I love you."

He rolled his eyes. "And now you're throwing around the *L* word. I already married you, lady." The edges of his lips tugged upward, but he didn't allow the smile to truly break free. "Come on, grab a box."

"We're going to need to make a lot of trips," she said, complying with his order. "Both our cars are pretty small."

"Devon's downstairs with Frankie's truck."

Of course he had organized a truck for her. That was her Moe. "That's why you're going to be the father of my kids. You'll remember the diaper bag."

She followed him down the narrow staircase that led to the street. Her earlier apprehension had been replaced by excitement. They were going to do this. She was going to be a mom, and everything was going to be wonderful. If they hadn't both been holding boxes, she would have given Moe a quick hug of appreciation.

"Where's Frankie?" she asked, as they dropped their boxes onto the open tailgate.

"He and Mandy are at the doctor's."

"Is everything okay?"

Moe shrugged and slid the boxes farther into the truck.

"Where's Devon?"

They both scanned the street, finding him a few doors down, chatting with Fran, the owner of a local boutique. With him as mayor, Amy was sure Devon's work was never done.

"Hey, Devon! You helping or what?" Moe called.

He waved, angling himself their way, but continuing to chat.

Moe dusted off his wrinkled T-shirt in the bright July sun and set a hand on his hip. "Looks like we're loading up ourselves," he muttered.

"Are you unpacked already?" Amy asked, as they climbed the stairs back to her apartment. She'd been so busy with the wedding and then putting her life in order, as well as packing, that she hadn't even helped him move in.

What if he'd already hung that awful painting of a cat he'd done in high school? The proportions were wrong, giving the feline a slightly demented look. It would break his heart if she asked him to take it down, but she couldn't live with it staring at her all the time.

"Not everything. I was waiting for you."

He'd declared their current apartments too small to raise kids in. But Amy knew it was more than that. He'd lived alone in a walk-out basement suite in a duplex overlooking the river for as long as she could remember, probably since the summer after he'd graduated from high school and his father and sister had left for South Carolina, leaving him behind. Her best guess was that with a new home, he was offering her a fresh start in a place deemed neutral ground. Neither of them would be stepping on each other's toes or messing with someone else's established territory.

New habits and all that. Couple's habits.

As she watched his shoulders flex when he lifted a box full of books, groaning and muttering about how it would have been nice for her to distribute the books' weight in a few boxes, she wondered what habits they would fall into as spouses. Would he offer her a chaste good-night kiss that would eventually become more? He sometimes gave her a passing peck on the cheek, one that felt very European, at the end of a long night in the pub.

She hoped that he would do that each night at home so she could accidentally move her head at the last moment, lining up their lips from time to time.

She smiled at the planned ploy and picked up a box in turn, following him down the stairs, eager to see where their new life would lead them. Because she knew that as long as she had Moe, she had everything.

~

MOE STACKED THE LAST BOX FROM THE TRUCK along the wall in the living room. None of Amy's boxes were labeled and he wondered if her unpacking system would simply be to open every one and dump the contents on the floor. He had a feeling it might be.

"That's everything," Devon said, handing Moe a rather sad-looking houseplant that had ridden in the cab of the truck.

"Thanks for your help. Can I buy you a beer?" He headed toward the fridge, ready to retrieve a cold one should his friend accept.

"Sorry, I promised Olivia I'd come straight home so I could watch Abigail while she puts some finishing touches on a dress." Devon and his wife had a busy, inquisitive toddler who kept the two of them running as they tried to balance their semi-new careers along with parenthood. "She's trying to get ahead before her parents come for a visit. Rain check?"

"Sounds like you'll need a double after the in-laws."

"Don't you know it," Devon said with a wry smile.

"How's Olivia liking making her own designs?"

"She's loving it. She makes my ears bleed talking about bodices, tulle and other stuff—but don't tell her I said that," he added quickly.

Despite Devon's complaints, his expression gave away that he loved every minute of it.

"Your secret's safe with me."

JEAN ORAM

"See you later, Amy!" Devon called into the house.

She peeked her head out of the first bedroom along the hall. Her eyes were lit with excitement and her white tank top brought out the early summer tan on her shoulders. "Thanks, Mr. Mayor!"

He gave a salute from his spot at the door. "Just doing my duty and making sure Blueberry Springs citizens get what they need."

Amy laughed and disappeared back into her room. Moe closed the door behind Devon and let out a slow exhalation. This was it. Spouse time.

Time to make some babies.

Well, make a fertility appointment.

Why did the idea of in vitro feel so disappointing?

Amy came out of her room, a box in her arms. Moe followed her swaying hips down the narrow hall into the sunny kitchen, where she dumped the box onto the counter, her tank top catching on an open flap and revealing a flash of bra that made his mind go straight to the process of making those babies she wanted.

Just act normal, dude. That kiss at the wedding went too far, and things are getting weird. You can't let a kiss like that happen again.

And those thoughts zinging around in your brain?

68

All she has to do is take one look to know they're as dirty as the oil in an old diesel engine. Don't make it awkward, man. Be cool.

"Kitchen stuff," she explained, her chin tipped down as she waited for him to start the job of unpacking.

"Right," he replied, thrusting his hand into the box, to retrieve a soup ladle. Standing beside her, inhaling the familiar scent of her shampoo, he had to block out the ping of lust that kept slamming up against his brain like a moth to a porch light. Maybe she had a box that would keep him busy in the garage for a few hours.

"What do you want to do with duplicates?" he asked, holding up the ladle.

She took it and plunged it handle-first into the jar on the counter that held his own serving utensils. "You can always do with having two," she explained.

She stopped and surveyed the room, her lips turning down. "You've unpacked all of your stuff, haven't you?"

"Do you need me to move anything?"

She mulled that over while he shoved her mixing bowls into a low cupboard.

"No, not yet," she said finally, her lack of decisiveness a sure sign that something was on her mind.

"You okay?"

"Yeah, just hungry."

Easy to solve. The pizza had arrived just before Devon left. It was sitting behind the big box she'd started to empty. She must be distracted if she hadn't noticed the white box or sniffed out its wonderful scent yet.

"Tell me what you need, and I'll make it happen," he said in a seductive tone, tugging the pizza box closer. Time to show her they could be like their old flirty selves without things getting weird or awkward.

Amy's chest expanded as she slowly inhaled, uncurling her hands, which had bunched into fists, and placing them flat on the counter. "Moe…"

He held up the pizza box and Amy's shoulders dropped, her lips twisting into an unimpressed grimace.

"Chill," he coaxed. "I know all you need is some DNA for your babies and someone to help change diapers." The look of fear and doubt returned to her gaze, and he tugged her into a loose hug. "We're going to create that family you want. Neither of us has any crazy romantic idealizations, which is why we're doing this. This is going to work out better than everyone else's marriage, I promise."

Amy hugged him tight, her body nestling into

the nooks and crannies of his own, making him think of a jigsaw puzzle.

"You always know what to say, don't you?" she murmured against his chest.

"I try. Now," he said, releasing her, "let's feed you."

She nodded and took the slice of plain pepperoni pizza he passed her way. Just pepperoni and cheese—her favorite. Unlike him. He might not be adventurous in life, but when it came to pizza he wanted all the fixings.

"I don't know why I'm so..." She waved the slice of pizza in the air as though trying to conjure up the right word.

"Nervous? Skittish? Chicken? Maybe it's a secret fear of change."

"Ha-ha," she said dryly.

"Don't give me that. I deserve a real laugh."

"Sometimes a woman fakes things."

"You weren't faking your reaction to that knee-weakening kiss I gave you at our wedding." He might as well head straight to the very thing she was trying to avoid talking about, because he'd bet that fantasy-inducing kiss was at least half the reason she was acting a bit off today.

"Yeah. What was that?" She put down her pizza, turning to look at him with such intensity he felt bad for their future children, envisioning them trying to squirm their way out of something.

"It got to you," he stated.

"It got to you, too." She picked up her slice of pizza again, aiming it at him like a weapon, her cheeks pink. "There was something…odd about it."

Odd wasn't the adjective he'd choose to describe the heat that had been present, ready to weld them together for all eternity.

"What was it?" she insisted.

"Quit badgering me."

"As your wife it's my right to nag and demand answers. We can't kiss like that or things are going to get complicated."

She reached up and pulled the elastic off her ponytail, setting her hair free to dance across her bare shoulders.

A shudder of attraction slammed into him and he let out a jerky breath. "I'll take this to the garage." He dumped the last items in the box on the counter and turned to flee.

"Moe." She grabbed his hand, her fingers sure and warm, like they'd been when she'd caressed the nape of his neck during that kiss. Another shudder ripped through him.

She wasn't going to let him go until he gave her a proper answer, was she?

And what was the proper answer? That he'd

wanted to consummate their marriage at their earliest convenience after that soul-searing kiss?

"It was probably just the moment getting to us," he replied.

She was searching his eyes for something, then, seeming to find it, she released him, saying, "Do you think our kids will find it strange that we have separate bedrooms?"

Don't think about bedrooms.

He gripped the empty box, heading to the attached garage, saying over his shoulder, "Not when I explain to them that you snore like a bulldozer."

"You said it was more like a transport truck."

"That, too."

He dropped the empty carton on the garage floor. His tools were still boxed, lined up against the wall. He needed shelves. A worktable where he could teach their kids how to hammer a nail in straight and use a power drill.

He picked up Amy's box and carefully peeled off the tape holding the bottom together, before collapsing the cardboard and stacking it with other boxes from his move, ready to go to the recycling depot.

"You haven't put up your posters yet," Amy said, when he returned to the house. She was in the living room, gesturing to the bare walls.

"I threw them out. They seemed a bit too…college."

She smiled, obviously agreeing. "What about your painting?"

"That one I did in high school?" he asked in surprise.

She nodded.

He didn't think she'd liked it. The thing was awful. "Dumpster."

"Dumpster! But you made it."

"Doesn't mean I have to keep it forever."

"You hung it on your wall forever."

"Because I didn't have anything to replace it with. And now I do."

"With what?"

"I thought we'd frame some of those photos you took of the mountains."

"Back when I wanted to be a photographer?" She laughed and shook her head, digging into a box of books. She stacked them on his coffee table.

"Don't say they're not good enough."

"They weren't good enough to get into a gallery."

"You tried just one and gave up."

"So?"

"So?" he retorted just as quickly.

"Are we fighting again?"

"Yup."

"How are we going to make up?" she teased, a flicker of raw temptation coursing through her smoky amber eyes.

This was it. A test. A pop quiz. One he had to take, but wasn't sure he could pass.

He allowed his gaze to trail over her bare legs, then up over her shorts, all the way to her smiling eyes. Her lips curved upward like those of the Cheshire cat.

"I have a few ideas," he said, his voice husky.

"Do you?" Her eyebrows darted upward, giving him the go-ahead.

Fun and games. His wife was back to the Amy he knew and loved. No weirdness. No awkwardness. Just best friends who could dish the heat without anything but a few laughs ever coming from it.

Perfect.

Perfectly unsatisfying.

He pushed another unopened box against her chest. "Unpack, then we'll make an appointment to get you knocked up."

Her expression dropped into a fake pout. "That's nowhere near as fun as I was imagining."

"You'll get used to it." There was no need to press their luck. Not yet, anyway.

"I hope not." She gave him a teasing, promising

laugh that sent shivers of anticipation down his spine.

It was going to be a very long marriage.

~

AMY WAS RELIEVED THAT THINGS WERE HEADING back to normal, and that she and Moe could still manage a touch of heat in each other's gaze without starting something that would lead to awkwardness.

They'd moved to the spare bedroom, which would serve as a small home office and guest room, and hopefully soon a nursery.

Moe had insisted on hanging her framed nursing degree and now stood back, making sure it was level. "I booked us a honeymoon."

Amy's heart picked up speed. "Honeymoon?"

"I mean a getaway," he said quickly, looking so uncomfortable she had to laugh. "My cousin Dallas over in Indigo Bay, South Carolina, gave us a steep discount on one of his resort's cottage rentals along the beach as a wedding gift. I booked us in for two days at the end of August."

How could they afford that?

No, Moe would have planned ahead, saved up.

Which was really sweet. So sweet it tugged at her heart.

"Are you falling for everyone's predictions about how our marriage is going to become real?" she asked.

Moe pursed his lips, but when he caught the mirth in her gaze, he let out a burst of laughter. "It is pretty nuts, isn't it?"

"It's like everyone has forgotten how every time we tried to make our friendship something more it fell flat." She tried to rub away the sharp sting of loss that had taken up residence in her chest. Moe was so perfect, it would have been great if it had worked out.

But it hadn't.

"What happened to us, anyway?" Moe asked, facing her more fully.

She shrugged. "We just sort of fizzled."

"Fizzled." He squinted into the distance, looking contemplative.

"We're too different."

"You like action and adventure."

"And you like steady and reliable." She squeezed his arm affectionately and he refocused his gaze on the shirts she'd used as padding around her framed items. He began folding them neatly.

"Anyway," he said, "I can cancel the 'honeymoon.' It was just a thought. A getaway before the kids start coming and it becomes harder to slip away."

"It's so cute that you're worried I'm going to think you're trying to woo me with this trip." She danced around him, letting her fingers trail across his shoulder blades. "Do you have a widdle crushy-wushy on your wifey?"

He dropped the shirt he was folding and reached for the phone in his back pocket. "I'm canceling."

"No." She laughed and placed her hands over his, blocking him from unlocking his phone. "I think we should go. It's a sweet idea. Wasn't Ginger there not too long ago? She said it was fabulous."

"Yeah, she went back. It's where she and Logan met, when she went for that workshop."

"How do you remember that stuff?" She'd bet if she quizzed him, he'd know where most of the couples in town had met.

"People tell me things. I listen." He spoke slowly and clearly, no doubt trying to annoy her. "I'm a good listener, in case you failed to notice."

"Is that why you get good tips at the pub, when all you do is pour beer without too much head?"

"I'm also good-looking, and show them a bit of leg every now and again."

Amy plunked herself on the guest bed, sitting cross-legged. "How did we meet?"

He frowned as though thinking. "I don't remember."

She grinned, knowing he would never forget the rather embarrassing incident. "Really? You don't remember falling on the ice so badly that you bruised your prostate and came into the ER because your bladder was full, and there wasn't a thing you could do about it?"

The incident had happened shortly after she'd taken the nursing job in Blueberry Springs—just one town over from where her parents had recently moved.

"I try to forget," he said, his cheeks an endearing shade of fire engine red.

She stood, grasping his shirt to tug him closer as she whispered against his ear, "I don't."

He shivered. Or maybe it was a shudder. She wasn't sure which.

He'd been such a good sport that she hadn't been able to help but like him. Especially since he'd been out on the glassy lake trying to save a poor yearling doe slipping and sliding on the ice, unable to get away from a pack of coyotes intent on having her as a midwinter meal. Moe had rushed to chase them off, and had ended up taking a hard spill.

"You really don't understand the concept of sexy talk, do you?" he said.

She still had his shirt bunched in her hand, keeping him close. He was warm and smelled heavenly—like good memories. She forced herself to release him instead of curling against him and kissing him, long and slow.

"So you're taking me to Indigo Bay to revive the spark in our dying relationship?"

"Ha," Moe deadpanned. "That spark died long ago. If there ever was one."

He pulled a frying pan from a nearby box, tossing it onto the bed as he continued his excavation. He seemed intent on getting her unpacked in less than twenty-four hours.

"You're no fun."

He didn't react, so she poked him in the ribs. Before she knew it he had gripped her around the waist and bent her backward, supporting her comfortably. "Oh, darling," he said in a crisp accent, his lips inches from hers. "I miss the days of yore where we went at it like rabbits, sparks flying, lighting our world on fire."

"Sounds dangerous, Mr. Days of Yore." Her words were coming out all breathy. "And where was I when all this rabbit business was happening?"

He swept her upright again.

"It's like driving down Main Street. You blink, you miss it." He went back to the kitchen to continue unpacking her things, and she followed. "What's this?" He held up a spray bottle half filled with liquid.

"Don't be so hard on yourself. You lasted much longer than a second or two." She took the container from his grip, trying to distract herself from the flood of intimate memories. "It's for dampening my hair to make my curls behave."

"Why was it in with all of this?" He was twisting the nozzle, testing the effect until the mist became a jet of spray. She'd have to remember to readjust it next time she did her hair or she'd shoot herself with a stream of water.

"Because it was in my kitchen."

He nodded, as if her packing system made sense. It didn't, but in some crazy way he likely understood it better than she did.

She breathed deeply, taking in their new home. A cute bungalow built in the nineties, it had a powder-blue-tiled backsplash behind the sink, and pink floral wallpaper borders at waist level in each hallway, as well as a foot down from the ceiling in the kitchen. Other than those dated touches, it was perfect. It even had a big fenced backyard, so there'd be no worries about bears wandering through while the kids were out playing.

And despite the boxes everywhere, she already felt at home. She pulled Moe into a spontaneous hug, and after a slight hesitation, his hands landed on her waist again.

"You're the best," she said against his chest.

"In bed?"

She lightly batted him away. "What is it with men always thinking about sex?"

"You started the innuendos."

She stuck out her tongue.

"Is that an offer?" He gave her a dark, hungry look. There was a flare of something that wasn't usually present in their playful banter, and she wasn't sure whether to hit the brakes or the gas pedal.

"What would you like it to be?" She twisted, rolling one shoulder and sending him a haughty, simmering look that drove most men a little bit wild.

Moe was after her in a second, and Amy squealed when he attacked her with the water bottle, the cold spray hitting her neck, then her bare legs.

Laughing, she tore through the house, seeking refuge as he continued to chase her. She ripped through the living room, stubbing her toe on the couch leg in the process. "Ouch!" she cried, lifting her foot and cradling it in her hands as she hopped on the other one. "Time-out! Time-out! I'm hurt."

She fell backward onto the sofa, her hair tumbling around her face.

"Are you faking?" Moe narrowed his eyes, the spray bottle directed ruthlessly at her chin.

"No!" she insisted, still clutching her toe.

He squirted her anyway, the stream of cool water wetting her cheek.

"Hey! No fair! I called time-out."

"That was in case you're trying to pull a fast one on me." He sat beside her. "Is this the poor widdle baby who got hurty-wurty?" He spared her toe the briefest glance.

"It hurts."

"This'll help." He secured her foot between his strong hands and began tickling her sensitive arch. She squirmed and bucked, laughing.

Fearing she'd void her bladder before Moe ever relented, she summoned her strength for a counterattack. When her fingers slipped under his shirt he jolted upright, slamming his arms to his sides in an attempt to block her from reaching his ticklish ribs.

"Not fair!"

"Totally fair." She pushed her fingers to the spots he was trying to protect, crawling over him to gain leverage. He tumbled against the arm of the couch as she continued her attack. He was clamping his mouth shut as though it was possible to keep the laughter inside, his breath coming out in deep huffs.

"I'm not ticklish!" he exclaimed, struggling to maintain a straight face. Then suddenly he was on the offense again, rolling her off him and onto the floor beside the couch, his long body pinning her to the rug with its delicious weight. She wrapped her legs around him, thinking she'd flip him over, but as he pressed closer to reduce her leverage, their hips meeting, their noses brushing as electricity arced between them, they both froze, the air stilling around them.

"Hi," she breathed.

"Hi yourself."

Was he going to kiss her?

Was she going to kiss him?

His solid body felt right pressed into her, and whatever it was that had appeared during their wedding kiss resurfaced, simmering between them, dark and dangerous, and entirely too tempting.

"You know we're in the perfect position to make out right now," Moe said.

She made a soft sound of agreement.

"And we're married." His tone was matter-of-fact, almost cavalier.

They stared at each other for a weighted moment, considering their options.

"You're a good kisser," Amy replied, unsure why she was nudging them toward the forbidden, slightly fraught territory of more-than-friends.

"It could make things complicated and awkward."

"It would be risky," she agreed.

His body had settled against hers and she wanted to keep him there forever. He tenderly brushed a lock of hair off her cheek as her body hummed a familiar tune. She had a feeling that when it came to the lyrics, Moe's soul knew every word.

"Are we ready for risk-taking?" he whispered. His mouth had drifted closer to hers and her eyelids fluttered. He lightly dragged a finger over her lower lip and she parted the tingling flesh.

"It would be foolish," she whispered back. She wanted to kiss him, but knew she had to hold back, though she was unsure she could.

"Utterly foolish."

She breathed her reply. "Completely."

"Entirely."

"Wholly."

"I can't think of another synonym," he said.

"Satisfyingly complex and erroneous?" she suggested, her eyes opening.

"That's more than one word."

They were coming back around, their brains reengaging and putting them back into the safety zone of friends, not lovers. She swallowed her disappointment, trying to find relief, so she could focus on it instead.

She was having trouble.

Moe blinked, then cleared his throat as he slid off her, the mood that had been building between them dissolving like it had never existed.

They were back in the friend zone. Right where they belonged.

But she found that it was the one place she didn't want to be. Not with Moe.

AMY FANNED HERSELF AS SHE TRAILED AFTER MOE, heading back to the kitchen. She'd almost kissed him. Almost let things go *way* too far. Deliciously far.

What was wrong with her? They were supposed to be *normal*. Not act like hormone-crazed lovers. If she gave in, what would she do if this time things didn't settle back into an amicable friendship? There was so much more than just their friendship at stake.

Was it the idea of making babies sending her brain into a tizzy? Because they didn't need to do *that* to create offspring. Nope. It was walk into the fertility clinic, have the qualified staff take care of a few things, then walk out pregnant.

She needed to put her head back on straight so this little attraction problem she seemed to be facing could fade away. Just like it always did.

No spouses with benefits. Nope. Not for them.

"It's hot in here," she said, when Moe caught her fanning herself.

"Nah, it's just you." He gave her a wink and she brushed his arm with a hand, a gesture meant to show that she was still cool with things, able to take their flirting in stride without it messing with her mind. But the touch electrified her flesh, sending tingles zinging all the way up her body, then back down again.

She cleared her throat and rolled her shoulders, trying to work away the attraction. Every time she thought she had it licked, it was there again like an addiction to cigarettes. Just one whiff of the sweet smoke and she was twitching for a drag even though she hadn't touched cigarettes in nearly fifteen years, having quickly outgrown the need to use the stinky things as a way to get under her parents' skin, and finding boyfriends a much healthier avenue.

Spying a stack of envelopes sitting on the edge of the kitchen counter, she attacked them, scooping one up, her gaze catching the mailing address. In surprise, she asked, "You're already getting your mail here?"

"I do live here."

Leaving her forwarding address with the postal service was still on her to-do list. That, among many other things. She was more behind than she'd thought, thanks to putting on that wedding.

She went to set the letter down, but the return address had her pulling the folded paper out of the envelope. She caught herself and asked, "May I?"

It was from Cesar Phipps's daughter, Kimi.

"Is this a bonus for all the work you've been doing at the pub?" she asked. She knew it was some sort of trial period set up by Cesar's estate, but did he really want to be a manager? She didn't think so. The new, extra work was making him cranky. But she could tell the lure of being in charge appealed to a part of him he usually tried to ignore, as it was too much like his father's way of thinking. She wasn't sure what would happen if he said no to managing the pub in September, but it probably wasn't much worse than having him run ragged taking care of everything.

Talking to him about the pub was just one more thing she hadn't had time to do over the past few weeks.

Moe shifted, opening the fridge and taking out a beer. "Want one?"

Amy shook her head. Then realizing her drinking days were likely numbered once they started trying to make a baby, she changed her mind and snatched Moe's after he took the inaugural sip.

She checked the label. "It still surprises me you don't stock beer brewed in the pub you manage."

"I'm not the manager."

"You have been for years. And will be officially until September—you've just never had the pay or the title. Cesar took advantage of you and still is." Amy flattened the letter and skimmed it.

"He didn't," Moe said sharply.

"He did."

"He was like a father." He pulled another beer from the fridge to replace the one she had commandeered, his expression unreadable. "He taught me a lot, as well as gave me a lot of responsibility and freedom. You can't put a price on that."

"I can." She dropped the letter onto the counter. "He took advantage of you and now Kimi wants to, as well."

Moe shot Amy a sour look that she ignored because she knew she was right.

"Kimi's proposing a managerial partnership where you help her and she helps you," she stated.

Moe didn't say anything, his gaze locked on the ceiling as he took a long swallow of beer.

"She's been running Brew, Too—the city's pub —into the ground. She wants to use you as a life raft."

"It was already languishing. Cesar wanted to

shut its doors, but she begged him to give her some time to turn it around."

"And?"

He shrugged. "She's still working on it. He conditionally bequeathed it to her, and she has three months to prove she's making headway or it's liquidated." He looked away again, taking another long pull of beer.

"So she wants to pick your brain so she can figure out how to keep her pub in Dakota. Nice. What's she offering you in return? Besides more work for nothing?"

"I don't know yet."

"Will she take over the work Cesar did? Will she make things go back to normal, like when he was still alive? Or is she just going to take, take, take, while you continue to run yourself ragged trying to do everything for that family?"

"Amy, it's not like that."

"Then what's it like?" He was too nice and she feared Kimi was going to walk all over him. There had been a balance with Moe and Cesar, even though Amy felt Moe should have been given more rewards and acknowledgment for all he did with the pub.

He was picking at the beer label, his expression uncharacteristically closed. She could sense he wasn't telling her everything, and she reminded herself that he was grieving and that men didn't always want to talk about every little detail. In time, she was sure that he'd tell her. Right now, everything to do with the pub was likely hurting him, as he missed Cesar. The man needed time and understanding.

"You know you can tell me anything," she said. She read the letter again. "If you're going to say yes to working with Kimi, can you request I get a raise first? I have that wedding to pay for." Amy took a swig of beer and added dryly, "Before she gets Brew Babies from the estate and runs it into the ground. Speaking of which, maybe we should find a way to keep the place out of her hands so she doesn't destroy it." She paused, remembering she was waiting for an answer to her question. "So can you?"

"No."

Amy jerked. "Why not? I work hard."

"You're my wife."

"Then why didn't you give me one last week before it was too late? My money is your money, remember."

"Last week you were my ex-girlfriend."

"Arrgh. Nepotism!" She banged her bottle on the countertop. "Why doesn't it ever work in my favor?"

Moe's lips twitched as he collected the old

newspaper she'd used to wrap her dishes, stuffing it into an empty box.

"So I'll never get a raise ever again?" She gave him a sly look as she sidled up to help. "What are the others getting?"

Moe straightened from his task and took a sip of his beer as though giving himself more time to answer.

"Does Marissa get paid more?" Amy pressed.

"She's been at the pub a long time."

"So have I."

"Technically, she has seniority."

"But I've worked there longer than she has." Marissa had been hired months after Amy first started at Brew Babies.

"And you've left the pub how many times to go work elsewhere? She has more hours, hence seniority."

Okay, so Amy had left the job a few times, but the point was she always returned, and nobody else on the team worked as well with Moe. He understood and supported her need for change, so what was the big deal?

"I'm here now with no plans to quit. Why don't you give me more responsibility, and then a raise?"

"I can't invest in training you just to have you leave."

"I'm not leaving."

"You're planning on a maternity leave within the year."

Oh, right. That.

She blinked back the slight burning in her eyes. "Are you discriminating against mothers?"

She'd always believed Moe understood, but seeing Marissa getting more because she'd stuck around all this time was a wake-up call. It made sense, but somehow still surprised her, especially since Moe hadn't ever entrusted Marissa with a key to the building, as he had Amy.

His voice was quiet and level as he said, "I love how you follow your heart, Amy. But the fact is, I can't count on you not to leave me high and dry."

"As a manager."

"As a...a man in charge of things."

Some of the tightness in her chest eased off. "I always come back," she said lightly.

She didn't miss the flash of uncertainty in his gaze, as though he expected that one day she might not.

CHAPTER 3

$\mathcal{M}$oe had come to the city to talk with Kimi. Amy had stumbled across Kimi's offer to partner with managing the pubs, and he knew Amy wouldn't accept shrugs and conversation deferrals on the topic forever. Which meant he needed to take action and figure things out so he could tell her what he was doing with the pub, their very livelihood. Once he figured that out himself, of course.

When she'd been busy with the wedding there'd never been time for a heart to heart on the subject, and anyway, he'd feared that talking about the pub's future, and the inherent upheaval no matter what happened, might cause her to nix everything, from their pledge, to the closed offer on the house, to the job itself. Now he didn't know how to broach the topic, because he didn't have a clue what was going to happen. He was supposed to be the man with the plan and he had nothing. Nothing but news that would shake her up. News that could change the unspoken promises he'd made to her—that everything would be just like it always had been.

"It's good to see you. Thanks for coming in." Kimi shook hands with Moe as she drew him into her father's large office. Her smooth fingers lingered in his, her gaze wandering over him in a not-so-subtle way that made him think of the pub's drunks ogling Amy around last call.

Kimi tucked her skirt under her to take a seat at her father's large mahogany desk.

Correction, her desk now. Her office.

A lump formed in Moe's throat. Things just weren't the same without Cesar.

"I'm sorry about your dad," Moe said, immediately wishing he hadn't. He'd expressed his condolences at the funeral, and then again at the reading of Cesar's last will and testament. He really didn't want to talk about his own grief at the moment, let alone anyone else's.

The day of the reading had been a surprising day of contradictory feelings. It had been Amy's thirtieth birthday, and he had returned from the reading of the will, still in shock over the late Cesar's generous and unexpected business proposition.

He could purchase the pub for approximately half its value—a little income for Kimi and Spencer to help placate them, Moe suspected, as they surely hadn't been very pleased about his possibility of inheriting Brew Babies.

After the reading he hadn't had time to change out of his dark suit before appearing at Amy's party, and the festive mood in the pub had been a welcome reprieve from a day of holding it all in. But instead of greeting Amy first, he'd headed straight for the bar. She'd been laughing off to his left, accepting birthday wishes from a group of women, radiant in a short sundress that showed off her legs and curves.

Moe had loosened his tie and poured himself a shot of whiskey. He'd knocked it back, set the empty shot glass upside down on the bar and savored the alcohol's burn.

The tension riding in his neck and shoulders had already begun to ease and he'd removed his suit jacket. Then carefully folded his shirtsleeves and started filling the more complex drink orders that were waiting for him, stacked up scraps of paper left by the waitresses.

Cesar had taught him everything from prioritizing to keeping customers happy. The man had felt like a father in so many ways, guiding and trusting Moe to expand his business, giving him a place within those four walls where he felt he was more than just a bartender. More than just some small-town guy without a future.

And now Moe had the opportunity to be more. He could say yes to clause fifteen. He could be the person his father had always insisted he wanted him to become—a business owner. A man with freedom, security and independence.

He'd never minded working under Cesar. Never minded it one bit. The man had been fair and generous, both in life and in death. More than he needed to be.

But now? Now what was going to happen? Moe needed to figure out how to run the place on his own or else let it go and find a whole new career. Start over.

Still at the bar, Moe had poured another shot, setting it beside his empty glass, leaving it untouched.

"Who's this for?" Marissa had asked, coming by with her tray.

He had given a minuscule shake of his head, and her mouth had formed a silent "oh" before she'd slipped away to take more orders from Amy's guests.

Moe had lowered his hands to the bar and let out a long sigh before straightening his spine once again and working his way through the drink orders, doing the one thing he knew how to do.

Kimi had rightfully expected to have both pubs bequeathed to her. She was Cesar's flesh and blood, after all, and had a business degree. She'd also been helping her dad at both pubs for the past year, introducing systems to boost efficiency and streamline profits. She'd been inseparable from her father, determined to become his right-hand man.

When the lawyer had read Cesar's wishes in regards to "the son who wasn't blood, but who was greatly responsible for the thriving success of the Blueberry Springs pub," Kimi, who had just been conditionally bequeathed the struggling Dakota city sister pub, had sat totally still, barely breathing. Moe had waved a hand in front of her eyes to make sure she wasn't having some sort of silent seizure. She'd snapped to, giving him such a pained look it had sliced a part of him open. He'd started to tell her he wouldn't accept the offer, but she'd stood abruptly, apologizing to everyone before fleeing from the room.

Instead of talking to her, making excuses for

the years of hard work he'd put in alongside her father, he'd returned to Blueberry Springs.

He'd mixed a Cuba libre and a chocolate vodka martini, placing them to his right.

"Thanks," Marissa had said, whisking by. At the end of the bar, she'd set the drinks in front of Amber Thompson and Jen Kulak. Moe should have known by the orders who they were for. He'd sent them a nod of acknowledgment when they looked up, then went back to work.

Once all the orders had been fulfilled, Moe had come out around the bar to greet the birthday gal.

"You were late," she'd scolded, after she'd thrown herself into his arms.

"I was at the reading of the will."

Her joyful expression had wavered and she'd stepped back, hands on his shoulders, so she could take him in. "How was it?"

He'd shrugged and pulled her back into his arms, needing the hug. "Happy thirtieth."

"Did he leave you anything?"

"Sort of." Moe hadn't said more, because what could he say? That the man had offered him the chance to take what wasn't rightfully his, for an amount he didn't possess? But if he didn't snag this chance, they'd both be looking for new jobs by September.

As if Amy had sensed his reluctance to talk, she'd said, "Did you find yourself a girlfriend in the city?"

Her palms had been resting on his chest, and he'd hooked his hands loosely around her wrists, still needing the physical contact. Her large brown eyes were almost amber with happiness, and he'd found that light spilling into him, making his worries drift away.

"Nope. No girlfriend."

"Even with that stunning suit that makes you look so hot?" She'd leaned into him and he'd reminded himself to find an excuse to wear the suit again someday soon.

"Nope. No takers. I even stood on a street corner and did a little dance in the June sunshine."

"Their loss."

"Tell me about it. I got all sweaty for nothing."

"Did you buy me a ring?"

"I brought you balloons. I shoved them all in your car. I also poured a few bags of confetti down your vent system and turned the fan on high. Have fun driving home."

"Girls want jewelry." She'd released a wrist from his loose grip and had flicked his somber tie. "No wonder you're still single, you prankster."

"And are you still single, Miss Amy Carrick?"

Her gaze had been slightly unfocused as she'd settled it on his lips. "You know I am. You cursed me three years ago with that pledge."

"So it's my fault now?"

"Always." She'd rested her head against his chest, and he'd moved his hands to her hips, steadying her even though she didn't seem to need it. She'd snuggled in and he'd found himself wishing he had a woman in his life. Not a friend in need of a warm body to prop herself against, but more.

"You do tend to surprise me."

"It's what you love best about me."

"True."

Her hands had drifted back up to his shoulders, then she'd hooked her arms around his neck, their embrace feeling more like a couple's than that of best friends.

"Here I am at the ripe old age of thirty. Single." She'd snuggled deeper into his arms, where she felt familiar and right. Like she belonged. Maybe it was simply their history, their comfort in being together, or maybe it was something else. That something that kept rearing up now and again, but never really blossoming into something they could hold on to.

"You're single, too." She'd lined up her hands

side by side on his chest, her face tipped up, so trusting and lovely.

"I am." He could have lowered his lips, given her a birthday kiss.

"Are you going to buy me a ring?"

The marriage pledge. They could hold on to moments like this and many more. He'd have someone to come home to, and so would she.

"What if Mr. Right is just around the corner, waiting for you?"

"He had his chance to find me."

"Amy?" Moving forward with their marriage pledge was a pretty big step.

"Rodney Harper—"

"Rodney?" He'd twisted his lips to illustrate his distaste over her using his legal name.

"—consider yourself off the market." And with that she had angled her face and placed a warm, dry kiss on his lips that had sent his head spinning and his mind into confusion.

They'd bought a house a week later, and gotten married two weeks after that.

It wasn't until everything had settled down a few days ago that he'd realized the bank probably would likely need an actual down payment for the loan he intended to apply for.

He was embarrassed. He was the planner in the relationship and he may have just messed up the livelihoods for himself and his wife, as well as several other employees.

Kimi was speaking to him, her tone suggesting he'd tuned her out during his little jaunt down memory lane. Moe brought his mind back into focus on her, the office, the papers spread out on her desk.

"My father had health issues for some time. His passing wasn't entirely unexpected." She swallowed hard before lifting her eyes and straightening her back. "You said you've looked over my proposal?"

And this was where his confusion lay like a tiger ready to pounce. There was no perfect solution. He obviously would be crazy to turn down purchasing the well-priced business that kept both himself and his wife employed. They had a wedding to pay for, a mortgage, and soon visits to the fertility clinic and a maternity leave. Their little family was going to need the stability and security his father was always harping about, and if Moe didn't buy the place they'd have nothing.

But at the same time, managing and running a pub, as well as coming up with yet more money when lately all he'd done was spend, plus finding time to help Kimi with her struggling pub, too, it all felt like too much. More than he could stretch to take care of.

"I did look it over," he replied finally, answering

her question. He needed Kimi's experience with Cesar's behind-the-scenes jobs, but feared she wouldn't be able to take on enough to be a true help.

"What do you think?"

"It's intriguing."

"Brew Babies wouldn't be where it is today without your ideas and hard work." Her voice was distant. "My proposal is that we join together to manage both pubs. You need help, and I can work with you to keep things on track. We both have too much to lose if we fail."

Moe shifted in his seat. "What about Spencer?" Kimi's brother had been given a payout, having never taken more than a passing interest in the business. Still, when it came to losing their father's legacy, he might find himself ready to step up.

"He's no help. He'd rather play video games all day and live off of his inheritance than be an adult." Kimi straightened the pens on her desk and cleared her throat. She laid her blue-painted nails atop a document and slid it across the desk. "Do you have any questions?"

"A few." Moe reached for the papers, buying time in hopes that his indecision would vanish and that the right path would show itself. He *knew* what was right, but there was this invisible force holding him back, preventing him from reaching out and accepting what he'd been bequeathed.

"That's new," Kimi stated, her gaze latched to his wedding band. She tried to smile, but her trembling lips wouldn't cooperate. "Congratulations."

"Thanks."

"Who's the lucky gal?"

"Amy Carrick."

"From the pub? Are you mixing business and pleasure?" she teased, in a low sultry voice. "You naughty man."

Moe opened his mouth, hesitating as he debated how honest he should be about the pleasure part of their marriage pledge.

"But I should have guessed," she said cheerily, flipping closed the file folder she'd laid out in front of her.

"Sorry?"

"Whenever she's around there's no room for other women." She gave a small wave and a laugh that was a bit too tight to be natural. "I hope someday I find someone who'll make me as happy as Amy obviously makes you."

Moe cleared his throat. "I'm sure you will."

She reopened the file folder, her tone becoming crisp and professional. "I'd like your input." She began handing him sheet after sheet. "Mostly in regards to money, duties, hours, etc. How we'll split the division of labor."

Moe felt an invisible band tighten around his forehead. "How long do you propose we work together? Just until we're through the trial period, or longer?"

"The next two months for sure. Possibly longer if things go well." In other words, if they didn't lose the pubs in September, they'd keep the partnership going.

He scanned the pages, hoping to see the jobs he despised assigned to her. Unfortunately, the proposal wasn't that specific. He tried to imagine himself fussing with orders, payroll, as well as inventory, shipments, promotions, negotiating deals with suppliers, not to mention developing recipes for new beers, instead of simply tapping other brewmasters' kegs.

What if he found a way to buy Brew Babies, then flipped it? Maybe he could work for the new owner without any headaches. Profits from the sale would cover the cost of in vitro, even creating a cushion so they could fail a time or two.

Why did he feel disappointed that in vitro might truly become a viable possibility?

He shook his head, dismissing thoughts of baby-making from his mind. He needed to think like an owner. Like The Man. And if he bought and sold Brew Babies, then what? He wasn't the man in control of his own destiny.

But if he bought it...headaches. And they'd all be his to deal with.

Moe's damp thumbprints were making the paper stretch and wrinkle, and he relaxed his grip, trying to keep the papers pristine.

"Barkeeping forty or more hours a week," he said, "along with all of this doesn't leave me with a lot of personal time."

That band around his forehead was getting mighty tight.

"Moe..." There was amusement in her tone, and he wasn't sure he liked the hint of condescension that came with it. "You would be the *owner*, the *manager*. You'd hire out barkeeping."

Moe cleared his throat again, feeling ridiculous for not thinking like someone above a bartender. You didn't do the lower level jobs if you could hire them out.

But the idea of no longer tending the bar left him feeling...well, it was similar to the idea of in vitro being possible again. As though his life wasn't quite in line with his inner feelings.

Before he could sort out the meaning of it all, Kimi began speaking. "You've added entertainment and a larger menu to Brew Babies, making the pub a part of the community. You've increased profits substantially over the past few years, and I'd love to hear your thoughts on what can be done here in the city."

"Yeah, of course." That was the easy stuff. The fun stuff.

If that was the stuff he got to do, he'd be okay. Plus, there'd be more money coming into their household. And Amy would be able to work part-time after the kids came, or go wherever her heart took her.

He should find the money and make the pub happen.

Be the owner. Be the boss. Take control of his financial future and not leave it to someone else to decide when and where he made his money.

"Yeah, let's figure this out and do it." He stood, shaking Kimi's hand.

She beamed at him. "Thank you, Moe. Thank you so much." She clamped both hands around his.

As he exited the office after discussing the specifics of their new partnership, he bumped into Kimi's brother. The pale, doughy man, who called himself a professional gamer, looked agitated, his eyebrows drawn low.

"Spencer, good to see you." He gave his hand a brisk shake.

Spencer angled a thumb toward Kimi's office. "She wants to manage your pub with you."

"She does."

"Why didn't you ask me?"

"I didn't realize you were interested." Or qualified. Moe scratched his cheek.

"Dad and I used to talk about the businesses a bit. I might know stuff that could help you guys out."

"Maybe you could help Kimi with her place?"

"You know how it is working with a sister. A super bossy one." He smiled. "But yeah, I'll help her where I can. Offer's open to you, too. It's been a rough month, hasn't it?"

"Yeah. And thanks."

"How long will you two work together?"

"Well, assuming I can scratch up the cash to buy this place, for however long it benefits us both."

Spencer was shifting from foot to foot, eating lint-covered gummy candies from the pocket of his jeans. "My dad always liked you. Wished you'd joined the family."

"Right," Moe said awkwardly.

"But you didn't."

"I didn't." He'd managed to dodge that one. Barely. He'd dated Kimi for a few months—just long enough for both of them to realize it would never work.

He excused himself, thoughts of Spencer falling from his mind as he tried to figure out where he was going to come up with approximately two hundred thousand dollars in two months and make himself both a manager and an owner.

~

AMY STARED AT DR. NASH LEHAM UNDER THE unforgiving lights of his office's exam room. When had artificial insemination become so expensive? All those add-on costs such as testing, the storage of extracted eggs and doctor visits added up. Especially since the success rate wasn't one hundred percent.

"Is there some sort of employee discount?" she asked hopefully, even though she knew there wouldn't be.

She'd asked Moe to marry her, then purchased a house to combine their two households and have room for a family, and she couldn't afford to make a baby, let alone two.

"We don't do in vitro here in Blueberry Springs," Nash replied. "You also don't work here any longer."

"I still have my nursing certificate. It's up-to-date."

Mark your calendars! She was officially pleading.

"Do you have a health plan at the pub?" Nash glanced at her with those bright blue eyes, obviously taking in more of her story than she figured the average doctor would.

"It's not good enough to cover this."

"You've been married less than a month. These things take time." His tone was even and kind. He was using his doctor's voice; the one reserved for patients who were quickly approaching the unhinged stage.

She didn't speak, unsure what to say to a man who assumed she had a traditional marriage. How did Nash always manage to stay out of the Blueberry Springs gossip circles when they swirled all around him like whirlpools?

"Do you expect to have issues with fertility?" he asked.

She gave a quick shrug.

"Have you been tested?"

She shook her head, her ears heating. She'd worked comfortably alongside Nash off and on for years, which was why she'd come to him. She didn't expect to feel this bashful or embarrassed.

"I assume everything is in order," she mumbled.

"Well then?" He was probing, and she'd counted on him simply setting her up and sending her off.

"Moe and I don't have that kind of marriage."

Nash remained silent, loosely clasping his clipboard, his head tilted to the side.

"Our plan is to have children together via artificial insemination."

Nash still didn't speak, giving her way too much conversational rope with which to hang herself. He didn't need to know the embarrassing truth about how her well-meaning best friend had swooped in to help her, when her love life kept pushing up daisies. She didn't have all the time in the world to have kids. She needed this to work. "It's a platonic marriage. A marriage between friends."

"But you two dated in the past?"

Why did everyone get hung up on that part?

She cleared her throat and rolled her hunched shoulders back. "We're in a good place right now. Sex would only complicate things."

"It would also provide children at no cost."

He handed her an ovulation-tracking calendar with a dry smile. She heaved a sigh, wondering how she was going to break it to her husband that the only way they could afford to conceive kids was the old-fashioned way—by getting naked.

Amy pulled a few pints of dark ale behind the bar in Brew Babies, her eyes drifting toward the back office, where Moe had been working all night.

He'd spent the afternoon with Kimi discussing her partnership offer, and Amy had spent the afternoon in the doctor's office. She hoped he had better news than she did. Maybe news that they were secretly wealthy, so she wouldn't have to go begging her parents for money to provide them with grandchildren. Perfect little beings full of love, laughter and joy.

She knew her folks didn't mind being asked to help, and that it made them feel needed, but she was getting tired of frequently finding herself in a position where she had to ask. Although with her mom having her pay for the wedding, she might be done saying yes to bailing Amy out.

Either way, she would sort something out. But in the meantime, she'd work on a fail-safe plan, like Moe always did.

Moe. Sweet Moe. He'd been uncharacteristically quiet, not even asking how her appointment had gone when she'd slipped in ten minutes late for her shift. She kept waiting for him to come out of the office and pour drafts alongside her, to ensure the beer flowed fast, like it always did on a profitable poker night. But instead he'd spent more time at his desk than usual, and she wondered if maybe things hadn't gone well for him today, either.

The pub, warm and boisterous, enveloped her

in its familiar buzz, from the *whoop* of a hand of cards being won to the kitchen bell dinging to indicate an order was up. The jukebox started, playing some tired old song from the seventies, which meant John Abcott would be up dancing with his new wife, Gloria, in no time.

Amy glanced to her right again, her attention pulled to the hallway that led to the alley, the washrooms, the small brew room and Moe's small office. He'd been popping out to chat with customers almost every hour on the hour, the tension easing off of him before he'd go back in again. He was due for another break soon.

Something cold spilled over Amy's hand and, sighing, she tipped the glass to pour off what Moe would certainly call too much head. He claimed it was her impatience that caused her to produce too much foam, but she knew it was because she didn't have the special knack he did. But tonight it was because there were way too many beers to pour, as they were understaffed without him out here. He needed to get that agreement in place with Kimi so he could download the dreary work to her and return to the bar and the life he loved.

Mary Alice Bernfield sat a few stools down, trying the new sampler of the latest brews Moe had tapped late last night.

"I do like this one," she told Marissa, pointing to a darker beer.

A loud whoop went up at the table behind her, causing her to jump.

"Amy! This round you're working on is on me!" Frankie Smith, the winner of the hand, called out.

She nodded, keeping an eye on the table beside him, which was full of smokejumpers in training. They were getting loud and she made a mental note to be a little slower in topping up their drinks.

"Want a pint of the dark?" Marissa asked Mary Alice, reaching up to pat at her glossy black bun and fix a hairpin.

The woman shook her head. "This'll do. I need to head home soon. Just closed up the store for the night and was in need of a nightcap."

"You came to the right place." Over her shoulder, Marissa asked Amy, "Did more soda come in? We're almost out."

"There's more in the brew room."

"Nope. This is it."

Amy glanced out at the crowd. They had a few designated drivers in the house tonight, such as Oz Reiter, who no longer drank. They all got free soda and refills upon refills. That combined with the rye and Cokes that were on special tonight meant they'd be out of soft drinks by tomorrow.

"Moe ordered some last week. Didn't it come in?"

Marissa shook her head. "Two shipments have come in, but no soda."

"Weird." Kimi really needed to step in and take care of these things for Moe, as they were slipping through the cracks. There was only so much one man could keep track of. "I'll see if he can put a rush on it."

Mary Alice turned to Amy. "Where *is* that hunky hubby of yours?"

"Hunky?" Amy had just picked up the tray holding the half-dozen beers she'd poured for Frankie's table, and nearly dropped it when she glanced up, spying the man in question leaning against the poster-covered wall where the hallway and pub's big room met.

Moe caught Amy's eye and winked before bending to hear what Gran, an elderly lady who liked to keep most people in town on their toes with her quick wit, was saying. Amy bet she was suggesting, once again, that Moe try his hand at distilling sherry, and that she, a seasoned connoisseur, could personally critique each new batch, pro bono.

Kind and casual as always, Moe was smiling, giving Gran as much time as she needed to state her case. Recently, the woman had become a bit of a night owl, a change in medications resetting her internal clock, and she found the pub a lively and fun place to spend her newfound energy, much to the chagrin of her granddaughters, Cynthia and Beth.

"I do like him with his shorter hair," Mary Alice stated, turning to study Amy's face.

The clean, crisp lines of his cheekbones still took her by surprise, and she half-expected an unruly lock to fall into his eyes. "Yeah, it's nice," Amy said noncommittally, hoisting the tray once again, determined not to provide any body language tells that would give the gossip something to go on where her attraction to Moe was concerned.

"Any more of those wedding kisses happening?" Mary Alice called, her voice carrying across the pub just as the jukebox song ended.

Amy nearly tripped, her eyes flying to Moe's. His glittered in amusement as he escorted Gran to the door where the town's new cab driver, Ahmed, was waiting to transport her back to the nursing home.

"Take care," Moe said, leaning down so Gran could place a dry kiss on his cheek. He disappeared back into his office as Amy neared Frankie's table.

It was poker night. Didn't Moe remember he was supposed to stay out on the floor to help handle things? *Real* things like mixing drinks and settling tabs.

How long would it take him to get Kimi on board and all this taken care of?

"You should get another poker table," suggested Dale, one of the men waiting for a turn to join the game.

"Ricky, I can see your cards," Amy called over her shoulder to the player with the royal flush. He instantly pulled his hand to his chest, eyes darting back and forth to see if anyone else had managed a peek.

"Moe just brought in a third one this week," she told Dale, weaving her way between chairs to deliver the beers.

"Why do we have to use a special table? Can't we just play wherever?"

"You can ask."

"No way," one of the men piped up, having overheard the conversation. "It's not the same without the felt-covered poker tables."

"Plus, they have cup holders so you don't knock your beer over," Ricky added, causing Dale to sigh.

Moe had found the latest poker table in a pawn shop. He had been slowly adding tables after Nicola Samuels-Haber, the town's community planner who also planned community events, had stopped running poker night in the community center. The weekly event at Brew Babies was the most profitable by far, with drink and appetizer sales going through the roof.

"I still say you need another," Dale replied, his arms crossed.

He was the only one who seemed to be waiting for a table to play at tonight and, according to Moe, a lineup increased demand.

"Can I get you another pale ale?" she asked him as she continued to weave between seated players to deliver fresh brews and retrieve empty glasses.

"Keep 'em coming," he replied with another sigh.

The table of smokejumpers behind her erupted in laughter just before one of the poker players laid down his cards and all the rest groaned in defeat. Frankie leaned back as Amy reached to place his fresh beer in the cup holder between him and Scott Malone. Frankie's elbow hit the glass, sending the frigid liquid splashing all over her.

He apologized and stood in one smooth move, poising a napkin over Amy's chest before catching himself.

"My fault," she said with a gasp, setting down her tray. Marissa tossed a small towel across the table on her way by. "Accidents happen."

"Too bad your shirt wasn't white," one of the smokejumpers joked as he pushed his chair aside so she could access the puddle that had dripped off of her and onto the floor.

"Yeah, I love getting beer stains out of white clothes."

"Dude, not cool," Scott replied, standing. The town's only law officer wasn't in uniform, but held himself with such authority it was as good as wearing a badge.

"Just saying," the smokejumper said. "A little wet T-shirt contest would keep things lively." He shot a grin to his buddies and elbowed the closest one, and their laughter hit headache levels. These guys had spent the day learning how to leap out of perfectly good planes into fire zones, and the mix of alcohol and residual adrenaline seemed to be amping up their testosterone levels.

Chair legs screeched on the floor as the men of Blueberry Springs stood in unison, facing the smokejumpers, a solid wall of support.

"Guys, it's all cool." Amy gave a light laugh. "Really. It's fine."

"You're not a piece of meat," Scott said.

"I know that," she said. "How about an appetizer? Anyone hungry?"

Her suggestion was ignored.

The jukebox was now pumping out something country, and the mouthy smokejumper snagged

Amy, tugging the towel from her grip. "As an apology, dance with me."

She pushed against his chest. "That's not an apology, and I'm working."

Before she could do anything more, Moe was there, forcing himself between the two of them.

"She's not interested," he said, his jaw flexing.

"Says who?" The smokejumper pushed out his chest, shoulders back. "I saw her first."

He gave Moe a shove, but Moe was right there in the guy's face, his spine straight, arms loose at his sides. The men from Blueberry Springs crowded behind him, jostling Amy out of the way.

Moe held up his left hand, fingers splayed to highlight the wedding band on his ring finger. Obviously grasping the significance, the man glanced uncertainly at Amy, a muscle twitching in his jaw.

"Didn't see her ring. Next time spring for a bigger one and mark your territory properly."

Frankie and Scott pressed forward again, and Amy, unable to reach Moe, snagged Frankie's elbow. She didn't quite dare to restrain the lawman.

Moe's neck had turned red and he shifted from foot to foot, his right fist clenching as though crushing a particularly thick beer can.

"Stay away from my wife." He glowered at the smokejumper, who lifted his hands to the sky, his expression one of mocking innocence.

Amy was certain Moe was going to swing.

But then the smokejumper begrudgingly took his seat. Moe continued glaring at the man's backup crew until they all sat as well, at which point the cluster of men from Blueberry Springs started easing back.

"You okay?" Moe led Amy away from the poker tables, and when he reached out to lightly touch her elbow, an arc of sparks zipped up her spine. A possessive blaze in his brown eyes suggested he wanted to kiss her madly, just to prove she was his. It made her want to believe, just for a second, that what they had was real, and that it wasn't going away. That maybe he *wanted* to make their children the old-fashioned way, and that together they would discover how to have what they'd always been seeking, but had never found.

Amy held her breath and leaned closer. Just in case he wanted to make a point to the people in the pub about whose wife she was.

His shirt brushed the bare skin of her arm as he moved into her personal space. She shivered in anticipation and tipped her head back so he'd have better access to her lips. She caught the subtle hint of his aftershave and inhaled deeply to capture the fullness of it, of him, of everything that came with that wonderful scent.

In the distance, under the sad guitar strumming from the jukebox, the office phone rang.

Moe blinked twice, then stepped away. "If you need anything…" He gave the table of firefighters a meaningful look. "I'll be in the office."

Amy nodded, feeling off center and as though she'd just missed a train. As if she'd been on the platform with the right ticket, waiting for the doors to open, but when they had, crowds had rushed around her, and when they'd thinned the train was already gone.

Trying to hide her disappointment, she scurried back to the bar to collect herself, ignoring the mess of spilled beer on the floor back at the table. Never, in all her years, had she seen that side of Moe. One where he looked ready to deck a guy.

And it had been over her.

What did it mean? And why did it seem to amp up the electricity inside her like their wedding kiss had?

It was as if the Moe she'd married was completely different than the one she'd dated all those years ago. He wasn't more daring or adventurous, not really. He was just more…primally attractive. More unexpected and take-charge, in a way that made her breath catch.

Anticipation. That's all it was. She was anticipating his next move like she was Jane and he was Tarzan, ready to sweep her away.

But she didn't want a kiss from him. She didn't want him to sweep her off her feet. He was Moe, her steady, reliable best friend, who was married to her so they could have children. He wasn't about to turn into the daredevil alpha she seemed to need in order to keep her interested, to settle her.

"What was that all about?" Mary Alice asked, her gaze tracking Amy as she moved to the dishwasher set under the bar.

"Just drunks."

"I meant with Moe."

Amy glanced up. "What do you mean?"

"He looked ready to devour you."

Amy opened her mouth to shoot down that comment, but found she had no argument. He *had* looked ready to devour her. So ready she'd leaned in like a fool. Just like she had last night on the floor by the couch.

She needed to get a grip, then somehow lock it down so she didn't lose it again.

"Don't you say I'm seeing things," Mary Alice crowed. "He was gonna kiss you so good your hair was going to curl!"

"It's already wavy," Amy retorted, a betraying heat pushing its way into her cheeks.

"And now I think I know why."

Amy found her gaze drifting toward the office. All she knew was that if she kept wanting her friend to kiss her and to make her weak at the knees, things were going to get awkward in ways that were *not* part of their marriage deal.

But then again, when it came to listing awkward things that were outside the parameters of their marriage pledge, so was their only currently viable plan for starting a family.

And she was soon going to have to break the news to her husband.

CHAPTER 4

"*S*orry for acting like that." The smokejumper who'd suggested he'd like to see through Amy's wet shirt tossed enough bills to cover his table's tab onto the bar, plus some, and met Moe's eye before cutting his gaze away.

"No harm, no foul," Moe said, trying to be polite. Hours later, he still wanted to grab the guy and do something uncharacteristically violent to him.

The man gave a sharp nod and exited after his friends. They'd been model customers from the "incident" until closing.

Moe placed most of the cash in Amy's tip jar, trying to reclaim control over his anger.

He needed to cool it. Let it all go.

Amy deserved better. Women as a whole deserved better.

"Did anyone do a sweep of the bathrooms?" he asked.

Marissa called out that she had, but Amy kept her head down as she cleared away empty glasses, avoiding his glances and not making eye contact as she moved past him with glassware for the dishwasher.

She'd had half the men in town backing her in a situation she'd been successfully laughing off, and he'd swept in and thumped his chest. She probably hated him right now.

But she was his wife. He'd been within bounds, hadn't he?

She seemed a bit off tonight, though. Had she noticed the way he'd almost kissed her, almost claimed her like a caveman for all to see?

Of course she had. He'd be a fool to think otherwise.

Although her awkwardness could also be due to the way he'd almost kissed her last night, too. He'd laid himself on top of her like he had the right to get intimate with her on the floor of their living room.

He was hopeless. Like a randy teenager all over again. Only worse, because he knew exactly what he was missing with Amy. How had they always slipped back into the "friend" zone when they'd had that heat?

Marissa had removed her fake lashes, leaving them on the bar, where they looked scarily similar to a pair of large dead spiders. She was counting out her tips, and Amy grabbed her own, trying to give Marissa some extra as thanks for helping her stay on top of one of her tables during a rush, as well as cleaning up the spilled beer.

"Nah, next time just wade in when I need it," she said, folding the bills back into Amy's hand. She tucked her tip money in her purse, and since she'd come in earlier than Amy, said good-night, leaving Moe to finish closing up with his wife.

He locked the doors after Marissa left and killed the jukebox, enjoying the abrupt silence.

"How was your night?" he asked, emptying the second dishwasher so they could reload it. "That big tip should help pay for the wedding."

"I don't think leaving the taps open on poker night is a good idea. And if you'd been out here instead of hiding in the office you would have made tips, too."

Moe caught himself stepping back. Was Amy, who never stressed over anything, freaking out about money? Was that what had her acting odd?

"You know I'm planning to pay half the wedding costs, and I'm sorry if I overstepped tonight."

She shrugged, her cheeks pinking. "It's fine."

"It was my wedding, too."

"Fine. Pay for half."

So was that it then? They were good? They were going to move past how he'd allowed his newfound, alpha, chest-thumping personality to come out and play? Because he had a feeling that if a guy treated her that way again he'd be right back in the ring. Only next time, maybe a little less restrained.

Amy still wasn't looking at him, and when he moved into her physical space, reaching high to place a margarita glass in the rack above her, she found a reason to sidle away and give him more room instead of owning it like usual.

Had she tuned in to the fact that he'd wanted to kiss her in front of those guys? Kiss her until her lips turned cherry red and they forgot about the outside world?

Moe sighed. Now all he could think of was kissing those perfect lips of hers.

He ran a hand down his face, then glanced around the pub. He didn't want to stare at the computer screen again, but staying out here with her was dangerous. Maybe if he concentrated on the cleanup he could pour his energy into that instead of imagining what it would be like to kiss her again. Lay her out over one of the poker tables, or press her up against the quiet jukebox. He bet her mouth tasted as sweet as the soda she'd been sipping all night to stay hydrated.

He ran his hand down his face again as if the move could sweep away his unwanted thoughts.

He cleared his throat. "I have some stuff to do in the office."

"You're going to leave me to deal with all of this?" She was looking at him now, all right. Hands on hips. Head tilted to the side, eyes narrowed.

He found himself moving outside her strike zone.

"I have work." He angled a thumb toward the office. She'd married him to help her, not to have him lusting after her. And if he stayed out here... Lust central.

"You always clean up with me. And I thought you talked to Kimi today about your workload."

Spying a cloth, he snatched it up and began furiously wiping at the rings staining the countertop.

Amy had her head quirked, studying him. "You're avoiding me, aren't you?"

There was a hint of uncertainty and vulnerability in her tone and he quickly said, "It's just stress. Lots of work." He waved toward the office. "If you want to head home I can finish cleaning up."

"What happened in the meeting with Kimi?" She took a step, breaching the safety zone of personal space he'd established. When he retreated, she moved forward yet again.

"What? Nothing."

There was no eye contact avoidance now as she stared at him, head-on.

She leaned into him, hands pressing against his chest, her large eyes focusing on his lips.

"Did she try to kiss you?"

"What?" Moe sputtered, at a loss. That question had come so far out of left field he felt like he was on the wrong field altogether.

"What were you thinking when you were facing down that smokejumper tonight?"

He struggled to change the direction of his thoughts in order to keep up with hers.

"That he'd crossed the line."

"You looked different than usual. More...primal."

"It's the haircut."

She was standing much too close, the scent of the spilled ale mixing with her perfume and feeling so familiar. So much like something he wanted.

She snugged up against him, and it was like someone had sucked all the oxygen from the room in order to supply him with enough willpower to keep from taking her into his arms and kissing her until their souls merged into one and the world settled into place around them.

"I'm fed up with guys treating women like a piece of meat." He sidestepped to adjust a stack of coasters, brushing her away. "Seriously. That's all."

Her shoulders dropped a notch and a flicker of something that looked like disappointment zipped through her brown eyes.

She returned her attention to the dishwasher, not glancing up as she said, "I can clean up."

"No, I can help. The office stuff isn't going anywhere."

"You were up past five, trying to catch up on everything."

"How do you know? You went home at two. And speaking of which, how are we going to deal with working this late-at-night thing when we have kids?"

She let out a sigh so long and laden with frustration that he leaned forward to try and catch her expression. "What?" he asked.

"In vitro is really expensive."

"Yes."

She looked up at him, her eyes filled with such pain his heart hurt just looking at her.

"We'll figure it out," he said quietly, his mind racing for an easy answer.

There wasn't one.

In vitro. Purchasing the pub. Their house. His

father's house. The wedding bills. How was he going to pay for it all?

"Did you finalize the agreement with Kimi at least?"

This would be the time to tell her about Cesar's ridiculous, generous offer to purchase the pub if Moe made his three months as the manager. About how the business would be liquidated if not.

But what if she told him to put their dream of having kids on a shelf—a shelf that might be forgotten until it was too late? He couldn't do that to her. He'd made a promise. One that was more important than owning a pub.

A pub that supplied their livelihoods.

"Kimi and I are going to work together." He quickly looked for a way to change the topic before Amy started a fight about Kimi taking over and claiming more ownership than she should. He had plenty to learn about this business, and would be getting more from Cesar's daughter than the equivalent of a few promotional ideas, in terms of reciprocation with their partnership. "You had your doctor's appointment today?"

"It's ridiculous that she's got you working two jobs in here. She needs to ask the estate to take care of the business end. You don't want or need this headache."

"Is there any chance you've been saving up for

in vitro?" he asked.

She winced, her right eye closing.

His stomach dropped. She hadn't planned for the cost.

"Nash suggested that if money was an issue... well..." She suddenly looked shy, her cheeks flaming red.

It took Moe a second to catch up, and then his mind stopped working completely.

Oh.

Oh.

Because when it came to making babies, there was only one way they could save a lot of money. And that meant breaking the first unwritten rule of their pledge.

AMY WAS SO EMBARRASSED. MOE HAD TURNED RED right up to the tips of his ears when he'd realized that neither of them had the money to make babies the way they'd planned, and that there was only one way to proceed. The way that cost them nothing but a few intimate moments together.

"I know you didn't sign on for this," she said.

"For making babies?" He cleared his throat a few times. His cheeks were pinking up again.

They were still cleaning up the pub; cleaning,

organizing, restocking with their usual flow.

"The agreement was always that it would be in vitro." She struggled to find the right words, a hitch in her chest preventing her from acting as casual as she wanted to. "I understand if this is a deal-breaking oversight and…and if you want to leave me."

Moe's movements slowed. "Right," he said, his voice flat.

"So?" she asked after an extended silence.

"I'm in this for the long haul." He looked at her, his eyes a kind, deep brown that made her think of happiness and trust. "Maybe there's a solution somewhere. Did Nash say how long we have until the risks and complications go up due to age?"

"He didn't have to. I already know." She let out a frustrated groan. "This wasn't how it was supposed to work out. I'm sorry I'm not more organized. I should have had a proper plan."

This was what her mother had been getting at. This was why Faith wanted Amy to be more like her sister. But Jillian had made mistakes, too, just none this big.

Moe grabbed Amy in a hug, holding her tight. "If you had a proper plan I'd probably ask to have your head checked." She tried to push out of his arms, but he refused to release her. "You know I'm your friend because I like you just the way you are.

Don't ever change. I shouldn't have assumed you'd have all the details taken care of. That's my thing, not yours, and I dropped the ball."

"Don't blame yourself." He'd loosened his hold and she was able to lean back so she could watch his expression.

"We will figure this out. Together."

"Are you trying to be my rock in the storm?"

"I believe it's an anchor." He released her to tap his chin and peer at the ceiling, as though trying to recall his wedding vows.

Amy let out a soft chuckle. "I love you."

"You always say that when I save the day."

"Well, it's true."

"For the record, I have not yet agreed to have sex with you."

"You can't refuse me for long. We live in the same house. All I have to do is walk across the living room in lingerie and you'll knock me up so fast our children will all grow up to be race car drivers."

He laughed, leaning against the counter, arms crossed. "You're mighty full of yourself."

She lifted her palms to the sky, and said, "Your fault. You've built up my ego by telling me repeatedly how hot I am."

"I might just have to knock you up the old-fashioned way so I can enjoy your hotness one or two last times." He lightly touched her lower back, nudging her aside. She inhaled sharply and arched away as sparks zipped through her. She whirled, hands on the bar behind her, chest out.

What was *that*?

Sparks. Seriously. Every time.

Why? Why now?

"You could say excuse me," she said, her voice faint and breathless.

"I could." He shifted to step past her. She echoed his move, blocking him.

He was watching her, trying to figure out what game she was playing. She wasn't sure herself, only that the talk of having babies had her pulling up a few choice memories. Hot memories of her and Moe locked in a sweaty embrace.

She licked her lips.

"You need a little manhandling from time to time," he said, his own voice rumbly and low. "It breaks your human-contact dry spell."

"My dry spell isn't as bad as yours. You're practically a monk."

"Hence my affinity for brewing things. I have all this…" he lowered his voice again "…*energy* to redirect."

"Really?"

"Really."

It was getting deliciously warm in the pub.

"Is there anything you like to do other than brew things?" She picked at a spot on his shirt where he'd been splashed by grenadine while mixing up an Alabama slammer for an early customer. When she looked up at him again, his eyes were dark pools. "To burn off that excess energy."

He allowed his gaze to travel down her torso, as if he was considering the possibilities. "I still haven't said yes, you know."

"You will."

And she swore her spine would melt the moment he did indeed say yes.

MOE SAT AT THE KITCHEN TABLE, WAITING FOR AMY to come home from a baby shower for who-knew-who. It seemed all their friends did was have kids these days, no doubt adding pressure to Amy's own quest to reproduce.

He'd looked over their medical insurance and hadn't found a single loophole they could leverage to go the artificial insemination route and have it covered.

Amy came in, slamming the front door behind her, a sure sign she was deep in thought. She entered the kitchen and stopped in the middle of the room.

"What?" she asked.

"In vitro is really expensive." She already knew that, obviously. "Our health plan doesn't cover it." He closed the binder where he kept his medical receipts and insurance papers. "Money's going to be a bit of an issue."

It was down to choosing between a baby and the pub. And they couldn't afford either one.

Amy joined him at the table, throwing herself into the chair across from him. "I'm sorry. I should have looked into this before we got married."

"I could cancel our honeymoon," Moe said, glancing at the sheet of numbers he'd been working on. "That'll save us a few hundred."

"I was looking forward to our getaway."

"You just want to be pampered."

"Of course. Plus, the adventure of going somewhere with my best friend who never seems to leave town adds a certain appeal."

"I leave town."

He glanced at the numbers again. Going on the trip wasn't going to make a big difference, and he had been looking forward to the freedom of traveling with Amy.

His wife reached over and snagged his sheet of calculations. She skimmed it, able to decipher his scrawls. She slid the paper back to him.

"Well?" he asked.

She gnawed on her pinkie nail before giving him a tentative look, her nose scrunched adorably. "Is it wrong that I want to vote that we keep the cheapo honeymoon and procreate the old-fashioned way?"

His mouth went dry, and it was as though his eyes had become a pair of runaway horses. No matter how hard he tried to pull up, they continued to drift down Amy's physique. He knew exactly what the old-fashioned way would feel like, sound like and taste like.

He inhaled swiftly and leaned back in his chair. She was his friend—his wife of convenience.

A wife who wanted him to hit the sheets with her like a real couple trying to conceive.

His mind was unable to find its way through the thick haze of longing in order to list pertinent questions he should ask so they could formulate a plan.

Amy leaned forward, her hand outstretched, her rose tattoo flexing as she quickly made her case. "We've always seamlessly fallen back into being friends any time we've gotten intimate. It was never uncomfortable or awkward. We could do it again."

"Twice."

She tipped her head to the side, confusion creasing her smooth forehead.

"Two kids. We'll have to do this twice."

Could he take her to bed, and then go back to being friends again? Sure, they'd accomplished it before, but this time felt different. *He* felt different. Like he might not be able to make that smooth transition back to the friend zone.

"I don't know." Moe pushed away from the table. He well remembered what it had been like living with two arguing parents before Lily was born and his mother ditched them. "It's risky if we can't settle back into being friends again. We live in one house. We're married. Kids will be coming into all of this and we work together at the same pub." There wasn't enough wiggle room in their situation if things went wrong this time.

"We'll keep our separate bedrooms," Amy said. "I mark off my ovulation on a calendar and we just… You know. Lights off, I come into your room and the magic happens."

Moe laughed despite himself. "The magic happens?"

She was blushing, and it was endearing. But it wasn't the magic that he was worried about. It was afterward, and wanting that magic at times when he shouldn't.

"Why don't you ask your parents for financial assistance?"

"I shouldn't still be going to my parents every

time I want something. I'm married. I'm thirty. It's time to grow up, settle down and act like an adult."

Moe felt his right eyebrow involuntarily quirk in question. She always went to her parents, and they never failed to help. Had she already asked them, or had she decided it was finally time for a bit more independence? "So you're not going to ask them?"

Amy sighed impatiently. She was definitely getting the whole wife thing down pat. "Do you have some fresh ideas that are better than mine?"

"Asking your parents was my better idea." He moved to the kitchen counter and began running water to wash the pots and pans, unable to stay still.

Amy followed.

"We didn't get married to have sex," he said.

Why did this feel like such a big deal? It wasn't as though they'd never seen each other naked or something.

Amy crossed her arms, her lower lip forming a tight line as she leaned a hip against the counter. "Was sharing a bed that much of a hardship in the past?"

Moe laughed so he wouldn't think about how much of a hardship it *hadn't* been, making love to her. They were good together. Just not quite the right fit for long-term, and pushing across that boundary again felt like tempting fate and trying to cash in on what could possibly be waning good luck.

"You aren't friends with any of your exes," he pointed out.

"Except you."

"Except me. And this time the stakes are pretty high if things don't settle out."

"We're going to make things unsettled?"

"You've spent time with me in the bedroom." He stepped into her space, lowering his voice. "Things are going to get *very* unsettled."

Amy giggled. "Is that a yes?"

"It means…" He'd leaned toward her like he was going to caress her, hold her, kiss her. He caught himself and straightened. "I'll think about it."

Probably a whole lot more than he should.

"We do still have that honeymoon booked…"

She was literally trying to kill him with his own impure thoughts, wasn't she?

"It's a getaway," he mumbled, his throat tight with longing.

The last thing he needed right now was to start thinking about a genuine honeymoon situation where he and his new wife created babies in the way nature had intended.

CHAPTER 5

When Amy answered the door, her mother pushed past her, entering the house with a large potted plant in her arms and a canvas bag slung over one shoulder.

"What are you doing?" Amy asked.

"Since you and Moe are planning to have kids right away, I thought I'd bring you something to practice on."

Amy peered out the door as though expecting a small child to come toddling in after her.

"This," Faith said, pushing the plant into Amy's arms, "needs watering at least once a week, fertilizer every two. It's nontoxic."

Responsibility and commitment. In plant form.

"I don't have a green thumb." Amy pointed to the languishing plant in the front window. It looked a tiny bit better than it had when she'd moved in, likely because Moe had babied it. In other words, actually cared for it a bit: watered it and trimmed back the dead parts. "And I hardly think a plant is the same thing as a child." Amy tried to hand the pot back to her mother. "Anyway, neither Moe nor I can afford to have kids."

He still hadn't given her an answer to her between-the-sheets solution. Sure, it had been less than thirty-six hours since her proposal, and he'd been working almost nonstop the entire time, but who was counting?

Her mother eyed her suspiciously, refusing to accept the plant. Amy gave up and set it on the coffee table.

"It needs more light." Her mother moved it closer to the window before facing Amy again. "You got married to have children. And you can't *afford* it?"

"Well, not in vitro, that's for sure."

Her mother shook her head. Her lips were pinched, thin and white. It was the I'm-not-impressed-but-don't-know-what-I'm-going-to-do-about-you look. Amy was quite familiar with it, as well as the burst of problem solving that typically followed.

She held her breath hopefully.

"Your father and I are no longer bailing you out."

"I didn't ask you to bail me out," Amy said indignantly.

"You think I don't recognize that cute and hopeful look you just gave me? It pulls at me, right here." Faith tapped her chest. Her shoulders were squared as she focused on adjusting her wedding band so the diamonds were facing outward. "You're a married woman now, and your father feels it's time I backed off and let you figure things out instead of jumping in to help. Especially if you plan on becoming a mother. The last thing you need is me hovering and telling you what to do. My own mom was like that and it drove me around the bend."

She placed her hands on her hips and surveyed the living room. After taking a few steps, she tipped her head to peer behind a tall bookcase. "You're going to need to attach this to the wall. I don't want my grandkids getting hurt if they climb it and it tips over on them."

"We can't afford artificial insemination. There will be no grandkids."

"I'm sure the two of you can figure something out," she said dryly. "You are married, after all."

She pointed to the framed mountain photos Moe had hung. "And I like this. It's about time you displayed a few of these, after all that work and expense you went to learning how to capture such stunning images. You were good, you know."

"Sex wasn't part of the deal." Amy sat on the couch, the weight of her failures settling over her.

Why couldn't she have turned out more like her sister? Jillian had made it look so easy to be perfect. She would never have ended up in a situation like this. "What's wrong with me?" Amy moaned.

"Is that a rhetorical question or do you want a real answer from someone who loves you and has known you all your life?"

Amy winced.

"Well, for one," her mother said lightly, as though Amy had chosen option number two, "you are the most scattered and unorganized person I have ever met. You also tend to expect other people to clean up your messes while you go your merry way, never learning from your mistakes. I feel as though I'm partly to blame for that, though."

Amy felt the sting of her mother's words strike deep inside. "Do you wish I was more like Jillian?" she asked softly, voicing what had been in her mind for decades.

Faith sat beside her on the couch, her face marked with sorrow. "Of course I want you to be more like she was. I don't want to be *worrying* about you all the time."

"You don't need to worry about me."

Her mom gave her a slightly exasperated look.

"Really," Amy stated, wishing she could say it with more conviction.

"Honey…" She pulled Amy's hands into her lap with a laugh. "You and your best friend got married, and you promised to give him children, but you didn't even think about how much it would cost. Of *course* I worry about you. You're paying for a wedding and a mortgage instead of making do in one of your old rentals, with a simple ceremony."

"The house was Moe's idea," she said, unable to keep the hurt from her voice. "And my rent was more than my share of the monthly mortgage."

"But Amy, honey, how's Moe going to buy the pub if the two of you are spending your money and tying up your credit on everything else?"

"He's not buying the pub. He's just the interim manager."

"That's not what I heard from his mother."

"His mom?" Moe hadn't spoken to her in years.

"She's been chatting with Lily, apparently. I ran into Farrah when I was in the city the other day. She was there for a conference and we got to talking. Anyway, Lily told her he was given an unreasonably lucrative offer, but he's not acting like he's going to take it."

Amy felt her mind stutter. Moe hadn't said a thing about buying the pub.

"What man doesn't want to own the place he's been building up over the years?" Her mother stood. "With things up in the air with the current ownership, I'm sure he'd like to take the offer and secure things."

That would explain why he'd been poring over their finances, and had suggested they cancel their honeymoon despite that flicker of hope and longing she'd seen in his expression.

Now Amy felt selfish, as though she was luring him away from what he might want most. "Why didn't he tell me?"

But things were starting to click. He wasn't happy managing the pub...and yet he was doing it. He'd accepted Kimi's help, which meant he wanted to figure out how to run the place, be the one in charge. The owner.

One of her mother's eyebrows lifted. "He made promises to you and..." She shrugged. "You can't always have it all. Money is a finite resource."

"But he shouldn't have chosen me! He should have chosen the pub, if that's what he wants."

What if she was wasting his life now instead of just her own? She had to find a way to make this work for him.

She shook her head. "This marriage isn't a mistake."

But she felt as though she was lying.

Faith slung the canvas sack over her shoulder.

"What's in the bag?" Amy asked, her mind still reeling with Moe's news.

"Baby books. But maybe I'm a bit ahead of myself."

MOE STARED AT THE VAT OF FERMENTING HOPS AND tried to think through his situation with Amy—rationally. The problem was he was far too willing to help his wife create those babies without medical assistance, and that was making it darn near impossible to methodically work through a pro/con list about changing up their plans.

They both wanted a family, and to have it all right here and now. Children, a spouse, a bustling cheery home. Secure and happy, surrounded by the sounds of people who were there for you, who loved you...

The problem was they didn't have all the time in the world to save up and make that dream happen. If they wanted it, they were going to have to amend their agenda.

And have sex.

Together.

Repeatedly.

He chuckled softly. Scarcely a hardship.

He was going to say yes to the new plan, wasn't he?

Of course he was going to say yes. Had there ever been any doubt?

But their friendship—that was going to be tricky to navigate successfully as things heated up, then cooled, then heated up again.

He held the container of pH strips in his hands and stared at the tank. For the life of him he couldn't recall what the levels should be for the mash at this stage of the beer's fermentation. There was supposed to be a chart on the wall, but he didn't see it. He set the strips aside, wishing Cesar was still alive. He could use his experience and advice right about now. In the past month, Moe's whole life had become super complicated. Down a father figure, up a wife, as well as an extra job.

His phone buzzed in his pocket. He lifted it out to check the screen and nearly dropped it.

There was a social-media friend request from a name he hadn't heard in years. The last time, it had been spoken with bitterness by his father.

Farrah Harper.

His mother.

His thumb hovered over the Accept button,

then wavered over to Decline. His phone screen was shaking. No, it was him experiencing the tremors.

Farrah hadn't sent a well-meaning birthday card a few months late for his birthday in several years. Why was she reaching out now?

She probably didn't even know he was married.

Or maybe she'd heard and she wanted to be a part of his life, of his kids' lives. His kids could have a grandmother. An unreliable one.

His trembling thumb hit the Accept button and he cursed at the slip. He wasn't done thinking this through.

"Well, what's the worst that could happen?" he muttered to himself, pocketing the phone again. He was now friends with his mother. He could probably anticipate another twenty years of being ignored.

He sat on an old bar stool with wobbly legs that had been placed in the back room where the odd vat of beer was brewed on-site.

"Now what?" he said to the empty room. He wasn't ready to go home and face Amy and her proposal. Not yet.

"Talking to yourself?" asked a female voice, making him jump. Seconds later, a long slender leg and pale blue high heel came into view. Kimi. She leaned against the doorjamb, arms crossed.

"I'm a good listener," Moe stated.

"I do remember that about you." She stepped into the room. "Everything all right?"

"I can't remember what the pH should be." He waved idly toward the test strips.

"You need me," she teased.

"You're a brewmaster?"

"Only if something fabulous comes with that title. Otherwise I prefer something with a bit more bite." She walked to the vat, putting a little extra sashay into her movements. With a few fluid motions she was testing the beer, as though she'd been born doing it. And maybe she had. She'd been tagging along behind her father since she was a kid, and even more so in the past several months. She likely missed her dad with every step she took these days.

Rightfully, she should have inherited both pubs.

"It's coming along fine," she announced, after a moment or two of efficient checking. She tidied up after herself, then faced Moe. "So? Spencer said you might be having troubles coming up with the money to buy this place?"

"I just bought a house for my dad, then myself. Got married."

"I could front the money."

"Why?" She'd get more in the short term if the place was liquidated—half of whatever was salvaged. If she tied herself to the pub, she'd be signing up for more work, more headaches, although a steady trickle of money.

"Why?" She laughed at his surprise. "For more equity. This is my daddy's baby. Why wouldn't I want to keep it in the family?"

He'd previously felt uncomfortable about Cesar's generous bequest, but now even more so.

"I front the money you need," she said, "and you make me a part owner."

"Is that allowed?"

"This is business. Of course it is." She was moving around the room, touching objects as she went, encircling him. "We continue to manage the place together like with our current agreement." She stopped in front of him. "Nothing changes except we own it."

He'd signed that management agreement with her. She wouldn't do everything Cesar had, but they'd share some duties, split the cost on some bulk orders to save money. It would be better than doing it all alone, and he had a better shot at winning over the estate's lawyers, who were judging his abilities to run this place.

Of course, in accepting her help he'd also signed on to work with her on Brew, Too in the city. They'd share any managerial bonuses from the pubs' profits during this quarter—although he didn't expect to gain much, since business at Brew, Too was still languishing, despite Kimi's constant efforts.

"We both win," she said smoothly. Her eyes narrowed. "You look tired."

"So do you." And she did. Sad, too. But she still had that same determined spark in her gaze that she'd always had. She'd turn that city pub around; he was certain of it.

"You've been working two jobs for the past month," she said, her tone undecipherable. Sympathy and understanding? An impatience for him to get with the program and become a super manager? "Is your new wife giving you troubles about not being home more? It's a tough adjustment, having someone in your space all the time."

"She's cool."

"And that's why you're in long before your shift starts?"

It was true he was avoiding Amy, but not for the reasons Kimi likely assumed.

"You're also here early."

She smiled. "Your inventory is low. I was coming to check on it."

"Check up on me, you mean?"

She smiled again. "You're new at this. Although not with taking care of inventory."

"A few orders haven't come in." The delay had

caused them to change a few upcoming specials to accommodate for items that had failed to arrive. He didn't recall that ever being an issue before, and the timing didn't make him look great. Moe knew every tick could add up when the estate lawyers looked over his trial period performance. But at least he now had Kimi, as well as her systems and experience, on his side. And possibly her equity. But did he want to co-own with his ex? He wasn't so sure about that.

She angled an ear closer to him as though hard of hearing. "I'm sorry?"

"We're waiting for a few orders."

"There are no outstanding orders."

"Sure there are." He led her to the office, fired up the computer and signed in to the software she'd set up for them to send and track orders, as well as manage inventory. "There's an order for soda, rye, nacho chips…" His voice trailed off as he clicked on the orders page, which should be nice and full as automatic restocking went through after their Sunday morning inventory. The page was blank. He clicked over to fulfillment, in case the items were already on their way. Nothing. "What the…?"

"Moe." Kimi's voice was loaded with exaggerated patience, a tone that made his back straighten and his hands bunch into fists. "If you forget to order things or take inventory, own up to it, don't hide it from me."

"I'm not. I placed the order. *Twice* for some things. I even phoned about the missing soda."

"Then where is it?"

He pushed his chair away from the desk and lifted his palms, indicating the screen in front of him. "How about you and your fancy software tell me."

"Moe." There was that tone again. "Computers don't screw up and forget things."

"This one did."

They stared at each other for a moment, reminding Moe of an old Western movie showdown. Any moment one of them would draw their weapon and shoot.

"Look," he said patiently, hoping to disarm her so they could sort this out. "I know I'm learning a lot about the things your father used to do, but I've been filling orders for years. This isn't me."

"You could lose Brew Babies if you don't prove you can run this place in the spirit in which it was established." Kimi's tone was equally patient, which was annoying, but it gave him hope that she wasn't about to blow their whole deal sky-high. "And you know how anal my uncle, the executor, is about following my father's guidelines when assessing this."

He stood, his frustration returning. When Cesar's will had been read he'd been floored, flattered, flabbergasted. His old boss obviously hadn't felt his kids should have Brew Babies, but now he wondered if maybe he hadn't wanted Moe to have it, either. Maybe he'd handed both him and Kimi impossible tasks with their respective pubs, so they'd fail but not feel passed over. They'd recognize on their own that the task was beyond them and that liquidating both pubs was truly for the best. Even though Moe would walk away empty-handed and jobless.

"You need to get on top of these orders."

He bristled. "I know."

"I know the soda guy," a voice announced from the doorway. Moe turned, to see Spencer giving his sister a sheepish smile. "I got tired of waiting in the car."

Kimi leaned closer to Moe, her voice low and urgent. "I don't want to work with my gamer brother, but we're going to have to if we don't start doing better."

"I can call him. Dad and I used to shoot pool with him on Saturdays," Spencer said, cracking his knuckles, his eyes bright as he took in the office. "What do you need done?"

"You…you know the guy?"

"Yeah, of course. Kimi would, too, if she wasn't

so full of herself and came out to play from time to time." Spencer gave his sister a teasing grin.

"I was *working*."

"The jukebox is broken," Spencer stated.

"It's always breaking," Moe replied. He wasn't sure he wanted yet another Phipps helping, but if Spencer could get the soda order here in time for opening tomorrow he'd be grateful.

"Music's important," Spencer said.

"And jukeboxes are expensive," Moe replied. "We have a makeshift sound system for when it breaks. Can you get the soda here for tomorrow, do you think?"

Spencer nodded and shrugged.

"You can't keep driving someone's car in here," Kimi said to Moe. "That's not up to code."

"No, we have something different." Although that had been fun the one time they'd brought in a car with a pumping sound system to liven up the pub. That had been the beginning of Cesar giving him free rein, as he'd been tickled by Moe's creative problem solving—and the way the profits that night had doubled any other that month.

"You need to get to the bottom of the inventory issue," Kimi said, moving toward the door, her tone light but firm. She paused in the doorway, one hand on the frame as she turned to look back at him, her gaze resting on him for a moment too long. "Until tomorrow."

"Tomorrow?" Moe asked in confusion. But she was already gone, leaving him in the room with Spencer, who was still chatting about jukeboxes.

"Jukeboxes rock, man. They get people moving and spending. Customers can't leave until their song plays."

Moe nodded.

Spencer added, "I'll look into getting a new one."

"Sure. Fine." Whatever. "Tell Kimi I'll email her a list of activities she can try in her pub to help attract a larger clientele."

"Awesome. And fix that inventory thing. Kimi's really ticked about it."

"Yeah, thanks for the heads-up on that."

Spencer winked and followed his sister out, promising him a soon-to-arrive soda order.

Moe shut down the computer again, figuring that in vitro baby making was definitely off the table now, because there was no way he wanted to work shoulder to shoulder with the Phippses for the rest of his life. He needed to come up with a down payment and own his livelihood.

AMY RUBBED HER EYES AND PLODDED INTO THE kitchen, where Moe was notably absent. Brew Babies was closed until late afternoon, but it wouldn't be odd to find him there, seeing how many hours he'd been putting in. More, it seemed, since she'd confessed she couldn't afford artificial insemination. She flicked on the TV, sipping the coffee Moe had made before going out.

Last night she hadn't been able to sleep. Moe's protective behavior in the pub, then his awkward avoidance, followed by her mother calling her selfish, as well as revealing that Moe was in line to buy the pub, had Amy's thoughts running faster than trains in and out of Grand Central Station.

But most of all, she needed an answer on the baby question, because if they weren't going through with things, then she needed to set him free.

The front door opened and Moe walked in, his cheeks rosy from the blustery July rainstorm pelting down. He was carrying a small white bag.

"Brownies?" she asked hopefully. Mandy tended to pack her café's takeout items in white bags just like that.

Moe glanced at the sack. "No. No whiskey and gumdrop brownies. Something else." He pulled out a tiny pale yellow onesie. "It's from Mandy's, though. I couldn't resist. They're selling them at the front counter. Burke and Jill are raising money to help stock the new Friendship Center with some pool tables, hockey games and that kind of stuff."

He turned the tiny garment to face her so she could read the front:

My Daddy Thinks I'm Cute.

"Aw…" Amy climbed off the couch and inspected the outfit. It was super soft cotton. "Who's it for?"

"Our firstborn."

A wave of heat flowed through her. Was he saying yes to their new—and only—plan?

"What if our firstborn isn't cute?" she asked.

He gave her a look as though she'd just confessed to something awful. "Parents never think their kids aren't cute. It's a good thing you have me on board, 'cause you're going to be a horrible mother."

He was on board.

All the way on board? She barely dared breathe as she awaited confirmation.

"You'll ensure our children will be cute," she said, "and ensure someone remembers to restock the diaper bag, too. But for your information I will be an awesome mother, and sometimes parents secretly think their babies look like aliens. I heard it all the time when I was a nurse."

"Well," he said, refolding the tiny garment,

"we're not having aliens. And yes, I'll be the one who remembers to feed the children three square meals a day. You can be the fun one. I'll be the disciplinarian."

"I'm sure you'll find it so rewarding teaching them how to play chess and tape their eyeglasses back together," she teased, finally daring to get her hopes up about what the onesie truly represented.

"More rewarding than jumping off a bridge with nothing but a rubber string tied to your ankles?" he retorted.

"They're going to love bungee jumping. It's better than planning their week on the calendar and balancing their checkbook."

"Come on. That was off side." He threw his arms out like he was insulted. "Nobody has a checkbook to balance anymore." But he was grinning, and Amy realized that he was looking forward to having kids as much as she was—no matter if it sent them into the dangerous, uncharted waters of lovers in the lead-up to conception.

She gave him a spontaneous hug. She could hear his heart beating, and found the sound reassuring.

She tipped her head back. "Does this mean we're doing it? The old-fashioned way?"

"We'll have to set a few ground rules, such as

you get to deal with medical issues. For example, if our kids accidentally rip off a toenail while riding their bikes barefoot you get to deal with it." He shuddered.

She laughed, happiness bubbling up inside her like champagne. His hand was gliding over her hair, the move a soothing comfort, and a feeling of contentedness swelled inside her.

"Have I told you I love you?" she murmured.

"I said *rules*."

"Rules are for breaking."

"Not these ones. Number one, no falling in love with me—no matter how amazing I am with our kids. And if you're already in love, fall out of it. We're not going there, because we're not doing complicated. And we're not breaking up."

"Okay. What's the next rule?" He still had his arms around her and she felt nothing but excitement.

"What happens in the bedroom stays in the bedroom."

"But what if I can't help myself? What if you look super sexy holding our wee infant?"

"Well, that's a given. I can't be held accountable for that."

She laughed. "Fair enough."

"Rule three—no letting things get weird."

"No weirdness. No awkwardness," she confirmed.

His fingers were tracing warm circles on her back. "We'll slide right back into the friend zone as soon as we've done the deed. We're just two friends making a family."

She kissed him, slowly and sweetly, to prevent him from saying anything more, because everything was already so perfect. In her mind, there was nothing left to say.

She bracketed his face with her hands as she broke the kiss. "You're going to be an awesome father."

"That kiss breaks rule two. No kissy stuff outside of the bedroom."

"Aw. You're no fun."

"Seriously. This isn't a game. We're bringing kids into this world, this marriage."

Her mother's words about causing a mess and leaving others to deal with it slammed through Amy's brain. She nodded solemnly.

"I was simply showing that we can kiss and still stay in the friend zone," she said defensively. "No awkwardness."

"Friends, huh?" he asked, nibbling on her earlobe. She sagged into his chest, her eyes fluttering closed.

"I can totally handle that," she said, her words coming out in a jagged rhythm.

"Good, because the golden rule is that we're friends first and foremost." He grazed her exposed neck with his lips and she shivered.

"I'm fine with that," she managed to say on an exhale. "Although I think you're breaking some rules right now with what you're up to…"

"I couldn't imagine doing this kids thing with anyone else. How soon are we going to start trying?"

She wanted to sink into his strength and start immediately.

"Amy?" He ended his assault, allowing her to come to.

Right. She was supposed to be the cool, unaffected friend who could totally handle this handsome man peppering her with sweet, irresistible kisses that made her joints stop working properly.

She pursed her lips and gave herself a little shake, straightening her spine and stepping back from him. Friends. Definitely not allowed to let herself envision what "trying" usually involved between married couples. But after those less-than-innocent kisses, she wanted to go there all too badly.

"Yes. Soon. I'll have to check my calendar. But soon. Very soon."

CHAPTER 6

$\mathcal{M}$oe slid onto the couch beside Amy, passing her the bowl of salt-and-vinegar chips, his knee resting against hers.

She inhaled his scent. He smelled good. "Don't change your aftershave. It smells nice. Like you."

"Hmm." He settled deeper into the cushions, watching her out of the corner of his eye.

Why was she blushing? She felt like a schoolgirl talking with her first crush. It was only Moe, and they were only talking about his aftershave. Totally platonic. Nothing at all to do with the fact that they were going to have babies together.

By getting naked.

Soon.

Not tonight, but soon.

She flicked on the TV, switching from a news

story about missing members of a British Mafia gang's family to the movie streaming from her phone. She shoved a chip in her mouth, savoring the sting of the vinegar.

"I was thinking about the pub and what will happen with it," he said, staring at the screen.

"I hope you told Kimi to hire someone, so you can get back to what you love." Amy angled herself toward him, shifting the bowl into his lap.

That was what he wanted, right? To ditch the hassle of managing Brew Babies.

"Cesar—in his will—gave me an offer to purchase the pub from his estate at a low price."

So it was true. The offer that her mother had mentioned was real.

"As the owner I'd be working daytime hours, which'll be handy for when we have kids. Better pay, too. More flexibility."

Amy sank lower into the cushions, matching Moe's slouch. His tone wasn't enthusiastic. He was being Planner Moe, listing everything on the pro side of his pro/con checklist. Couldn't he see the substantial cons of being pinned to a business that was at the mercy of the economic ups and downs of a small town like Blueberry Springs?

"We'd be in control of our own lives," he added.

"We *are* in control of our own lives." He was starting to sound like his father. The next thing he'd say was that they were taking their lives back from The Man.

"We wouldn't have anyone dictating the way we run things, who we hire or fire. We could be autonomous."

There it was. Hidden in his words: Kimi and Spencer as The Man.

"There's security in being the owner." Moe hooked his hand in Amy's, giving it a squeeze. "We might even be able to afford in vitro for our second child if we owned the pub."

She pulled her hand away. For some reason using kids as an excuse to take a path that would surely leave him overburdened and unhappy felt wrong.

"You could stay home with our kids," he continued. "We'd have freedom."

"What's the deal? Specifically?"

"I can buy the pub for approximately half of its market value."

"Half?" No wonder he was tempted.

"Cesar considered each year I worked at the pub as a form of sweat equity and is bequeathing me that half. I could own the pub for a bit less than two hundred thousand."

That was still a sizable chunk of cash.

"Kimi must be upset you've been offered the prize pig."

"She's offered to front the money for the half I would need to purchase."

"She'd be half owner?"

"Yeah."

"Why not take the amount you were left and run?"

"I only get it if I buy the pub."

"Then buy it, flip it."

"Thought of that. Who'd I sell to? Kimi? Someone else? Then we'd be right back where we are now, but with new owners and even less control."

He made a good point. As it stood they were able to set their own hours, within reason, decide on specials and discounts, plus more or less had a say in almost everything.

"So you buy it and wear yourself out trying to run it."

"Kimi's offered to help me manage it indefinitely if need be."

"We'd work for Kimi?" There was no way. Amy had seen enough of her in the pub over the years to know she'd be right in there as top dog—even if she was only a half owner who lived out of town. She'd want to own it, run it, not listen to their thoughts and ideas on how to make it the best local hang out for their small community.

"*With* Kimi. But what if I found a way to buy it on my own—"

"Our own."

"And then in a few months, after we've learned how to make it float, we go out on our own without her help? No shared ownership or management with anyone. I'd—we'd—be the owner." There was a flash of worry in his expression, but it was gone before she could put a finger on whether it was about money, managing the business or something else.

"So you're going to buy it?"

He didn't answer.

"Moe?"

His focus was on the bowl of chips resting in his lap. Finally he looked up. "I'm not sure I can come up with the money."

Because he'd bought a house and was paying for a wedding he hadn't wanted. Add in the discounted honeymoon…

She *was* selfish.

No, he'd wanted those things, too. Maybe not the wedding, but the house. It made financial sense for them to own a place together.

But was he really considering owning and running Brew Babies? He was miserable with his current duties, which were a mere preview of the future. His future.

Was she acting selfishly by wanting something different for him?

And why hadn't he spoken up about this sooner if it was what he wanted? If she'd known, she would have skipped the house, the wedding and the trip, for now, and simply had them later.

"I'm sure Wini would say yes to the bank loaning you the funds to buy the pub." Although he'd just signed into a twenty-five-year mortgage, so there might not be any cash left in the lending pot, seeing as he'd used up his savings getting his dad into a place, too. "We can ask my parents." Borrowing a bit for equity was different than being bailed out. Way different.

"Maybe it *is* time to try something new," he said thoughtfully.

She sat up. Now he was talking.

"I'd be a manager," Moe said. "No more bartending."

Amy stared at him as though needing to confirm his identity. "But you like being a bartender." How could he give up making drinks and mingling with the locals? It was his thing, and it had been his identity for a third of his life. He wasn't as jovial with that office work tying him in knots, and he was dropping balls as the manager.

"Technically," she said, "you *have* been trying something new. And you don't like it. You're stressed and keep escaping from your little office to come shoot the breeze with customers."

He didn't say anything.

"Is this about money?"

"I'd be a better manager if I wasn't trying to take care of everything *and* tend the bar. I could run the place in the spirit in which it was established over the years if I had help."

"Of course you could, but there's more to life than money." This was why she'd left nursing time and again. It made for a great, secure income, but the job had killed her.

"More?" he challenged. "Such as having kids and being parents who are present? Having a spouse at home when the kids are awake, having your husband there to help you put them to bed? Maybe fold some laundry and mow the lawn at a semidecent hour of the day?"

"That all counts for squat if you're not happy. Happiness is more important." Amy took a breath, speaking more calmly. "I appreciate how you're trying to do this for our future family, but I can't be selfish and let you sacrifice so much. There are two of us in this relationship. If we need money or a better work schedule I can go back to nursing. We don't have to buy the pub."

"You hated nursing."

"It wasn't the right fit for where I was at the

time. But it was a much better fit for me than managing is for you. We don't need a ton of money to be happy. Not when it comes with oodles of stress."

They had never fought before, but this was starting to feel close.

"Wouldn't it be better if that dad wasn't some middle-of-the-night bartender and could take time off during the day instead of sleeping, make his own hours, and afford things like hockey and the kid's first car? It's important for a dad to be there for his son."

"When did this stuff start mattering to you?" Amy retorted, then she winced. Of course it mattered. His own father had been working in the mines every day, and hadn't been around after school or even for supper. It had often been Moe and Lily at the supper table alone—eating whatever they'd managed to create. His dad hadn't been able to fly out for the wedding, and she wasn't even sure when Moe had last seen him in person.

"I'm sorry. I know you want to be there for your kids. But what is this really about?" One of the things she liked most about Moe was that he didn't get tied up in the "proper" stuff like money and job titles like her parents did. Despite all they said about wanting her to be happy, she knew they weren't pleased that she'd settled on waitressing. Now Moe wanted more, too?

"It's just good sense, Amy."

"You can't change because everyone else thinks it's a good idea." She placed her hand over his knee. His gaze zeroed in on her ring.

"I'm not changing, and I think it's a good, smart, solid plan."

"You can't take a job you hate. It'll slowly kill you." She stood, hands on her hips, her mind made up. "You're saying no to Kimi's money. We make an okay income and yeah, the hours aren't great, but the stress is minimal. You've been tense all month and—"

"Because I've been working two jobs and learning how to take over Cesar's tasks."

"This won't change if you buy the pub. You can't stay away from pouring drinks and chatting up our customers. Try it for one night. You'll die." She sat again, her earlier anger gone, replaced by a quiet assurance that she was right. She only had to convince him that the status quo was totally fine.

"Amy, this is what'll be the best for our family."

"I get a say in what's best for our family, too, and you taking on a job you despise just for better hours and more money isn't for the best."

"So you want Kimi to own half, manage half and be your boss?"

"No. We have other options. This isn't the only town or the only jobs in the world."

"We just bought a house."

"So?"

"Buying the pub is the best plan."

"It can't be the best, and you know how I know?"

He wouldn't look at her, his anger and frustration mounting, turning his cheeks pink. She had a feeling she wasn't as close to convincing him as she'd like to be.

"You and I, Moe?" she said gently. "We don't need much because we already have more than most people."

"Yeah? And what's that?" he asked dutifully.

"Jobs we love and a friendship that can get us through anything. Including babies made the old-fashioned way and crappy working hours."

She shifted so her legs were under her, and pressed a hand to his chest, feeling a bit emotional and tender about the fact that he'd make these changes to his life for her, for their family. "You don't need to make a sacrifice for us to have kids. That isn't how love works."

His brows pinched together. "Who said anything about love? This is about reality."

WHAT WAS MOE SUPPOSED TO DO? HE HAD TO provide for the family they were planning. He had to be there for them and not working late hours in some stinky bar his kids wouldn't even be able to walk into until they were adults. He'd grown up in a household where there hadn't been a parental unit tag-teaming him and Lily. His father hadn't had support from a wife, and he'd gone it alone in a job that kept him away from his kids. He'd done the best he could, but Moe wanted to do better.

So if that was true, then why wasn't he asking Wini if the Blueberry Springs bank would give him a loan? Why wasn't he prepping to sign his name on the purchase agreement should it be extended once his trial period was up, in less than two months?

The learning curve was proving steep, but he could do this job. He could manage the place. He had to.

If he didn't, the whole pub would be sold out from under them, and he'd have to sort out a new career for both himself and his wife.

A wife who was still in the dark about what would happen to the pub if he didn't purchase it.

"You all right?" Marissa was standing beside him at the bar, giving him a strange look, her eye shadow so dark tonight she almost looked Goth.

She pointed to the slosh of lager he'd just pulled

into a glass he'd already set up with grenadine for a cocktail. He contemplated the mess he'd made before pouring it out, struggling to recall what he was supposed to be making.

Be the owner.

"I heard you and Amy are going to make some babies." She waggled her eyebrows. "Looks like it's got you a wee bit distracted."

I appreciate how you're trying to do this for our future family, but I can't be selfish and let you sacrifice so much. There are two of us in this relationship.

Everything felt so complicated.

You don't need to make a sacrifice for us to have kids. That isn't how love works.

"Either that or time in the office has made me rusty," he said, trying to keep his jaw clenched so he wouldn't add something revealing.

"Ha. That'll be the day." Her voice lowered as though expressing great doubt as she added, "You? Rusty behind the bar?" She chuckled and took a tray of fries out to Luke and Emma, who had their heads bent together, no doubt plotting something that would make their all-natural cosmetics company another few million.

Moe just needed to make some babies, and then be there for them as they grew up. It should be simple.

But in five days everything was due to change.

He'd seen Amy's ovulation calendar—how could he not? She'd tacked it to the bare fridge, which they hoped would one day be covered in finger paintings and tiny handprints. Amy was on countdown mode and he still didn't know how he was going to be the man she needed. He felt it deep in his bones to provide not only financial support, but emotional and physical support, too.

She couldn't go back to nursing. She'd left the career enough times for him to know it made her unhappy.

Which all counts for squat if you're not happy. Happiness is more important.

Amy sidled up on the other side of the bar, sliding her tray into a bowl of peanuts.

"Look at that jukebox. Broken again." She sighed theatrically. "You don't want to own this place. Nothing but headaches."

Moe clenched his jaw and grabbed a green olive and, not caring if she was ready to catch it in her mouth or not, lobbed it at her. She opened her mouth too late, the olive bouncing off her nose.

"Your point was made last night," he grumbled. "Sufficiently." He was still pretty ticked about how she'd threatened to go back to her old career.

She was ready for the next olive, but again, missed it.

"Come on. My mouth is right here," she taunted.

He gave a disgruntled grumble of frustration, wondering if she might be afraid of him owning something and being tied down. Maybe a business was too much for her free spirit, but owning a home was okay. It just seemed like there wasn't a right choice. He could be an overworked, stressed-out owner, or give up on all of it and try to find another decent job—with nothing but his high school education and drink-pouring experience as backup.

"You need me to help?" Amy asked when he spilled soda over his hand while mixing a rum and Coke, missing the glass with the stream of soda. "Maybe I could stand behind you like a golf instructor and place my hands over the soda gun, directing it into the glass."

Why did that sound dirty to him? Was it the way she'd lowered her voice? Or was he just that muddled?

He needed help. He needed to wash his ears out with soap, scrub his brain and stop thinking about his best friend like she was some kind of porn star about to fulfill his fantasies come ovulation day. He was worse than a hormonal teenager with his first crush.

She started to come around the bar, but he

scowled at her as he poured two lagers. "I've got it." In his haste to prove it, he spilled beer over his hands as he banged the glasses down on the counter in front of her so she could take them away.

"An awful lot of head on these beers. You're losing your touch."

"Maybe I'm just picking up your poor habits."

She stuck her tongue out at him, wrinkling her freckled nose in the most adorable way before she spun on her heel, spilling not a drop as she carried the brews over to the table of intent poker players.

As she chatted with the customers, her tanned arms revealed by her tank top moving gracefully as she gestured and laughed, he wondered what sounds she would make if he kissed the skin at the base of her neck.

Why was he thinking about that? He had a pub problem to solve.

He jerked as he overfilled a glass of soda for Oz.

"Seriously. You okay?" Marissa asked, slipping by. She tapped the list of drinks she needed him to make, while giving him a concerned look.

"Just lost in thought."

"About impregnating Amy? Yeah, I can see how that might be a tad distracting."

Moe shot Marissa a look. He should cut his losses tonight and go work in the office. Except he knew Amy would chew him out for abandoning the bar on one of the busiest nights of the week. And then there was also that small part of him that wanted to be on watch in case the smokejumpers came back.

"Or is it something else?" Marissa leaned against the counter, her back to their customers. "I heard you're thinking of buying this place even though that Kimi Phipps thinks she has a right to Brew Babies and its income just because her daddy owned it."

"Would it be that bad if she bought Brew Babies? She's currently helping manage things."

"Would it be that bad?" Marissa reached out, placing a palm against his forehead as she frowned. "Strange. You don't seem to be burning up. You know she told me to pay for the soda I was drinking on my shift?"

"She'll learn that it's not about every penny, but about happy customers and happy staff."

"She won't ever learn that."

"Sure she will. I'm helping her just like she's helping me." She'd already somehow sorted out his mysterious inventory issue like it had never existed.

"She's not one of us, and she doesn't care about the little guy. She's a princess who wants every penny possible going into her fat little purse. You can't let her buy this place. If you do, I'll quit."

"Don't be so dramatic." He nodded to his sister, who'd come in, spotted him and was marching over.

"You're my boss, not Kimi," Marissa said. "And before you start saying this place is her father's legacy, it's *yours*. You're the one here late at night. You're the one trying specials and working with Nicola to bring in events so this town has a night life. There was *nothing* like this in Blueberry Springs until a few years ago."

"What if I can't keep running it in the spirit in which it was established?"

"Are you seriously asking me that? You *are* the spirit of this place. It's in your blood."

He was touched by her words, and a feeling of inspiration buoyed him. "You really think so?"

"I know so. And why are you defending Kimi, anyway? She's an entitled bossy pants."

Lily slid onto a stool across from Moe and Marissa, stating matter-of-factly, "Because that little princess is the woman who got away, and he never got over her."

"Get your head checked," Moe said in disgust. He'd gotten over Kimi just fine.

Marissa sucked in a breath and leaned back, pointing a finger at him. "You used to date her?"

She dropped her hands on her knees. "Why didn't I know that?"

Moe shrugged. He'd dated an out-of-towner a decade ago and it hadn't hit the gossip circles because the whole relationship had failed to flourish and hadn't become anything more than a quiet breakup. Not much in the way of news there.

"Heartbroken men don't like to talk about their feelings," Lily announced and Moe let out a snort. "So, what does a woman have to do to get a drink in this place?"

"Go drink in your own establishment," Moe retorted.

"We're not licensed."

"Since when?"

"Since they changed the renewal process and I messed up." She waved a hand. "I'll have it sorted in a week or two. In the meantime, something girlie with an umbrella, please."

"It all makes sense now," Marissa was saying, as though in awe. "You still love her, and are upset because I'm dissing her."

"She's a manager and that demands respect," Moe said, as he began creating a unique drink for his sister. A little root beer. Grenadine. Rum. Splash of lemon-lime soda.

"You should know she's already asking about Amy like a jealous ex," Marissa confided.

Moe's head jerked up, his body going on high alert. "What do you mean?"

"You know, typical can-I-fire-her stuff. She wants to sink her hooks into this business. You, too, if she can."

"She can't fire anyone without my authorization." At least he was fairly certain that was how it worked. Although maybe not. He dropped an umbrella in Lily's drink and put it down in front of her.

Her lips twisted in disgust. "It's brown."

"Yup. I hope you hate it."

She scowled indignantly, but took a sip, pausing to consider the flavors. "It's decent, actually."

"You serious?" Moe stole a sip. It did sort of work. It wasn't something he'd make again, but wasn't nearly as gross as he'd hoped.

"Kimi's the reason for the marriage pledge, you know," Lily said, taking back her drink. "Moe thinks he'll never be able to love again."

"My heart is just fine. Don't you have food burning on your stove or something?"

"Was it a bad breakup?" Marissa asked Lily, leaning over the counter and resting her chin in her hands.

"I was in South Carolina, so I'm not sure, but he didn't really date after that," Lily said quietly.

"Because I realized how nutso the opposite sex

is." He turned to Marissa. "Don't you have customers to serve?"

She picked up her tray. "I've heard about your three-month trial period, and if there's a way for Kimi to benefit by shooting you down, she'll find it."

Moe jerked the soda gun too hard, kinking the hose. "There's no way for her to benefit if I fail. She'll get more over the long term by co-managing a thriving pub."

"Keep an eye on her."

"Marissa…"

"I know her type, Moe. Watch your back."

AMY WIPED DROPS OF WATER FROM THE CLEAN BAR counter in preparation for opening and tried to focus on work and not the fact that tonight was the night.

The Night.

Moe trailed a finger across Amy's shoulder blades as he passed, looking way too satisfied with himself when she shivered in response. Today was baby-making day. Moe knew it, and so did every cell in her body.

They'd been going in opposite directions all day, frustrating her to no end. Now they were locked into an eight-hour shift together, and into what was surely going to be an all-too-tempting dance as the tension built between them when they neared closing time.

"If you need to practice, let me know and I'll meet you in the brewing room." He gave her a wink as he moved farther down the bar, collecting a stack of cardboard coasters as he went.

"It's been a while, but I don't think I've forgotten how," she retorted.

She wasn't sure if his subtle teasing was to help them cross their "just friends" line after their shift tonight, or if he thought acting like a tease was hilarious because they were still "just friends." Married friends.

She gestured to the pub's front doors. "Are you going to unlock the place and let people in?"

"That's your job."

"Since when?"

"Since I'm the manager and get to tell you what to do. It's also your job to turn on the TV."

"Pulling the boss card?" She didn't recall him ever going for the dominant role, but now wondered if over the years he'd been holding back, and what might be in store for her tonight. She shook off her thoughts and flipped the dead bolt to unlock the main door. "It's not as sexy as you think, by the way."

"It's sexy."

"If you hold your managerial position above me and keep teasing me about ovulation-related activities, I swear I'm going to either kidnap you and move us to a new town, with new jobs, or I'm going to take out a loan to pay for in vitro."

He pretended to be aghast. "You wouldn't."

She aimed the remote at the TV, which Moe turned off more frequently than he left it on, stating that customers came to socialize, not watch what they could at home.

"You'll be celibate for life." She pointed a finger at him, before realizing that in a way, they both had signed up for that, outside of the few ovulation times when they'd come together. She wrinkled her nose, her shoulders sagging. "That's actually kind of depressing."

"Don't worry, I can platonically snuggle with you, to make you feel less alone in our mutual celibacy."

She strode across the pub, grabbed the soda dispenser and threatened to spray him with it. He held up a tray as a shield.

"What are you? Captain America?"

He stuck out his chest, adopting a heroic stance. She squirted a thin stream of soda at him.

"Hey! I was striking a pose."

"Actually, with your short haircut you almost look like him."

"My hair's darker."

"I said *almost*." She put down the dispenser and gave him a poke in the gut. His stomach was firmer than she remembered. "Have you been working out?" She made a grab for the hem of his shirt, trying to lift it, but he blocked her with a sweep of his arm.

"I'm not a piece of meat."

"I'll be running my hands all over you soon enough," she said in a sultry tone. "Very soon. Then I'll know the complete and utter truth."

She tossed her hair over her shoulder and strutted away, only to find his arms wrapping around her waist, lifting her off the ground. She squealed and reached for something to anchor herself as he pulled her out from behind the bar.

"It's going to kill us waiting all night," he growled, sending tingles of anticipation throughout her body. "I think we'd better move quickly in case that ovulation window closes."

"Does the office door lock?"

"Let's find out."

She turned in his arms as her feet hit the ground, kissing him as they made their way into the small office.

The room was a mess of papers and filing cabinets. A small desk. One chair. But it would do just fine for her purposes, as she'd never been so ready in all her life.

Moe backed her against the door as he fiddled with the doorknob.

"It doesn't lock," he announced.

"Then I guess we'd better make sure we lean against it."

"I could lock the pub's doors."

"Who's going to come in this early?" She clutched his face, angling her mouth across his.

Moe gripped her behind the knees, lifting her so she could wrap her legs around his waist as she leaned against the door for support.

This was it.

Baby making time.

She giggled, feeling bubbly inside. She felt light and free. This time, she could let herself go and just be in the moment. Let nature take its course instead of worrying about consequences.

"Are you nervous?" He gave a teasing eyebrow waggle that settled her apprehension.

She'd hesitated, hadn't she? Thought about things for one second too long, allowing a thin edge of doubt to slip in.

"No." She locked her lips on his, the kiss firm and demanding. No doubts. They'd planned for this. This was Moe. Her best friend. The most trustworthy person she knew.

Their kisses slowed and deepened before urgency and longing fought to control the pace of their moves. Moe's hands ran from her hips up to her ribs. She softened against him, moaning as his moves became more insistent.

She'd forgotten how good he felt. How patient and thorough he was.

He had her shirt off before she realized it, his own already gone, their warm flesh touching. This was what she needed. Contact. Release. She tightened her legs around his hips as he leaned into her.

"What if we can't conceive?" she blurted out as his lips moved down her neck. Her eyes fluttered open. What if after all this she couldn't bring the dream alive?

"We save up for in vitro," he said, his lips not deterring from their course.

She laughed and kissed him hard, running her hands over his back, their bodies kicking into high gear.

"I'd stay with you even if we can't have children," she murmured, realizing it was true.

He replied by taking her mouth with his own, his kisses impatient, demanding. Her feet slid to the floor and his fingers worked her jeans lower on her hips.

A thump on the door behind her made her eyes fly open. Another thump sounded; from someone trying to enter?

Amy gasped and let go of Moe, hands flying to cover her bra.

His eyes darkened, his jaw tightening as he leaned into the door with both palms.

"Who's there?" he called.

"Moe? It's Kimi."

Both Amy and Moe cursed under their breath, their eyes meeting in mutual panic.

"What are you doing in there?" Kimi called. "You have customers and there's no staff out front."

"Just a minute," Moe answered, his voice too husky to pass as normal.

He kept his hands on the door while Amy dived for their discarded clothing. She scrambled into her shirt, then yanked at her pants to do up the fly, while Moe did the same, turning his back against the door. He was shaking his head and looking ticked off.

Amy straightened her clothes and finally nodded at Moe. *"Sorry,"* she mouthed.

"Later," he mouthed back, tapping the end of her nose. Then he gripped the back of her neck and yanked her into a fast kiss, before slipping out of the office, saying, "What's up, Kimi?"

He closed the door behind him, allowing Amy a moment to herself.

She leaned against the paneling and tipped her head back, trying to slow her heartbeat, her thoughts, her desire.

Those few minutes of kissing had revved her up in a way she'd never been before. Was it the anticipation of baby-making that was acting as an aphrodisiac? Too much time thinking about it, anticipating the moment? Probably.

It couldn't be Moe, her best friend, her rock.

She took a long, soothing breath, running her fingertips over her tingling lips and wondering how she could sneak off with Moe before their shift was over.

"You have to have someone present up front at all times," Kimi said, while Spencer marched around behind the bar as if he owned it.

There were no customers and Moe had a suspicion that Kimi had known what was going on behind the office door only moments ago.

"What if someone had come in—someone underage—and helped themselves to some liquor? Who would be liable? My father's estate is legally responsible for what goes on here, and so am I as a managing partner."

Moe shifted uncomfortably.

Spencer came over and joined the conversation, arms crossed. "Maybe you're not fit to be manager. Even with help."

"Spencer, don't interrupt," Kimi snapped, before turning back to Moe. "What were you doing in there?"

"Having a private conversation."

"With...?"

"Amy."

Spencer let out a delighted bark, his face lighting up. He nodded and grinned at Moe.

Kimi's eyes flashed as she demanded, "Where is she?"

"Probably finishing up with things."

Behind his sister's back, Spencer gave another grin and nod, along with a subtle thumbs-up.

"She is *not* authorized to act in a managerial role," Kimi warned, as though she expected Amy to be in the office hiring and firing people.

"She knows that."

Kimi went stalking toward the office, her brother following with a self-important swagger. Amy met them in the hall, looking cool and un-affected.

Moe felt affected. Completely. He wanted to

push Kimi and Spencer out the door, throw the dead bolt and get busy with Amy on any available surface. Or preferably, all of them. Something had set fire within him and he had no idea where to find an extinguisher.

Assuming he even wanted one.

"Kimi. What a pleasant surprise," Amy said mildly.

"The two of you know better than to leave the bar unattended."

"We were talking in the office."

Moe didn't dare check Spencer's reaction.

"With the door closed?" Kimi narrowed her eyes at Amy, her gaze no doubt locked on her well-kissed, pouty red lips. "You're on the clock. You don't spend the estate's time getting intimate with your husband."

"I knew it," Spencer announced, receiving a dirty look from his sister.

Amy raised her eyebrows and stepped closer to Kimi. "I'm sorry?"

"This isn't your personal playground." Kimi's head had angled upward in an attempt to match Amy's height. "You two need to take your responsibilities seriously."

"I'd say Moe is taking them so seriously he's likely to have a heart attack because of the way you're abusing and overworking him."

Moe caught Amy by the arm and tugged her away. When she shot him a look so dirty bleach couldn't ever clean it, he gave her a kiss on the temple in a feeble attempt to placate her. She could easily—and quickly—reach the point of no return with Kimi, who was out for power and control. The woman was grieving both for her father and for losing this pub—Marissa was correct about that —and it was coming out in a way that made her nearly impossible to be around. But now was not the time to burn bridges.

"We'll be more careful about making sure there's someone up front during opening hours," he said.

"Don't you have something to tell Kimi about buying the pub?" Amy asked.

"What did you want to say?" Kimi's face lit up.

"It's nothing. We've just been hashing out ideas is all." Moe gave Amy a warning look. She still didn't know the full story about what would happen if he didn't buy the pub. The problem was, if he told her, he didn't think she'd change her mind about him owning and managing the place. He feared she'd fly into a reactionary panic and give up—say the place was going down anyway— and take off on some new adventure instead of staying here, with him, where she belonged.

"And?" Kimi prompted.

"Still just brainstorming. No conclusions yet."

Amy sent him another cold and peeved look while turning on her heel. "I'm going to go finish what I was working on. Alone."

As she returned to the office, Moe's brain stopped working. What did she mean, "finish"? Didn't she need him to follow? She'd said alone, but he'd been a big part of what she'd started, and he knew she wasn't talking about work.

He glanced at Kimi. Could he get away with kicking her out, locking the front door and running back to Amy? She might be a managing partner, but he was still the one responsible for the spirit in which it was run.

"I just came to drop this off." Kimi laid a document on the bar. Moe wasn't sure what it was, but he was certain it could have been emailed.

"I'm still looking into a new jukebox," Spencer said, as his sister marched across the room toward the outer door. "Think I might have a line on a sweet deal."

"Great."

"That soda arrive for you?"

"It did, thanks."

"Who's your man?" Spencer shot him a grin. "I am!" he called triumphantly as he headed out into the sunshine.

Moe mentally fist-pumped the air as the two

departed and whirled to head to the office. He knocked lightly on the closed door before letting himself in, uncertain whether he'd find an angry Amy or one who needed his help. Intimate help.

She was sitting on his desk, fully clothed.

"I'm sorry about Kimi," he said.

"Why don't you just tell her you don't want this place?"

"Saying no is pretty final."

"So is yes." She pushed herself farther back onto the desk so her feet dangled. She gave him a mischievous look, her gaze sending him an invitation.

He began to close the door.

"You better leave it open or we'll get in trouble from Kimi."

"How about I lock the front door?"

"You wouldn't dare." There was a glimmer of something in her eyes that made his blood pound a little faster. Amy always made him feel alive, but this…this was a challenge that could change his life.

"Maybe I would."

Kimi wasn't coming back; she'd delivered her daily dose of you-can't-handle-this-job. And nobody in town would blink if the pub didn't open for another few minutes.

"You're husband material," Amy said, a hint of daring in her voice, "not Mr. Wild Child."

"Opening a little later isn't being wild."

"What if she returns?"

"Are you afraid of her?"

"Are you afraid I'll get bored if I have to wait until later?" she asked.

"Maybe I'm the right man to finally keep you from getting bored. Any time of day."

"Let's see, shall we?"

Moe set a new land speed record as he crossed the pub, leaping over chairs on his way to lock the front doors, before returning to his waiting wife and rising to the challenge.

CHAPTER 7

$\mathcal{A}$my followed Moe up the sidewalk, watching the way his strides ate up the space between his truck and their home. It was three in the morning, their shift having gone on longer than eight hours. Even though she should be exhausted and ready for bed, she was amped up, with energy running through her veins from their little make-a-baby session in the pub's office hours ago.

Moe had ignored Kimi.

He had gone ahead and used the office as his own personal playground, opening the pub a good thirty minutes late, smile firmly in place.

Hers, too.

Moe was a good husband.

Very good.

But hopefully not so good that he'd knocked her up tonight, because she was anticipating having to keep on trying.

There had been an undercurrent of urgency to their coupling, but also an awareness that this was something they weren't going to do very often. Tonight could have been one of the last times they got to enjoy each other so intimately. It had made her savor every touch, cherish every movement.

It had also made her want more, and as Moe unlocked the front door she struggled with the urge to jump on him, wrap her legs around his hips and kiss him thoroughly.

"You know," she said, as he pulled his key from the lock, "I heard it's rare to conceive the first time."

"Yeah?" Moe slid her a quick look. Under the porch light she picked a piece of lint off his sweater. The air around them was mountain-fresh and cool. As he turned to face her more fully, she watched him through her lashes, trying to read his expression.

He gently brushed her cheek with a thumb, the move so tender that she leaned into him, face tipped up, hoping for a kiss. Hoping he'd be tempted to keep on trying and trying with her.

"I don't think that doing it again would break any of our rules," Moe said. "In fact, I think it would be the practical thing to do. A few marathon days would be less likely to test our friendship than trying once a month from now until conception."

She murmured in agreement. His lips were almost upon hers and her eyelids fluttered shut. When his mouth failed to land, she opened her eyes, worried that she was taking things further than he was willing to go.

"Are we going to kiss?" she whispered.

"Yes. All week."

He placed his hands on her hips, the warmth of his touch seeping through her jeans. She wanted to be closer.

His lips dusted hers with a kiss, and she nudged the door open. "We should go inside before things get X-rated."

She flicked on the interior lights, her back to the house as she kept her attention on Moe, drawing him in, drawing him closer. No distractions. No interruptions. He was going to be hers.

"Seriously?" He stopped abruptly, his tone unimpressed.

"We don't have to," she said quickly, waiting for a clue as to his sudden change.

He was staring beyond her and she turned to see what he was focused on.

Someone had sneaked in and rearranged their furniture as per a Blueberry Springs tradition that struck newlyweds. Nobody had been pranked in years and she thought the tradition had died.

But apparently not. Their electric stove was in the middle of the living room. The toilet seat was sitting on a patio chair, a roll of toilet paper on the bedroom dresser beside it. The room was littered with balloons, and wedding streamers hung from the ceiling.

"Everything's out of place," she said stupidly. She'd been part of such a prank before, but had never really thought about how it would feel to have someone slip into your home and rearrange your possessions.

She glanced at Moe. The situation was obviously serving as a wet blanket rather than an aphrodisiac for him, too.

"We've been pranked," Moe said, his voice flat and lacking humor.

"We could ignore it?" she suggested hopefully, despite knowing the mood had been officially killed.

Amy hurried to her bedroom. Her best lingerie was tied to helium balloons and was drifting near the ceiling.

And her bed was missing.

She'd really been hoping to use that bed tonight. For several different reasons.

She marched toward the front door, determined to get even for the invasion. That and the interruption. "I'll bet you anything it was Devon."

"Where are you going?"

"To retaliate." She marched back to the cluster of things in the middle of the room and snatched the roll of toilet paper, while noting that the plant her mother had given her was doing quite well in its spot by the window. She mentally stuck her tongue out. See? She was responsible. About to go TP the mayor's house, but that didn't negate the fact that she had a handle on her life and was ready to live it her way.

"Middle of the night." Moe's tone held a light warning as he listed all the reasons not to issue revenge. "New baby. Plus we're not even sure it was him."

"Lame reasons. All of them." She snatched up a few other items she might need, stuffing them into a shoulder bag. "And little Abby is a toddler now. It's payback time."

"We're in our thirties."

"Barely. Do we have more toilet paper?"

"I bought the good stuff," Moe protested.

"I'll wear heels during my shift tomorrow night and get extra tips to replace it. Are you coming?" She waited, hand on the door.

"We might get caught by Scott and charged for public mischief or vandalism or trespassing or something. He's been taking his job a lot more seriously these days."

"When have we ever been caught?" They'd played pranks on Devon and even the used-to-be-grumpy Ethan several times over the years. Mary Alice was also on that list, as were Jen and Rob—they'd switched the newly planted spruce tree in their front yard for a poplar. Mandy had found pink flamingos littering her yard on her thirtieth birthday. Frankie's precious 1987 Mustang Shelby went up on blocks for his. That had been epic. They'd put together a treasure hunt through town so he could reclaim the expensive, special-order rims. They'd even tricked Scott once. And gotten away with each and every one. Sure, people suspected, but nothing had ever been pinned on them.

"We don't even have a plan," Moe said.

He was tempted, and that's all she needed.

"You're lame and old," she said, taunting him.

"You're young and immature."

"You don't have to come."

But as she left the house, he was hot on her tail.

"HOW DO YOU THINK THEY GOT IN?" MOE whispered.

He was holding Amy's smooth calves as she sat

balanced on his shoulders, carefully loosening the bulb in Ethan and Lily's front porch light. They'd already taken care of Devon's with the toilet paper. Now they were covering their bases with some small pranks at the homes of those most likely to be Devon's accomplices.

"Who got in where?" Amy asked. She freed the bulb and passed it to him. "Sweet. LED. They're going to miss these pricey babies."

Moe slipped the bulb into his back pocket, reminding himself not to sit down before he found a place for it. Getting glass in his butt would certainly lead to an ER visit, as well as being busted as he tried to explain what had happened.

"Dawn's coming," he remarked, as she tinkered with something else from her perch. It looked like she was rigging up a fake spider to swing in the doorway. "John'll be out soon." The town's lawyer normally jogged the streets around six in the morning. It was five fifteen. "By the way, nice touch with the spider. Lily hates them."

"I know, right?" She tapped his shoulder. "Okay, let me down."

She slid down his body, his hands fitting into the curves of her narrow waist, reminding him of unfinished business and their plan to preserve their friendship by making this week count in regards to conception. Her palms lingered against his chest for a moment and she gave a satisfied hum of contentment. "You *have* been working out, Moe Harper. I like it."

"I haven't given anyone a key to our place," he said, clearing his throat and wishing it was as easy to clear his mind of the images of what he and Amy could get up to if they had a little privacy.

"And you have your keys," she said. "Think they took mine?"

"Do you know where yours are?"

She shrugged and he shook his head affectionately. That was Amy, frequently misplacing stuff.

"Maybe we left a window open?" he said, holding the lid to a jar of honey as she smeared the contents on the doorknob.

"But my guess is they snatched my keys at work, borrowed them for a few hours, then returned them. That's what I'd do." She took back the lid. "Have you ever noticed it's usually a Mattson at the root of all pranks?"

"Shh!" he warned, as her voice rose above a whisper. "And here I thought it was us."

She grinned and turned, her jaw going slack. Moe spun to look behind him. Logan Stone was standing on the walkway, arms crossed.

"Um, hi." Amy smoothly slipped the honey jar behind her back. "They're still asleep." She jabbed a thumb toward the front door. "Working nights really messes with a person's sense of time."

Logan merely lifted his eyebrows a fraction of an inch in the predawn light.

"Oh! What's that? I think it's a chicken!" Amy broke off to the side, sprinting through the yard and into the neighbor's, even though Logan's steady gaze never left her.

"I'll just go see what she's up to," Moe said casually, placing his hands in his pockets and sauntering off after his wife.

He caught up with her half a block away on the alley side of a picket fence in dire need of a paint job. "I told you we're too old for this," he said, dropping into a crouch beside her and taking a pile of peeling white paint with him. "We've lost our touch." He slipped the lightbulb from his back pocket and handed it to her before sitting in the dewy grass.

"Logan used to be a spy. Of course he caught us." Her eyes lit up as she said excitedly, "Imagine if we got him onside? Our pranks would be legendary!" She leaned back against the slats, her chest heaving as she tried to hold in her laughter.

"It's not funny," Moe said darkly, determined not to give in and let her whimsical side rule the day on this one. They *were* too old for this. They were trying to become parents, and mature adults starting a family didn't act like this, stirring up trouble.

Although he had to admit he felt full of life and had enjoyed every moment of it. No matter how a day went, Amy always made it a fun one worth repeating.

He opened his mouth to say something, but closed it again, worried he'd say something that made him sound like a sap.

"Did you see his face?" She deepened her voice, putting on a macho act. "So serious."

"Like you said, he used to be a spy. He could kill us or frame us in about nine hundred ways without even having to get imaginative."

"Oh, Moe." She placed a hand on his arm, her touch sending a spark of longing through him, her face glowing in the soft morning light. "It's okay to let loose sometimes."

Her lips were a pale pink, her expression so full of life and affection that he didn't want to be anywhere else but with her. Ever.

He gently slipped a hand under her ponytail and brought her in for a tender kiss that would surely break some rules about this not being a necessary bedroom act of intimacy. But it felt so right he let go and gave in. The something he hadn't been able to pinpoint that had been in their wedding kiss was still there, simmering under the surface. He tried to coax it out as their kiss became more needy, but it stayed out of reach, tempting and teasing him to fully let go, to give in and lose himself in kissing his best friend.

AMY HOPPED OUT OF MOE'S EMPTY BED, WONDERING where her husband had gone. After that amazing kiss at dawn, with adrenaline and life flowing through her, they'd come home and fallen into his bed—hers was still AWOL. With the sun streaming into the room they'd moved together as partners, friends, and something much larger and stronger than either of those two things combined. She could have almost sworn it was love. The real deal.

But that could have also been the anticipation talking. Anticipation of their life together as a growing family, of a life that finally made sense and didn't make her want to run or shake things up. One where she could just be herself and be loved for every quirk she had.

She padded into the living room, a smile curving her lips as she spotted Moe stretched out on the couch.

"Good morning," he mumbled, his voice hoarse with sleep. One arm partially covered his eyes. "Feeling pregnant?"

"You think you're that good?"

"Are you saying I didn't give one hundred percent?" He groaned as he got off the couch, then placed his hands on his lower back and arched with a grimace.

"Why did you sleep out here?"

"You snore."

"Do not."

He grinned at her quick defense. "We have rules, remember?"

Right. Rules. Keep it in the bedroom. Don't pretend it's real and start snuggling and sharing a bed. Even if hers was missing and they planned to fill the calendar with bedroom activities in hopes of getting her pregnant.

"We need to find my bed," Amy said, hoping the sudden disappointment that had seeped in, dimming her glow, wasn't apparent to Moe.

"If we don't I guess we'll just have to share mine tonight, so this couch doesn't wreck me. We can break a rule in the name of ovulation." He lifted a brow in question.

She shook away images of them curled together, his strong arms cocooning her. Like a real couple.

"Yes," she said, nodding seriously, "I think that would be prudent."

"Prudent?" Moe laughed at her word choice.

"Shush, you. It's just one small rule we're breaking. And it's not even a real rule." It was a perfectly valid excuse for having him wrapped around her in the night like she craved. Giving in a little bit for now wouldn't change things between them.

"So...does that mean you didn't fall in love with me last night?" Moe shook his head as though disappointed in himself. "I'll have to try harder next time."

Amy rubbed her stomach. "Maybe there won't be a next time. Maybe I'm pregnant."

Moe shook out the blanket he'd slept under and folded it into a perfect square. "I thought you wanted to have more than one kid?"

"Maybe you gave it two hundred percent last night and I'm carrying twins?"

Moe's expression softened as he crouched in front of her. "If there's a little baby in there already, remember that dads are always the favorites. Moms are all about rules. Dads are about fun."

"Except in our case," Amy said, bending to speak to her stomach. "Dad is going to be the rule man, Mom is the fun one."

She felt a flush of self-conscious heat wash her cheeks as she gave Moe a bashful smile. This felt so domestic, and somehow so *right*.

He chuckled, then checked the time. "I've got to head in and bottle some beer."

"You're taking your role pretty seriously for someone who's going to say no to buying the place." They were going to have to chat about him telling Kimi eventually, and if he couldn't, then maybe they just needed to pick up and move somewhere else, find new careers and new adventures.

"I still have a job to do. What are you up to today?"

"Thinking pregnant thoughts."

"You do seem to be glowing. But I can't tell if that's pregnancy or from me rocking your world yesterday. Twice."

Amy snorted and waved Moe away. He disappeared into his bedroom to get changed out of his pajamas.

She went to the kitchen to begin brewing coffee, wondering how it was that after one night with Moe she felt content, calm and at peace with her life. *Was* it afterglow? Or was it just some great sex and a fun night of pulling pranks and feeling as though she had Moe on her side, which always made her feel a little bit invincible?

She might not even be pregnant. And they were still nothing more than two friends trying to put together something that looked like domesticity. She needed to find her bed and get her head put on straight again, or she was going to start thinking this was something it wasn't.

"You okay?" Moe was leaning in the kitchen doorway, watching her.

"Yeah, of course. Just remembering to keep my expectations in check. You know me." She focused on finding the lid to Moe's travel cup. "Something new and I'm all in, as usual."

He stood beside her, his arm brushing hers as he took the prepared beverage. "You know this is going to be good, right?" he asked. "This won't be like nursing or anything else. It's only going to get better and better with time."

She nodded, the words she wanted to say locked inside her like a secret. She wanted to thank him for trusting her. For going along with her crazy plan that even her parents, who were desperate for grandchildren, didn't fully approve of. But most of all, for being him and for wordlessly understanding the things she couldn't seem to say.

This wasn't a mistake, because mistakes didn't feel this good, this *right*.

She opened her mouth to speak, to force the words out. Instead, she threw her arms around him.

When she released him, after the hug, he studied her face with a questioning gaze. She flashed him a quick smile, hoping to cover her insecurities, her worries that she'd get more out of this marriage than he ever would.

~

MOE STOOD STARING AT THE VAT OF BEER. THE instructions on the wall were ones he had followed before, but today he couldn't seem to wrap his mind around the simple step-by-step directions.

Open the vat. Test. Check against the newly replaced chart. Act accordingly.

Last night had gotten to him. He'd wanted to stay in bed with Amy. So much that he'd forced himself to move to the couch after she'd fallen asleep.

Get her pregnant. Raise kids.

Nothing more.

When they'd come together in his office, he'd expected it to be perfunctory, slightly rushed and awkward. Instead, they'd picked up right where they'd left off years ago, but with things being better than ever. Much better. It had been the kind of night where a man didn't care if this was the last woman he was ever with because he knew he wouldn't ever tire of her. Every time was different from the last, and he found himself wanting more leisurely, intimate nights filled with laughter and passion. He'd forgotten how freeing and powerful it was getting lost in a woman you knew so well— knew her like a best friend.

And that was likely the issue. He'd lost his head,

and if he wasn't careful, he'd lose his heart and lose her, too.

He plucked a three-legged stool from its spot near the wall, spinning it under him as he sat in the cool room.

He needed to get his head on straight. Their relationship was supposed to be a friendship and nothing beyond that. Although his thoughts last night had been *very* friendly.

She didn't have a bed and the couch was a back-wrecker.

So what was he going to do?

Moe put away the testing equipment. He still had a lot of beer to bottle, as well as kegs to fill.

But Amy's ovulation window was likely still open. So why was he still here?

They had a plan to increase their odds by making full use of that window. It was his duty as a husband to finish his work and go home as soon as humanly possible, so they could get the job done and put this behind them. Then they could move on as parents, partners, friends. No fuss, no muss.

He abandoned his tasks and headed out into the bright July sunshine, his phone ringing as he hit the parking lot. He contemplated not answering it.

"Moe here." He inhaled, trying to put the past behind so he could have a decent conversation with his father, who was finally reaching out to him.

"I was just talking to Amy—I called to welcome her to the family and apologize for not flying out for the wedding—and heard the news," his dad said, acting as though everything was fine between him and his son.

Moe perked up. She was pregnant already? He stumbled over the flash of disappointment at not being needed again until baby number two. No, wait. It would be too soon to know if she was pregnant, wouldn't it?

"I hear you're going to buy the bar."

"What?" Amy had been adamant he *not* buy it. What was going on?

"You're tired of working for The Man and are going to own the place despite what Amy thinks is best. That's my boy. Be the owner and take charge of your own life and destiny."

Moe leaned against his black truck, quickly pulling away when the hot metal burned his back.

"When do you take ownership?"

"I'm not sure I—"

"Not sure? Why not?" demanded his father.

"I'm not sure I can afford it."

"Have you tried? Crunched the numbers? I can sell this place, get you your money back. Before you and Lily swooped in I was just fine renting."

He hadn't been. He needed to retire from his factory job—the one he'd left mining in Blueberry Springs for a decade ago—as it had nearly caused him a stroke earlier in the year. He was still working only because he'd needed to cover his rent. Lily and Moe had set him up in a nice, small place of his own where his monthly bills were miniscule. He wasn't going to take a step back and return to renting.

"You're expendable," his father warned, his voice sharp with the upcoming lecture Moe knew by heart. He mouthed the words as his dad spoke. "They could fire you in a heartbeat. One screwup and you're out on your ear. How are you gonna provide? You can't support a family on nothing but a high school education."

Moe felt the pressure in his chest, expanding, pressing, insisting on taking up the space his lungs needed in order to do their job.

His father was right. He was in a precarious position, with nothing to fall back on.

Why hadn't he found a way to go to college? Night school or online courses?

He hadn't taken the path to higher education and instead had stayed in Blueberry Springs at the same job, happy and satisfied. And now he didn't have time to improve himself before he and Amy had a family. He was in a position where his job could be gone in less than two months.

His father was right. He had to secure his future—their future—and pursuing the pub was the path he needed to take. For the next several weeks, it was more important than getting Amy knocked up. He'd lost sight of his responsibilities.

"Thanks, Dad."

He ended the call, knowing what he needed to do.

Amy had married him because he took care of things. He was the steady guy with a plan, and owning the pub—he'd figure out the management aspect later—would put them in the future they'd envisioned. One where he was there for his kids. *That* was what was important. How had he allowed himself to get swept up in Amy's fun-loving side and forgotten that?

Moe pinched the bridge of his nose and closed his eyes, refocusing.

He didn't want to worry about money for the rest of his life. He didn't need much, but he wanted to be able to buy his kids the nice shoes, and to be there at suppertime, his children secure in knowing they could depend upon him. Same with Amy. He wanted her to know he was there, taking care of things so she could be herself. So she could settle down.

And Moe knew how to do that.

He flexed his hands a few times, then dialed Wini's direct line at the bank, leaving a message.

"Wini? It's Moe. I'd like to make an appointment to see about taking out a loan to buy Brew Babies."

CHAPTER 8

$\mathcal{A}$my found yet another excuse to walk past the brewing room during her early afternoon shift. Moe and Kimi had been in there for half an hour and something felt off. Moe had turned serious since their night together, and there hadn't been a repeat of their intimacy despite their marathon plan. Last night, Moe had slipped into bed with her after she'd fallen asleep, then slipped back out as soon as he'd woken up.

Sharing a bed was nice, but she'd hoped to share more. A lot more. Especially since her ovulation window wouldn't stay open forever.

"How can there be something wrong with the beer?" Moe asked Kimi as Amy passed by, causing her to pause in the doorway. "It was fine when you checked the pH a few days ago."

"Is something wrong?" Amy asked.

The color had left Kimi's lips and she focused intently on the chart resting on her lap. "We have to dump it."

"Can't we save it?" Moe asked. "Turn it around somehow?"

"What's wrong?" Amy stepped into the room.

"The pale ale's gone skunky," Moe told her.

"This is going to cut into profits, and there's no way to hide this from the estate," Kimi said. "Your poker nights consume a lot of pale ale, and the extra lot fermenting at the offsite brewery won't be ready until September. Once we run out, it'll be weeks before we have it in stock again."

"They can drink something else then," Amy said, unsure why Kimi was taking this so hard. Surely the estate lawyers knew things went wrong from time to time and wouldn't do more than express their frustration over the loss.

Kimi hooked a hose to the vat, feeding one end into a floor drain that led to the sewer.

"Do I have to pay for this?" Moe asked. His voice was flat, masking the worry Amy knew was there.

Amy readied a glare should she say yes.

"No," Kimi said, inhaling as though the word had hurt her. "These things happen and you're not the owner—the estate is. But because you're acting as a manager in this interim period, the cost could possibly impact your managerial bonus, as well as the estate's assessment of your ability to run Brew Babies." Her voice was small and tight as she added, "Even though I was in charge."

In other words, it looked as though it was going to reflect poorly on both of them.

Moe and Kimi had a similar expression of loss as they watched the beer slide through the clear hose and down the drain. It was filling the room with the stale scent of things gone wrong.

"But come September all errors will come out of your profits and hence your pay," Kimi said. There was something in her tone that made Amy turn to face Moe.

"September?" she asked.

"He's buying the pub." Kimi was smiling faintly as though relieved. Her smile faltered. "Alone."

Moe's eyes met Amy's, then cut away as he fiddled with the hose.

"You're what?" she asked him.

They'd talked about this. She'd offered to go back to nursing, but because he'd disagreed, he was buying the place behind her back instead of discussing it with her further? Anger and adrenaline flowed through her veins, making her muscles twitch.

"He didn't tell you?" Kimi's satisfied look of being in the know fueled Amy's anger even further.

Moe winced, giving Amy a sidelong look filled with remorse. *"Sorry,"* he mouthed, then added quietly, "I just decided and I'm still figuring things out. I meant to tell you tonight when we had some time to chat and sort out a plan."

She inhaled slowly, trying to keep a lid on her emotions, which were threatening to boil over.

He was doing this—buying the pub—for her.

Her.

She knew that. That was all she had to remember. He was the planner and had figured things out.

Such as working himself to death.

It wasn't worth it. Why couldn't he understand that?

And now Kimi was trying to use the pub as a wedge, her sledgehammer at the ready to drive it home and break the two of them apart.

"We'd talked about it, but we've been...*busy*..." Amy lowered her tone so it was confiding, barely masking a hint of intimacy. She curved her lips in a slow, warm smile that included her husband, but not Kimi. "Not just with this place, of course," she added in an offhand manner. "We're newlyweds. You know how it is."

Moe looked embarrassed, but also relieved that she wasn't going to blow up.

At least not in front of Kimi. She was still furious that he had gone behind her back. They were married. Partners. Friends.

But she still hadn't earned the right to know everything in his world, had she?

Their marriage and partnership, no matter how real it felt, was still just a pledge between friends, and he was welcome to do what he wanted with his life, his money. If he wanted to slowly kill himself as a manager and owner, trying to be home for his kids but also be present at the pub dealing with everything from staffing to management stuff, then she supposed they'd figure it out, because they were just friends.

Even if she felt bitter about the way he'd gone about it.

Friends first. Always.

But man, she was angry.

"So in late September it's all yours?"

At least if Moe bought it he would be the owner and boss, not Kimi. Amy could hardly wait for the woman's certain and impending swift exit.

Moe said, "If the estate determines that I've been able to maintain the pub's standards and run it in the spirit in which it was established, yes. Then I can buy it."

Great. No problem. He could do that.

Kimi pointedly fiddled with the hose draining the ruined beer.

Well, the spoiled beer might be a small hiccup, but things happened, right? Surely that wouldn't be held against him.

Kimi sniffed. Her eyes had filled with what Amy was fairly certain were fake tears and she tipped her gaze down and to the side. Before she could call her out, Moe's hand was on the woman's shoulder, giving it a supportive squeeze. Kimi folded herself into Moe's arms, and jealousy, unwanted and pure, reared up inside Amy.

She knew the game the woman was playing. And Kimi looked way too comfortable in Amy's husband's arms.

"It's okay," Moe said, his voice thick.

"I just wanted my father's legacy to—to…"

"I know." He shushed her gently, like she was a heartbroken child.

"You still have the other pub, right, Kimi?" Amy said.

Moe gave her a harsh look, drawing her up short. So instead of doing what she wanted, which was to drag Kimi out of Moe's embrace and give him a possessive kiss, Amy made a feeble excuse about customers, and let herself back into the empty pub.

Man, Kimi had game. She had Moe feeling bad

for standing up to take what he'd earned, and then managed to get him to hold and console her to boot. And, of course, Amy was made out to be the bad guy who lacked sympathy and understanding.

At the other end of the pub, Spencer was shoving the old jukebox out of the way, having installed a new one in its spot.

"What's this?" Amy asked.

"Ta-da!" Spencer smiled and held out his arms, showcasing the new machine. "Moe approved it."

"It's nice." She picked up the surge protector the old jukebox had been plugged into, handing it to him. "The wiring is a little glitchy over on that wall. Plug it into this so it doesn't get fried."

A fritzed-out new jukebox would be the last thing Moe needed.

"Isn't it a beauty?" Spencer set down the surge protector and ran his hands over the new piece of tech as though it was a beautiful car.

"It's nice." It was gorgeous and shiny, with lots of current hits as well as classics. "Who pays for it?"

"It was pretty expensive, but I knew a guy who pointed me to it. He said it's a good brand. So I don't know, but it should last a long time. Quality counts, right?"

"As long as its warranty covers spilled beer."

"No warranty."

"Moe approved that?"

"I bought it on an auction site. Saved him tons of money."

"It's used?" She moved closer. It looked brand-new. No scratches or anything.

"It's new, though it didn't have a manual or box. Floor model, maybe? Why does it smell like funky beer in here?"

"They're dumping a batch that went bad."

"Moe's having trouble keeping up with being the man in charge of everything, isn't he?"

"Moe's doing just fine."

"He should have had Kimi take care of it. She knows about that stuff. Even I don't," Spencer said.

"He put her in charge of it."

"Well, not every batch turns out." Spencer shrugged. "For their sakes, I hope they figure it out so the place doesn't get liquidated. It's a nice pub."

"I'm sorry…what?"

"Moe has to prove he can run Brew Babies like my dad never left or it gets liquidated."

Whoa. That was harsh. Although Cesar had always been a bit protective of his business, quick and ready to close Brew, Too when it had failed to perform immediately.

"Wouldn't Kimi just buy the place if it came to that?"

"Can't. Those are the conditions. He makes it and buys it, or it's gone."

Amy blinked, still wrapping her head around the situation. "You're sure?"

"I heard the will being read, listened to all the answers when Kimi asked a million questions. I was lucky I just got cash. Talk about pressure for those guys, huh?" He bent over the machine, jabbing at buttons. "So we can set how much people pay per song. What do you think is a good rate? We've got to get this thing paying for itself." He pressed a few more buttons, making all the lights turn red.

Amy, lost in her thoughts, ignored Spencer's question and headed over to the bar to fill the peanut bowls. The way she saw it, Moe not only had to rock his current job as manager, but also had to find the money to buy Brew Babies, or they were both out a job and Blueberry Springs was out one thriving hangout.

Why hadn't Moe told her the full details? Did he worry she'd freak out and run off to find a new job? The idea was a tempting one. Just ditch the whole thing.

But Moe loved this place. Surely he understood that she'd do whatever she could to help him preserve it, own it. That's what friends were for.

She set out the filled peanut bowls, resolved on figuring out how to help Moe manage the place like the rock star he'd always been, as well as find enough money to pay for it.

~

AMY WATCHED MOE SLEEP. HE HAD PROPPED himself up against the bar, head resting on his fists, a pile of financials spread out before him. Kimi and Spencer had stayed for most of the shift, helping out, dispensing advice.

Kimi had been nitpicking, in other words. While Spencer mowed his way through bags of chips and acted like he knew what he was talking about. But Amy figured Kimi was trying to prove she was indispensable so Moe wouldn't cut her out of the equation. Then again, Amy had always been a tad more cynical than Moe.

They'd also worn on him. She'd caught him massaging his temples once or twice as though warding off a sure-to-come headache while dealing with Spencer. The dude acted as though the pub was his own personal bar and kitchen, helping himself without ringing his orders through. She had a feeling he would never settle his growing tab. Sure, he'd found a jukebox and hired someone to paint the pub's front door, but other than that, he was mostly in the way. Cheerful and willing to be helpful, but more of a drain than anything.

Just like the beer Kimi had dumped earlier. At least the funky beer smell had dissipated quickly.

"It's time to go home," Amy said, nudging Moe.

He snorted as she nudged him again.

"Accounting puts me to sleep every time, too," she said, as he stretched and yawned.

"I wasn't sleeping," he said, his voice groggy.

"You need to go home and get a proper night's sleep if you're going to prove you have earned the complete rights to buying this place."

He looked up at her, his eyes sleepy. "I'm sorry I didn't tell you. I was worried—"

"That I wouldn't understand?" She placed her hands on her hips. "Knowing that the other option was to have this place liquidated may have swayed me into saying yes to buying it, you know." She sat beside him and leaned over the bar, snagging two glasses and the soda sprayer. She hit the button to pour water, filling the glasses, sliding one to Moe.

He reached over the counter's edge and fished around for the sliced lemons kept in a bowl.

"Already in the fridge for tomorrow," she said.

"Sorry I fell asleep."

"It's fine."

"I was going to tell you about wanting to buy the pub after I talked to Wini about a loan tomorrow. Or is it the day after?" He was bleary-eyed and adorable, his short hair sticking up. "I've lost track of what day it is."

She sipped her water, then said, "I hate that I had to learn the details from Kimi and Spencer first. That you didn't feel you could tell me."

Her stomach ached whenever she thought about how he hadn't been able to trust her with everything going on in his life.

"I'm sorry. It just feels like everything I thought I had under control, isn't." Moe shuffled the stack of papers back into a pile and stood up. "I spent hours inputting stuff, but where is it all?" He held handfuls of paper in the air and sighed. "I know some of this input stuff is new to me, but I learned the old stuff easily enough."

"I'm sure it's in there somewhere. You're a details man. Just working really hard. I have faith this'll all work out and that Wini will give you the loan."

"I'm hopeful, but I don't have a down payment. Just the promised equity if she says yes."

"She'll say yes. But if she says no we'll round up some investors. Burke and Jill maybe? No, they're just getting going with things. Luke and Emma? Even Mandy's flush these days. We'll sort this out, Moe. Blueberry Springs is a good town. We'll hold a fundraiser if we need to."

"Why are you so awesome?" he asked, his tired smile crooked and genuine.

She pushed off her stool, collecting her purse and ignoring the warm feeling she'd gotten in her gut from the way he'd looked at her. "I asked Scott to run the serial number on the jukebox, by the way."

Moe's head snapped up. "What? Why?"

"Just a feeling." She couldn't put her finger on it, just that something with the jukebox felt off. "Come on. I think I hear your pillow calling you home."

She needed him to get some sleep. She also needed to decide how she was going to help him save the pub while still continuing to be the man she adored. The real Moe. Not the manager who was tired all the time, not an owner who was stressed out over everything. The man who was her best friend and told her everything. The man behind the bar without a worry or care, and a special smile reserved just for her.

It had been a busy week getting the pub's annual statements, as well as a copy of Cesar's will, to Wini so he could make his plea for a loan. As well, since dumping the vat of beer, Kimi had been extra vigilant with the latest brew, coming in almost daily to check on things despite having her own pub to run. Today he'd told her to go home, get some rest. She wouldn't be much good to either of them or either place if she was worn-out. She had hired someone to help manage events in her pub, though, special ones such as open mic nights and poker games like those held at Brew Babies. It was tempting to find someone to take over that aspect of things here in town, too, so Moe could concentrate on other higher-level management issues.

The two of them had been working hard as a team, both of them learning a ton. Things had to get better soon. They had to.

Moe wandered the house, looking for Amy, finding her in her room even though they had yet to track down her missing bed. She was sitting on the floor, nose-deep in a book about the women of the Klondike.

"Hey."

"Hey." She looked up, went back to her book.

He sat beside her, imitating her cross-legged pose. They hadn't had a chance to marathon their way through her ovulation cycle, thanks to him. He'd been messing up with her left, right and center lately.

"When can you take a pregnancy test?" he asked.

"Hoping you need to do the deed with me again?" she asked, her eyes twinkling.

He shrugged. He was exhausted, as well as racked with guilt over not keeping his end of their marathon agreement. "I promised you two kids."

"Is sex all men ever think about?"

He leaned back on his hands, still cross-legged. "We think about boobs, too. And sports. Beer. Sometimes cars."

Amy gave him an exaggerated eye roll.

"We're very deep."

Amy leaned left, picking up a crumpled white pharmacy bag from a pile of laundry. She pulled out a rectangular box that looked a little battered, as though it had been dragged around town all week. He lifted his eyebrows in question. "Pregnancy test?"

"I've been waiting for you."

The guilt hit him hard. He'd been a horrible husband, horrible friend and partner lately. He'd been keeping her in the dark about things, working constantly and taking her for granted. He hoped once he had the pub securely in his name that things would change, that the pressures would let up.

"Lucky for you, I have to pee." She got up and went to the bathroom, calling through the door, "Set a timer."

He fished out his phone as he waited in the hall. "How long?"

"Two minutes." She came out of the bathroom, trying to bite back a smile.

"So? Any predictions?" he asked. He felt nervous. Uncertain. And not completely ready.

She shook her head. "I don't dare. What if I jinx it?"

"There's not a lot you can do to change the reading on that test at this point."

She held the white plastic stick, staring at the little window where he assumed lines or words would magically appear like they did in commercials. He looked over Amy's head, gently resting his hands on her shoulders as they stood in the hall, waiting. "What will it say if you're knocked up?"

"I think it'll say, 'Congratulations, your life is over.'"

"And if you're not?"

"'Sorry. Try again.'"

He chuckled, the vision of what that would entail coming to mind way too readily. He wanted to snuggle closer to Amy, but stepped back instead. One little snuggle could break so many rules. He'd already woken more than once this week with his body curled around hers, or their foreheads touching, hands clasped. He'd found himself doing whatever possible to head to bed after her, wake up before her so he wouldn't let himself go too far. But sleeping with her had led to some of his best nights of sleep. No tossing, no turning. Just restful sleep, like all was well in his world.

"Something's coming," she said, her body practically vibrating.

"What does it say?" The excitement built within him. He needed to own that pub. He needed to be there for Amy. They needed a crib. A stroller. A high chair. There was so much. He pushed his hands through his hair and stepped away to pace, but caught himself. There'd be time for pacing later. Right now Amy needed him present, not jumping ahead.

He glanced at her, and suddenly, staying still wasn't difficult. She was wearing the saddest frown he'd ever seen.

Instinctively, he stepped closer, resting a hand on her arm. "Are you okay? What does it say?" He glanced down at the device, not sure what the little lines meant, whether she was spooked at the prospect of being a mom-to-be, or saddened by their failure.

"Not pregnant." Her voice was choked despite her attempt at being cheery.

He tenderly pulled her into his arms. "The good news is we can share a drink to drown our sorrows."

She shoved him away. "Not funny."

"It's okay. We'll try again next month."

"I always fail at what I truly want. This is why I never try." She threw the plastic stick down the hall. It tumbled and slid, coming to a rest under the living room couch.

Moe froze for a second, processing her outburst.

"What have you ever failed at? And babies don't just happen the first time," he stated. She was one of the most accomplished people he knew, un-afraid to try something new, to go all out.

"I *know*," she said, her voice as irregular as a car with a clogged fuel filter. "I had to marry my best friend so I could have a family. That has failure stamped all over it."

"That's not because of failure. That's a creative solution to a very common problem. You didn't settle for someone you didn't love, like most people would due to a fear of being alone. You found someone you enjoy being with, and are making it happen. I think that's admirable."

She sucked in a big breath, her body wavering. Moe had a feeling she might be talking about something deeper, something bigger.

"Just… Never mind."

"No, tell me. We tell each other everything, don't we?"

She met his gaze with eyes filled with such pain it felt as though the narrow hallway was closing in on them as she said, "I used to think so."

He sucked in a breath, her meaning all too clear.

She moved to her room, and he caught the door before she closed it. "I'm sorry I haven't been telling you everything, regarding the will and the pub."

"We're just friends. They don't always tell each other *everything*," she said coolly. But the hurt in her eyes hit him in the gut. It was like watching a child deal with rejection from a loved one.

"Because sometimes friends named Moe have stupid fears," he muttered.

"I'm tired of people not trusting me. I'm not a flake. I'm responsible and you can tell me stuff."

"I know."

"You could have told me Cesar bequeathed half the pub to you and that we'll be out of jobs if you fail to make a profit. I could have been helping you manage the pub for over a month."

"I know."

"I wouldn't have run away, Moe. I wouldn't have asked for a wedding and I would have had us hold off on the house so you could make this happen."

"I didn't want to let you down or make this

your problem. I made a promise to you," he insisted.

"My mom thinks this is all a mistake," she whispered. "That I'm selfish and going to hurt you."

"She's said that?"

"She doesn't have to. It's right there in her words and looks and…everything."

"Well, she's wrong."

"I know." Amy's bottom lip began to tremble. "I'm just tired of having to live up to Jillian's life. I'm not her."

He gently pushed the door open and took Amy in his arms. "I chose you because you're you and nobody else."

She shuddered, clinging tightly to him.

"And because of who you are, I know that you'll cherish, honor and celebrate our children's passions and interests without telling them who to be. Because of that, I know you're going to be the best mother I could ever choose for my kids, Amy. We're going to make this happen. We're a team."

AMY CRIED INTO MOE'S PILLOW, UNSURE WHY SHE felt so broken up over the negative test and Moe's sweet words. He always knew what to say, how to be there for her.

What if she couldn't get pregnant? What if it was one more thing she reached for and failed to fully secure? Everyone thought she was amazing because she'd learned all sort of things, like photography and scuba diving, as well as earning a nursing degree and then adding on to it. But she wasn't a nurse. She was a waitress who'd married her best friend because she couldn't find anyone to love her and she was swiftly exiting her baby-making years.

Moe's bedroom door creaked open and she groaned.

"Let me wallow in my sorrows," she said into the pillow, her words muffled.

"I brought you something."

Amy rolled over, her tears stopping as Moe placed a massive sundae on the bedside table. Leave it to him to serve up bananas, three kinds of ice cream, syrup, cherries, crushed toasted peanuts and whipped cream to cheer her up. She didn't even know they'd had all those ingredients.

She sat up to take a better look, her mood lifting. "Are those chocolate chip cookie crumbles on the top?"

He handed her a spoon. He'd brought one for himself, as well, and she realized that he might be feeling a bit broken up, too. Because she'd let him down. She hadn't been someone he could trust with the information about the pub, and she wasn't someone who could give him the family he so rightly deserved on the first try. Yes, she knew these things took time, but she hated to feel as though she'd let him down.

"I'm sorry," she said around a spoonful of ice cream, whipped cream and syrup, her sorrows welling up again.

He'd settled onto the bed, sitting cross-legged, the sundae nestled into the bedding that was crumpled between them.

"For what? Talking with your mouth full?" He made a face and she laughed, a spurt of melted ice cream dribbling down her chin. She wiped it with her hand, then ran her fingers across her wet lashes.

"For not getting pregnant." She shoved another spoonful into her mouth, keeping her focus on snagging the last of the three cherries he'd set on the mounds of whipped cream. The first time they'd shared a sundae had been about a decade ago, after he'd broken up with someone from the city. They were just becoming friends and she'd made him one similar to this.

"I hope when you get pregnant that you have really weird cravings so I can bug you about them for the rest of your life. Like wanting dill pickles and whipped cream together."

"Actually, that sounds really good." She made fake gagging sounds. "No matter what happens, promise we'll always be friends?"

He held out his hand, offering his pinkie. She hooked her own in his, giving a small shake in a pinkie swear.

"Friends," he said.

She smiled even though she didn't feel it.

They went back to eating the sundae, a comfortable silence settling over them.

"So? When do we try again?" he asked.

She reached over and shoved a spoonful of ice cream in his mouth.

"Seriously, Moe."

"What? I'm a planner."

"Is sex really all men ever think about?" She gave an exasperated shake of her head, then shoveled more than her fair share of whipped cream into her mouth.

"Yes. We're also problem solvers." He battled her spoon for the last piece of banana. "The current problem is that you're not in the family way even though you'd like to be. It's a problem I would like to solve for you."

"You would, would you?"

"I would."

"In a platonic, manly, problem-solving kind of way?"

"Of course."

"Maybe my calendar is wrong." They'd finished the sundae and she set the dish on her bedside table, rolling up onto her knees. "Or maybe we weren't warmed up enough after our mutual dry spells, and we were a bit rusty."

"It didn't feel rusty."

True. It hadn't. It had felt natural and as though it had brought them closer.

She placed her cold fingers on his warm cheeks, pulling his face closer so she could give him a slow, sweet kiss that tasted like maraschino cherries and whipped cream.

"Are you seducing your husband?" he murmured against her lips. "I think that might be against the rules."

"I'm making sure you don't have chocolate sauce on your lips."

"That's something only a best friend would do."

"And I intend to always be *your* very…" she gave him another deep kiss "…very best friend."

He made a sound of agreement and she gave him one more soulful kiss before pulling back, resting her hands on his broad, strong chest, wishing she could take things a little further, a little deeper.

But when he gently caressed her cheek, kissing the trail her earlier tears had taken, she let herself go, savoring the way he felt, the way he cared, the way he let her lean on him when she didn't feel strong enough on her own. And when he took them across the line, she welcomed him, enveloping the intimacy and strength she drew from the man who'd always have her heart.

CHAPTER 9

*I*t had been a few days since Moe had watched helplessly as Amy broke apart when she'd discovered she wasn't pregnant. Several days since he'd put her back together, then proceeded to step across their friendship line. He'd like to convince himself that he'd only been acting as a friend, caressing her, kissing her. Taking things into the sweet zone where he wanted to stay, never returning to their status of just-friends.

Amy had welcomed him, given her wounded, emotional state. But he feared he should have been a better man and pulled back. Instead, they'd come together in his bed with no prospect of making a baby, and the whole thing had simply felt right. It had felt like the very thing he'd always wanted in his life. It had been like coming home, like an easy laugh with a friend who knew you and your back-story, like a favorite home-cooked meal after being away at war.

Being with Amy had quieted everything inside him down to the things that truly mattered. To happiness and contentment. To having that someone in your life who made everything make sense, made everything *better*. That someone who had found her way into your life so deeply, who had intertwined themselves into your every fiber, that you could no longer imagine life without her in it.

As Amy walked past him, an onion ring double burger held high on a tray in her right hand, she gently let her left glide across the waistband at his spine, as though letting him know where she was so he wouldn't back into her. Except she'd gone out of her way to move through his space, to deliver the intimate caress.

He watched her go, his heart pounding. It had been a natural, casual check-in lovers made.

Had the other night meant a lot to her, too? Even in her fragile state, had it been what she wanted, what she craved?

Logan Stone handed over his debit card, his gaze locked on the soccer game playing on the TV above the bar, and Moe mindlessly swiped it through the machine before handing it back.

"I'm so glad you two got over your fears," Logan's wife, Ginger, said to Moe, her gaze leading his to Amy. She was wearing a dark pink V-neck that hugged her curves and brought out a healthy glow in her cheeks. She was gorgeous, and she was his in name.

But he wanted more. He wanted it all. Her heart. Her love.

He didn't have that.

Not yet.

"Our fears?" he asked, unable to fully focus on Ginger's words.

"You two have everything you need for a strong, happy, healthy marriage."

"Except one big thing," Moe tactfully pointed out, pulling the empty beer steins from in front of Logan and his business partner, Zach, who was seated to his right. Moe kept the glasses in front of him, ready to use them as part of his "I'm busy" escape routine if need be. The dishwasher was enough steps away that it would break the conversation.

Ginger quirked her head. "Are you kidding me? Are you two still acting like this?"

"Like what?"

Logan gave him a look as if to say, "Don't play cute, it won't work, mate."

"You two are still too afraid to acknowledge the big *L* word?"

"Ginge, you need glasses." And maybe fewer drinks with her meal next time.

She took the two empty beer steins he'd been keeping in front of him, and held them up, looking through their bottoms. "I can see just fine, thanks."

Moe chuckled. "Keep dreaming, girl."

She pouted. "Oh, come on. I'm never wrong. Even the one time I thought I might be with Ashton and Zoe, back in Indigo Bay, it turned out I was right." She banged a fist into her palm. "Come on, man. Make it happen! Let go. Tell her you love her. You're putting up this wall like you're afraid if you show her that you love her, she'll leave you."

Moe shoved a fresh stick of gum in his mouth. "You're seeing things that aren't there." He picked up the empty steins. Logan and Zach gave a simultaneous groan over something happening in the soccer match.

"It's my superpower to see things couples can't. Just wait and see. I'm right!" Ginger insisted.

"Is she always like this after two drinks?" Moe asked Logan, knowing she was.

"Right about couples?" he asked, his attention back on them, his Australian accent thicker, as it usually was when he thought about his "sheila." He leaned over to place a kiss on his wife's cheek. "Uncannily so."

So much for the support Moe was seeking.

"She hasn't found me anyone yet," Zach complained from his spot beside Logan.

"I'm working on it," she said, leaning around her husband to address him. "You're a tough one."

"I'm going to order a nice wife from Russia," Zach proclaimed, pushing his sizable build off his stool. He clapped Logan on the shoulder. "Thanks for the drinks."

"Stay away from the internet until they've worn off," he suggested.

"I'm fine." The man wobbled on his feet before correcting his balance.

"He driving?" Moe asked.

Logan dangled a ring of keys from his fingers. "Good."

"He's having a tough time with the career change," Logan said with a heavy sigh. "Been handling it with a heavy dose of online shopping and the gym."

Moe nodded as though he understood. He didn't know Zach's full story, but the fact that life wasn't going the way he needed it to was obvious to anyone familiar with the human race.

"You two are so happy together," Ginger said, taking up the topic of Moe and Amy again like she was a bulldog with a particularly tasty bone. "You're the right fit and I can see you getting closer. This is where you guys always pull away from each other, but you won't this time. I can feel it. I can see it."

This was indeed about the time he and Amy usually slipped back into the friend zone. Which was what they needed, and wanted. This time and every time. No proclamations of love.

"Plus," she added, "it's harder to pull away from each other when you have to share a bed each night."

Wait. She knew Amy's bed was missing? Sure, lots of locals did, since they'd been trying to track it down. But the way she'd said it… "What was that about her bed?"

Ginger turned redder than her auburn curls.

"You stole Amy's bed!" Moe leaned against the bar. "What do we have to do to get it back?"

She bit her bottom lip, eyes shooting to the side, obviously hopeful that her husband would step in and save her.

"Um. We know nothing," Ginger said.

"That's true," Logan said, standing up and tucking his wallet in his back pocket. They probably didn't have room for it in the cramped apartment above Ginger's bridal shop, but that didn't mean they were innocent.

"So where is it?" Moe asked.

Ginger shrugged.

"How do we get it back?"

She darted away and Logan gave Moe a sympathetic look. He began ushering his wife toward the doors, but she hurried back, saying quickly, "Devon has it. They had company coming and figured Amy wouldn't need it." She gave him a sheepish look, her nose scrunching. "You know. Newlyweds. No need for a second bed...kind of like a little nudge in the right direction..."

"How thoughtful."

"Come on, babe," Logan said, having come to retrieve her.

"It'll be back soon!" Ginger called from the doorway.

Moe cleared their glasses while shaking his head. Amy came to stand at his side, close enough that their shoulders brushed.

"Ginger was in rare matchmaking form tonight, wasn't she?" Amy asked. "I heard her giving you the gears."

"This," he said, pointing to her shoulder, then his own, illustrating how she was well within his personal zone, "is why she thinks we're meant to be."

"So I should stand farther away?" Amy sidestepped, putting at least a foot of space between them.

Moe moved nearer so that their shoulders touched again. "I like it when you stand close. Don't change for her."

"Okay." Amy smiled, then rolled up onto her toes and placed a big kiss on his forehead.

"What's that for?"

"Why do you always ask that?"

"Because I want to figure out how to get more of them." He winked and lowered his voice so it was nice and gravelly. "And then how to get you to aim lower so they land right here." He tapped his mouth.

Amy gave a sassy shoulder sway that made him want to grab her and tickle her. Anything to be close to her, to inhale her scent and feel her bubbly laugh.

"But I think I have a plan for that," he said.

She had been reaching for a glass on the rack under the bar, and paused, head quirked to the side. "Oh?"

"Babies. I'm starting to think we need to have about twenty of them. And as for that fertility calendar you have? I believe it's wrong. I think we ought to cover our bases and go at it all the time. Just in case."

Amy laughed, her cheeks pink, her grin wide.

She picked up the soda dispenser, squeezing the handle and sending a stream of club soda at him.

He ducked and laughed. "You did *not* just do that!"

He lunged at her and she squealed, dropping the dispenser as she bolted to the end of the bar. This wasn't the first time they'd gotten into a sprayer fight. And it wouldn't be the last.

He shook the soda out of his hair and slowly moved toward her as though stalking prey. She was trembling, her eyes dancing. He loved it when they played, and it felt like they hadn't for ages. Everything had been too serious lately, and being with Amy like this always allowed reality to fall away, until it was just the two of them riding on a wave of giddy happiness.

He picked up the abandoned soda dispenser and aimed it at Amy. "How far do you think this thing can spray?"

"Not this far," she said confidently. It was true. She should be securely in the safe zone. But what she didn't know was that he had upped the pressure earlier in the day, having a feeling that their banter might land them here before the end of their shift.

"How sure are you?" he taunted.

"So sure that if you spray me from there, I'll kiss you. On the lips. In front of everyone."

It was a good thing Ginger had left, or she'd get the wrong idea about what was about to happen.

The people lined up at the bar hooted and cheered, with Mary Alice immediately taking bets. She slapped down a twenty and the pile of cash immediately grew.

"What are the odds?" Moe asked.

"Who cares? We just want to see you two kiss," Mary Alice proclaimed.

Moe set down the dispenser and everyone booed.

"I'm not sure Amy knows what she's getting herself into." Kissing in public would definitely break a few of their rules. Not just the kiss, but the fact that they might not be able to stop.

Amy began clucking like a chicken, her hands tucked in her armpits to form wings. She began doing an adorable little head bob, her knees coming up in time with her bobbing head.

In a flash, Moe lifted the dispenser and shot a stream straight at her.

She squealed, the shot getting her in the eye. Moe was at her side in a flash.

"Are you okay?" He began dabbing her face with the hem of his shirt, but she pushed him off, shielding her eye.

"Did you increase the pressure? That causes leaks in the hose!"

It had seemed like a good idea at the time.

"I'm so sorry. Are you okay?" He looked around the pub, wondering if Nash was still in the room and could take a peek to make sure her eye was all right.

"No. It hurts and stings. Who shoots somebody in the eye with soda?"

"Would this be a bad time to cash in on that kiss you owe me?"

Amy scowled and Moe stepped back, hands raised in defeat. Behind them Mary Alice was distributing the bet money, shushing those who were complaining about the fact that there'd been no kiss.

Moe heard her say, "Give them time, give them time. It's coming."

"What's going on?" The voice he heard next quieted the bar. It was cool, commanding, and definitely Kimi. She was wearing a pale blue business suit that made her look serious and in charge. Or maybe it was how the crowd gathered at the bar had parted for her, and the way she stood there with her hands on her hips.

AMY WAS MILKING HER HURT EYE TO THE FULLEST extent. After Kimi had panicked about the two of them wasting inventory—did that woman ever actually work in her own pub? She kept insisting if she spent enough time at Brew Babies she could absorb the vibe and somehow bring it to Brew, Too—Nash had prescribed Amy some eyedrops, as well as a patch to wear for a day or two, just to be safe. While Nash had been caring for Amy, she'd overheard Moe gently sending Kimi back to her own pub, giving her a list of business suggestions that would keep her busy and out of their hair for at least a day or two.

"Aye, matey," Moe said rather sheepishly, joining her in the living room. "Time for your eyedrops?"

"Will you put them in for me?"

He sat beside her on the couch and she put her head in his lap, looking up at him. He gently lifted her patch, then delicately pinning her eyelids so he could squeeze in two drops. She flinched at the coldness.

"Are you okay?" Moe asked.

She nodded and relaxed again, enjoying being cozied up against him. "You're going to make a great dad."

"If we can get you knocked up." He replaced the patch over her eye, his expression so serious and tender it made her feel inexplicably shy.

"It has been fun trying, right?" Heat spread to

her cheeks as she thought of the last time and how intimate and special it had felt. The trust and love that had been present had rocked her sideways. It was as though getting married had somehow amplified all her emotions. At the same time, her need to prove herself and go looking for the next exciting thing seemed to have waned. But she still couldn't seem to help wondering if Moe felt the same way—that this was good, special.

"What are you thinking?" he asked, screwing the cap back on the drops.

She hesitated for a moment, then said, "Kimi's a bit of a killjoy."

The woman was so afraid the estate was going to deem Moe a poor and wasteful manager, stealing away her partnership with the one pub most likely to survive the estate's mandated trial period. If she lost this partnership, she also lost the ability to latch on to this income stream—even though he was planning to bump her out once he had a firm grasp on the reins. Kimi didn't realize that the two of them spraying each other with soda was the kind of shenanigans that had always made the pub a fun and thriving place when Cesar had been alive, and that surely the estate's executor wouldn't get his undies in a twist over something so minor.

She also probably didn't realize that if she let

her hair down and had some fun over at Brew, Too, the business might turn around a little faster.

"Try dating her," Moe said wryly. He reached over Amy to place the drops on the coffee table.

"You two dated?"

He glanced at her thoughtfully, then away. "I never told you?"

"No." She sat up. It kind of felt like a big deal. One of those things you tell your wife. Even with a marriage pledge.

"When did you date?"

"Almost ten years ago."

The first breakup sundae. It had been about a decade ago, and she'd made it after he'd broken up with someone from the city. *Kimi.*

"How long did you date?"

"About a year."

A year. That was a lot longer than she and Moe had ever lasted.

"You two are very much alike," she teased. "The perfect couple."

Moe made a face.

"What happened?"

"She wanted more."

"More?"

"Marriage," he said, shifting uncomfortably and clearing his throat.

"And you said no?"

"I said no."

"That must have been awkward with you and Cesar."

"He was cool about it and seemed to understand."

"She'd be back in your pants in a heartbeat if you let her."

The surprise on Moe's face couldn't be faked and almost made her laugh, it was so sincere. "The only one allowed in my pants is my wife."

"You know if you find someone…"

"If you're going to say I can step out on you," Moe warned, his eyes flashing, "save your breath. It doesn't matter what our marriage is like, our kids will not grow up thinking it's okay for the man in the family to have a woman on the side. How can we teach our children to respect the opposite sex and honor commitment and relationships if I'm out gallivanting?"

His earnestness made her heart swell with gratitude. "What if you discover true love?"

A small voice inside her asked why she couldn't be his true love. Why couldn't they stay in a relationship for longer than a month or two?

Because it always fizzles, not sizzles, she reminded herself. He was perfect, just not the perfect man for her.

Although lately things *had* been sizzling. Here

and there. When they didn't put a stop to it. Why did they do that, anyway?

Stupid marriage pledge rules.

"If I fall in love, I'll let you know and we'll deal with it then," he said, his tone making it clear that he didn't like the topic. He linked his fingers with hers, his voice losing its irritated edge. "In the meantime, I'm here and I'm yours."

That statement shouldn't make her shoulders relax and her heart beat faster, but it did. Even though she knew he meant only as friends and pledge partners.

"Now, are you gonna do those dishes since I cooked supper, or do I have to make you walk the plank?" Moe asked, tapping her plastic patch.

She leaned closer, her knee pressing against his. "I bet you're hoping I still have this when it's ovulation time again."

"I'm pretty sure acting on any fetishes or role-playing in the sack would break a bunch of our rules." His chest had expanded, everything about him tightening as his eyes darkened with what she could have sworn was something. Something she'd love to explore.

"You need to live a little," she said. They were watching each other, a spell quietly weaving around them. She knew she should look away, get off the couch, but she didn't want to. She was ensnared, mesmerized by their closeness, curious about what would happen next.

"That's the Amy I love," he said warmly. "Always up for an adventure."

"And the Moe I love is a stable life force who makes me feel as though the world is a wonderful place."

"Uh-oh."

"What?"

"You just keep on breaking those rules, like the naughty pirate you are."

"What rule?"

"You said the Moe I love."

"As a friend!" She sat back, the spell breaking. "And you said it first."

"Admit it." He tilted his body closer, his arms holding her tight so she couldn't move, his breath warm on her shoulder and all too tempting. "I'm the man of your dreams. You just haven't let go yet. You crave and need a stable, wonderful man in your life."

She shivered, the anticipation and longing building inside her. "And you need more adventure."

"I agree."

Someone rang the doorbell and she sucked in a breath. Neither of them moved.

Finally she said, "Are you going to answer that?"

"Nope."

She slipped off the couch and out of his arms, heading for the door. If she wasn't careful, she was going to find herself in bed with him. She flung open the door. Nobody was there. But on the front walk was her queen-size bed.

"My bed's back." Her voice sounded hollow to her own ears, and tinged with disappointment. Moe had come up beside her, resting a hand on her shoulder. She wanted to joke, but his tender look of loss took the temptation away. She watched him silently, trying to sort out the weighty mix of feelings pulling at her.

She tucked her arms around Moe's waist, setting her head against his chest. What she had with him, those moments when she let go and didn't think, felt a lot like what she believed love might feel like. A contented peace inside her where everything just felt big and wonderful and wholly right in her world.

But if this was love, then why wasn't she freaking out and looking for the door?

Because real love didn't make you want to run, it made you want to settle in and enjoy it. Love with someone you trusted, someone you wanted to spend every hour with, was the very definition of contentment, wasn't it?

"I'll miss you stealing the blankets," Moe said,

his voice full of affection as he placed his chin on the top of her head. "Shall we set you up in your room again?"

His voice was cheery, and as she slid from his arms, her contentment waned and worries set in. Still, she couldn't help but wonder if this time there might be a way to give each other what they needed in order to make it past whatever had held them back the last time.

Maybe this time they could figure out how to find love. Together.

~

MOE PACED THE BREW ROOM BEFORE LEAVING THE pub for the night. There was no reason for him to be in here, but as he'd been waiting for Amy to finish mopping the hallway he'd begun to fear he was going to kiss her, make love to her, make things way too real. And not just because of the sweet pirate look she had going on with her eye patch, freckles and wavy hair. That contradictory combo had definitely amped things up inside him.

No, it was more about the look she'd given him when her bed had been returned the day before yesterday. The way she'd fitted into his arms and relaxed, as if there was nowhere else on the planet that she belonged. As if she was solely his, heart and soul. For a brief moment there'd been nothing held back, and he'd seen the flash of emotion in her eyes, a look that had echoed how he felt inside.

He didn't want to lose her. He didn't want her to run, to leave him like she had so many times before, because this time, somewhere along the line, he'd let go and fallen for her. And he knew what happened to men who fell in love with Amy.

There was one very good reason that she'd married him. Because he was safe. He wasn't going to fall for her and complicate matters.

But he had. When she'd said that if he found true love he could leave her, it had hurt. It had actually physically hurt as if someone was sliding something sharp into his chest. She hadn't even considered that he'd already found what she'd been talking about.

It was possible that she felt the same way, but was too afraid to say anything, to make a move. Sometimes he felt as though she wanted to say to heck with their rules and go all out and see where it led.

Was she just afraid? Or was hope simply blinding him in a very major way, twisting reality so it fit what he wanted?

"Completed your end-of-day checklist?" she called from the doorway.

"In record time." He turned, catching her with

the eye patch and mop. "Finishing swabbing the decks, matey?"

She flipped up the patch, leaving a red mark circling her eye. "I'm done with this thing. You know how many jokes I got tonight about being a pirate?"

"Besides mine?"

"Besides yours."

"I think it's cute. Adorable." Sexy.

She rolled her eyes. "I'll be ready in two." She disappeared to rinse out the mop.

Moe grabbed his keys and headed for the door, where he waited, his hand on the bank of light switches. Tonight would be the second one not sharing a bed with Amy. Last night he'd tossed and turned until his alarm went off. Then he'd pulled his groggy body out of bed to find Amy looking as defeated by her restless sleep as he was. She'd claimed her bed wasn't the same anymore, but he knew what the problem was. They were sleeping alone.

Amy was checking things as she passed the cleared tables, dusting a fleck of something off one. Her patch was back over her eye, her lips upturned as she made her way toward him, graceful and beautiful. *His.*

He flipped off the lights.

"You're such a jerk," she grumbled as the room plunged into darkness.

"If I wait for you I will be waiting all night."

"I'm five feet from the door!"

"Lock up," he said, pushing his way outside. He held the door for her as she dug through her purse.

"Can you? I can't find my keys. I must have left them on the bar or in the office, and I'm too tired to go back and look."

"You sure Devon didn't sneak off with them again?" Moe placed a hand on her lower back, ushering her out into the warm July night so he could lock up.

"I swear I've kept them tucked away since then. We don't need more furniture going missing."

"Maybe you need to leave your house keys in your purse, and put the pub keys on one of those coil string things around your wrist." Less to lose, and easier to keep track of.

"I like that idea."

"Have I mentioned lately that I am brilliant and a fabulous problem solver?"

"I don't need to inflate that ego."

He chuckled as he locked the pub, engaging its alarm system with his fob. It wouldn't be long until dawn. They really were going to have to figure out how to handle their hours once they had kids.

"It's a good thing I have you," Amy said, as they walked to his truck.

"I love it when you're right and admit to it."

"You're in full form tonight, aren't you?"

"All I'm saying is that you got lucky in the marriage pledge department. Not a lot of women end up with a great guy like me. You should count your blessings."

He opened the passenger side door for her, and she grasped his chin between her thumb and forefinger. The light kiss she gave him on the lips made his heart swell.

He'd do just about anything for more of those.

"I told you you'd soon be kissing me on the lips."

"Well, if we're going to be taking into account everything you say, then why don't I see more women falling at your feet due to your amazing good looks?"

He ran a hand through his still-shorter-than-usual hair. "I've been beating them off when you're not looking."

"In your imagination?" she asked, full of pretend innocence.

He acted wounded as he closed the door for her and walked around the front of the truck, staggering as though clutching a knife pushed into his chest, and grasping the hood for support. He was rewarded with laughter.

He straightened and climbed into the driver's seat.

"Although I could see some women swooning now, since you no longer have that crappy haircut."

"I can't believe you think my old haircut was crappy."

She shifted in her seat to study him, reaching out to brush the hair at the back of his neck. The gentle touch sent shivers down his spine. "You were cute then. You're handsome now."

"Is that why I got a lip kiss?" He started the truck, feeling as though tonight had potential. The potential to go somewhere, cross new lines that they wouldn't backtrack over.

"Maybe it's because we're actually getting out of the pub before dawn for once. Honestly, though, we *are* married. Spouses kiss."

"Even marriage pledge spouses?"

"I can stop kissing you if you'd like."

"I don't want to curtail your hobbies. I'm not that kind of husband."

She awarded him a laugh that filled the cab and lifted his heart.

"Cute babies, I tell you."

"Speaking of babies," she said with excitement, "did you hear the news? Mandy Mattson is *pregnant!*" Amy flattened her hands against her thighs and broke into a huge grin. "I can't believe it. After all of those years of infertility and going so far as to adopt Axel, and now she's pregnant."

"That's awesome. They must be pumped." Moe shook his head, pleased for his old high school friends.

"Mandy's still in shock."

"I'll bet."

He drove down the empty streets until he reached their own, only to spot a vehicle taking the corner to the next block too fast, its wheels squealing.

He shook his head, angered. "Seriously. How are we going to let our kids play on the street if there are yahoos ripping it up?"

"It's the middle of the night. People drive nicely in the daytime."

"They'd better," Moe said, gripping the steering wheel. He parked in front of the house, his pickup being a tight fit in the double garage. At the moment he'd rather spend his energy concentrating on something else.

"Carry me," Amy begged as she opened her door. "My feet are killing me."

"Don't be a baby."

"I should pull out my orthopedic nursing shoes."

Moe grimaced. "Those awful white leather old-lady shoes? Talk about a good way to reduce your tips."

"People aren't that shallow."

"Experiment. I bet that your tips would be..." He paused to calculate some mental math. "...at least 20 percent higher if you wore heels over your old nursing shoes."

Amy scoffed. "Get real."

"Bet?" He turned, ready to shake her smooth hand.

"Yeah? What's at stake?"

"Other than your sex appeal?"

"I'm a married woman. Sex appeal went out the door."

Moe gestured to her eye patch. "Oh, trust me, your sex appeal hasn't left the building."

She put her hands on her hips, the pale light from a streetlight highlighting her cheekbones and perfect lips.

"Fine. I'll wear heels for one shift. A Friday."

Moe winced. Those were busy nights and her feet would be killing her by the end of it.

"You'll wear the same outfit both nights to make sure there's no bias in that regard?" He stooped to pick up their empty recycling bin from the curb.

"I'll wear my Playboy bunny outfit both nights." She began walking up the sidewalk and Moe couldn't help but visualize what her backside would look like in the cute little black bodysuit and fluffy white tail.

"You have a bunny suit?" he asked, hurrying to catch up with her.

Amy stopped walking, and he stumbled into her. He dropped the plastic bin, his arms going around her to catch himself. "Will you wear your eye patch, too?"

She inhaled sharply, her body stiffening as he enjoyed the scent of her neck and hair. A nice blend of Amy and garlic butter from the kitchen.

Tonight was definitely full of potential.

"Moe?"

Something was wrong.

"Why is our front door open?"

CHAPTER 10

*A*my couldn't stop shaking. When she'd lived alone it wouldn't have been out of the question for her to forget to ensure the door was latched all the way, or even to lock it. But Moe always made sure the house was locked up, the windows closed and the stove burners turned off. Open doors did not happen under his watch even when he was tired or distracted by work.

"Were you the last one out of the house?" he asked gently, a slight teasing tone masking what she knew was unease.

"You locked up. I was tossing the recycling out on the curb." She closed her eyes, feeling to blame even though she knew it hadn't been her.

Moe already had his phone in hand. "I'm calling Scott."

As much as Amy didn't like the idea of getting their friend out of bed for what could be nothing, she really didn't want to go into the house until someone who was trained in this sort of thing had checked it out.

"It's probably nothing. I probably forgot."

"You just said it was me." Moe said into his phone, "Sorry to get you out of bed, Scott. Amy and I are pretty sure we locked the front door before going to work, and we just got home to find it wide open. She also couldn't find her keys at the end of her shift."

"They're on the bar, right where I put them down while grabbing my jacket." She gave Moe a dirty look. Her so-called missing keys were not related to this.

Amy was standing close enough she could hear Scott on the other end of the line. "Any evidence of foul play?"

She shivered and Moe put him on speaker as he replied, "We haven't taken a close look. We're still on the sidewalk."

"Don't go inside. I'm on my way." Amy could hear him say something quietly in the background, likely to his wife, Amber, who had undoubtedly also been woken up by the call.

"Tell him I'm sorry. It's probably fine. Stay in

bed. It was likely just Devon sneaking in to pull another prank or something."

Moe hesitated, then said to Scott, "We'll wait for you. There was a car speeding off our street when we came home."

"I'm already up and half dressed," Scott said, obviously having heard them. "None of us are going to sleep if there's any lingering doubt. Hang tight. I'll be there in under five."

Moe's words about her keys had created doubt in Amy's mind and she tried to think whether she'd had an eye on her keys all day. But the shifts and hours blended together and she wasn't sure.

Moe went to tuck his phone into his pocket but then changed his mind, keeping it in his hand instead. He was nervous, something that made Amy even more anxious.

The street was quiet, empty. The vehicle that had squealed around the corner was now nothing more than a memory, and possibly a clue.

"Did you recognize the car?" she asked.

He shook his head. "Did you?"

"What make and model was it?"

"It was an SUV."

"Ethan maybe?" she suggested. Their brother-in-law, the computer guru, would pull a prank on them, but after he'd had a car accident that was no fault of his own, Amy couldn't really see him driving that recklessly, even on an empty street.

"You know how many SUVs there are around town? I know at least ten people with similar models. And his is a darker color."

"Well, it was *someone* and maybe they broke in, or maybe they saw something."

"Or maybe it's a coincidence. We've been distracted and busy lately."

Amy glanced around at the nearby houses. Nobody's lights were on. No witnesses were on hand to help them out.

A bush rustled across the street and Amy stepped closer to Moe. He turned toward the sound and a chubby animal waddled out of the shrubs, its rounded flat tail dragging behind it.

"It's just Beavis," Moe said, letting out a breath as the local legend, a beaver, made his way across the street. He came out every spring and took a few trees from yards near the river, adding to his dam. He was an annoyance, but nobody seemed to mind too much.

Moments after Beavis vanished into a culvert, Scott pulled up in his police truck.

"Hey, guys. Anything new?"

They both shook their heads while Scott did a double take after seeing Amy.

"What happened to your eye?" He glanced at

Moe. "That's from the soda sprayer?" Scott winced and shook his head, easing toward the doorway, drawing his gun. He called into the house, identifying himself. Amy half hoped there were pranksters in there and that they were peeing their pants.

As Scott called out one more time, Amy tried not to giggle, knowing her reaction was ridiculous. But thinking of their friend acting all serious and ready to protect them felt silly somehow. She and Scott used to take turns acting silly in the school's bear mascot costume during high school football games, in between sneaking sips of whiskey under the bleachers. It was still a bit strange to see Scott acting like an official adult with some sizeable responsibilities.

Scott checked out the house interior and returned to the entryway, holstering his gun. "All clear." He crouched to examine the front door's latch.

Moe had his arm around Amy and she shivered again.

"Did someone break in?" Moe asked.

"Hard to say. These older locks are easy to pop without causing damage. They also don't always latch properly."

Moe had moved toward Scott, slowly disengaging from Amy, who clung to his hand. She felt the need to keep looking over her shoulder. When she got to the front door, she almost hoped to see the wood frame damaged by a crowbar, as having no signs of damage seemed eerier.

"Check for anything missing." Scott stepped aside so Moe and Amy could do a walk-through.

Amy visually swept the front room, noting nothing missing or out of place. She hurried to her bedroom, checking for missing jewelry. She didn't own anything fancy or expensive, mostly sentimental items or spontaneous drugstore purchases. Everything seemed to be in place, even her bed. Her tablet was still on the kitchen counter, nothing disturbed.

But still…something didn't feel quite right. She couldn't explain it. It was like the subtle smell of cigarette smoke lingering in the air, or the feeling that someone had been there, that something had been meddled with.

She met up with Moe by the front door. "Anything?" she asked.

He shook his head.

"Do you smell anything?"

Moe sniffed, and shook his head again. "Just your shampoo." He smiled.

"No cigarette smoke?"

"Did you start up again?"

She shook her own head and rubbed her arms.

She had imagined the scent then, as Moe, never a smoker, would have picked up on it immediately.

"Think that car was involved? Like there was a lookout who told them to get out?" She shivered once more, the thought of being watched making her feel as though her life and privacy had been invaded.

"If someone *did* enter, chances are they didn't find what they wanted, or were interrupted. Do you want me to keep watch outside for the rest of the night?" Scott asked.

"I think we're okay," Moe said, giving Amy a squeeze. "But thanks. A few long nights have made us paranoid, probably."

With her arms wrapped tightly across her chest, Amy nodded, even though her gut still told her something wasn't quite right. It wasn't anything big and scary with alarm bells, just something that wasn't lining up properly.

Scott lifted an eyebrow at Moe, who gave a small shrug.

"You know what? I know who can make you feel safer tonight," Scott said. He had his phone to his ear in seconds, calling in Logan, the local security expert, and making everything feel all too real.

~

MOE FELT AS THOUGH HE HAD FAILED AMY—FAILED at keeping her feeling safe in their home. She was scared, trembling against his side, and it made him want to lash out at the world. Yes, the front door had been open when they'd gotten home, but there had been no signs of entry, forced or otherwise. Yes, there had been a car whizzing around the corner of their quiet street when they'd come home a bit earlier than normal. But it was also late at night, when the most unruly teenagers had the run of the town.

He didn't know what to think, say or do. Had there been a break-in? He only knew that Amy was upset, and that had him seeing red, and revved up to slay anything that tried to harm her.

Logan and his associate, Zach, were crouched like boulders in the front doorway, barely uttering a sound as they swiftly installed a new lock set. Just in case.

That middle-of-the-night service was going to set Moe and Amy back a few bucks.

But if it helped settle her nerves, then it was worth it.

Moe continued to hold her against him, wondering if she felt as exhausted and as wired as he did.

By the time the two men had replaced the locks on both the front and back doors, as well as installed a makeshift security system, dawn was lighting the eastern sky.

"You're all set," Logan said. "We can come by and tweak things later. But you're safe enough for tonight." He glanced outside. "Or for this morning."

Zach appeared from the basement, munching on a bag of candy.

"Anything?"

"It's clean." He held out the bag. "Want some?"

Everyone shook their heads.

"What does that mean—clean?" Amy asked, sidling deeper into Moe's arms.

"He did a sweep for…" Logan paused, choosing his words. "…for anything amiss."

"Like someone adding a spy camera?" she asked.

"Exactly."

"Who would do that? This is Blueberry Springs!"

"Things happen everywhere." The two men shared a look Moe didn't like. He had a feeling they knew a lot more about the underbelly of the world than the general population could ever begin to believe. No wonder Zach was having a tough time finding a woman—he lived in an alternate reality where nothing was rose-tinted.

Moe shivered, thinking what that reality might involve, and causing Amy to shrink into his embrace even further.

Zach had picked up the tools, moving outside to wait for Logan.

"I really appreciate you coming in the middle of the night like this," Moe told Logan, after he'd done a quick run-through on how to use the new system.

Logan shook his hand, and said with a grin, "I'll send you a bill, mate."

"I'm sure you will." Eventually. He'd heard through the grapevine that sending timely invoices wasn't a strong suit for the two men. He'd heard about it long and hard from Mary Alice who despised owing people money. "Thanks again."

Scott had gone home to catch some more sleep before his shift officially started in a few hours, and soon Amy and Moe were alone again. The house felt large and vulnerable despite the new security system. Amy's paranoia was starting to wear off on him.

"You okay?" he asked her. The alarm's light was glowing, showing it was engaged. He had made her a cup of chamomile tea earlier, but she'd left it untouched. He was starting to think maybe she needed a shot of something stronger.

"I feel so..."

Violated.

"Want to stay in my room tonight?"

"Are you putting the moves on me?" she teased,

her voice flat, telling him that the incident had hit her more deeply than she was letting on. "Taking advantage of the situation?"

He hooked his fingers in hers, leading her toward his room. "Come on. We'll snuggle with my baseball bat."

"Is that what you're calling it? Rather conceited, don't you think?"

He chuckled at the innuendo. "I was actually referring to the bat I take with me when I coach for the Bears since I don't like the brand the school uses for practices."

Not bothering to undress, Moe pulled back the covers, kicked off his shoes and tugged Amy onto the bed beside him, wrapping them in the comforter. He cradled her in his arms and stroked her hair.

"You're safe," he said. "The security system is set."

"And you're here."

Something swelled in his chest, blocking his ability to speak for a moment.

"Yes, and I'm here." Her body fitted against his, her grip on him slackening as fatigue pulled at her.

Unable to sleep himself, still on hyper alert, he took solace in knowing that she felt protected in his arms and could rest—right where she belonged, in his embrace.

~

SUNSHINE WAS STREAMING THROUGH THE BEDROOM windows when Moe woke up, his hands intertwined with Amy's. Her eyes were drifting open, and he wondered if something had woken them or if they were simply in sync.

"Good morning," he said.

"Did you hear something?" Amy asked, her eyes wide.

"Just the squirrels in our eaves. We're safe."

She snuggled a little deeper into the covers. "Thanks for letting me sleep in here."

"You're welcome to until you feel safer."

"That was really nice of Zach and Logan to change our locks in the middle of the night."

"Are you okay?"

Amy shook her head as though trying to shake off thoughts. "It's the what-ifs, you know? I *know* we probably just forgot to latch the door properly and I'm spooking myself because of the car in the neighborhood. But it's like my mind keeps running down that what-if alley. What if someone knew we would still be at work so they busted in? What were they looking for? Did they take something? Why did they leave the door open?"

"Maybe Logan ratted us out to Devon and the others, and they were in the middle of pulling a new prank. You know, to get even for when we retaliated after they rearranged all of our furniture and took your bed," Moe offered. "Although without Logan saying anything, it was pretty obvious it was us due to the timing of our pranks. But Devon did take your keys before—or so we figure. Maybe this was all just nothing. Just a prank."

It had to be. Otherwise she was going to have him looking over his shoulder all the time if they kept talking like this.

She sighed. "If it was a break-in we probably interrupted it—they likely had a lookout who alerted them and they hightailed it out before getting a chance to do whatever they had planned."

"So all is well?"

"That ends well. I would've lost my mind last night if you hadn't been here," she said, her voice quiet and uneven. "My imagination is way too willing to make something of this."

"We have a security system now, and Logan and Zach did a sweep."

"I know." She gave his hand a squeeze. "You take care of things. And me. You're the best, you know that?"

Moe wasn't sure what to say, the sincerity of her words making him feel unsettled inside.

"Why didn't we ever fall in love with each other?" she asked.

She was watching him, with a serious look in her eyes, he'd never seen before. It was intense but vulnerable, too. He cleared his throat. "I guess because you love the idea of love, not the long-term reality of it?"

"I don't mind the long-term. I just haven't found a man who loves me for who I am." She tapped him on the chest with a heavy sigh. "And you don't count because you don't love me. Not in that way."

"And that's why we have the pledge," he said, stroking her mess of bed-head curls, his chest so tight it was difficult to speak normally. "Plus I can't find a woman who wants boring old Mr. Reliable."

He rolled over, throwing his legs off the side of the bed.

"Maybe more of them do than you realize," she said softly.

As he turned to size her up, he couldn't help but feel as though their relationship had some serious potential this time. The problem was, somewhere between potential and long-term something always happened, leading them back to just friends.

IT HAD BEEN A FEW NIGHTS SINCE THEY'D FOUND THE front door open, and Amy knew she could go back to her bedroom, but it felt empty and cold without Moe. She felt safe curled up against his side, and he didn't seem to mind the company, even though she was pretty sure he didn't believe that anyone had been in their house. She wasn't so sure she did, either.

But it was nice pretending that she and Moe had what everyone else did. It was nice having someone beside her, someone to chat with when she woke up in the morning. And someone to turn to in the dark hours of the night, with slow kisses, warm hands, bodies pressed together.

Amy felt a nudge. Ginger was waving a hand in front of her face. "Earth to Amy. You have that dreamy look in your eyes again."

"Don't be ridiculous. We're just friends making babies together." She did a quick scan of the pub, checking people's drink levels in case anyone needed a refill. Unfortunately, nobody seemed to, which meant she had no easy escape from Ginger.

"Who mentioned anything about Moe?" she asked. "And as for the friends part, have you ever kept track of how many times you kiss that man? Back when you were 'just friends' you'd find every sweet reason to plant one on his forehead or cheek in just about every conversation."

"Did not."

"Did so." Ginger whacked a thick booklet of

raffle tickets on the counter. "Have you got your tickets yet? All proceeds go to the senior center."

Amy sighed and went to the back room to find her purse. She hauled it up front while digging around for a twenty. She rarely won raffles, but hoped that if she did this time she'd get the adorable hand-knitted baby blanket, and have a reason to keep it instead of tucking it away as gift for her prolifically reproducing friends.

She held the twenty out to Ginger, just about pulling it back at the last second. Moe's request for a loan to buy the pub had been conditionally approved this morning. All he had to do was come up with ten grand as a good faith payment, should the estate grant him approval.

He should be in a better mood, although maybe his edginess was due to the spot check made by the estate's executor.

Then again, did they have ten grand? If not, she should be saving up instead of buying a raffle ticket.

Ginger snagged the bill. "Just one?"

"Please."

Ginger tore a ticket off her bundle and Amy shoved it in her purse, then tucked the bag under the bar after double-checking that her house keys were still inside, the pub keys still secured to her wrist by a coiled rubber band. The other night her keys had been right where she'd thought they were —on the bar. Safe and sound. But that didn't make her any less paranoid.

"And for the record," Ginger said, "making babies is what people do when they're in love with each other."

"Do you think he loves me?" Amy asked, immediately regretting have verbalized the question.

"Honey, he's loved you for years. You're both just too afraid to let go and dive in."

"We're just really good friends." Friends who had yet to slip back into the friend zone since they'd begun trying for a baby. Last night they'd even made love, slow and sweet. No calendars or plans, just that easy togetherness that brought them closer.

She was getting in too deep.

And it felt wonderful.

"Give me all your excuses," Ginger said, fingers waving in a "gimme" motion.

Amy shot her a "get real" look, but her friend leaned forward, all ears. "Come on."

"Fine." She sighed and placed her hands on her hips, daring Ginger to dispute all the reasons Amy had for why men didn't stick with her. "I'm not long-term, deep-love lovable. Men want a wife who doesn't take off on scuba vacations on a whim, or change careers. I'm too...selfish. That doesn't make for a good partner." She raised her arms and stepped back with a sigh.

"Moe married you," Ginger replied simply.

"Because we had a pledge."

"He's the one you always come back to. He's always been in your life."

"Because he's my best friend. We always drift back to friends when we try to go for more than that. We fail at doing the whole real relationship thing."

"Because you're afraid to lose the friendship part," she said with a "well, duh!" tone. "You two are making love like hot little monkeys—"

"Are not!" Amy lied indignantly.

Ginger gave her a try-me-again-you-liar look and continued, "You're living together, married, working together, and are still best friends. In fact, you two seem closer than ever."

Amy pressed her fingertips against her eyebrows. It was all true, but this time she worried it wasn't going to end well. They'd come further into this than ever before and she didn't believe they would be able to drift back to mere friendship. Their relationship had a very high potential for crashing and burning, like two planets colliding.

Ginger was furiously shaking her head. "Oh no, you don't! Don't you dare pull back from what's good. I can see you freaking out. This is what's *right* for both of you."

"Ginger…"

"Seriously, girl. Let go. Tell him you love him." She pulled herself over the bar and clenched Amy's hands. "This was meant to be." The ferocious truth blazing in Ginger's eyes—the woman who never failed with her matchmaking—struck Amy in her solar plexus. She believed in them. Believed in their love.

Amy's breath hitched and she stepped back, her throat thick with a mix of fear and hope. "You really think…"

Loud voices filtered out of the back room and into the pub distracting her. She couldn't think of a time when Moe had ever spoken so loudly.

She hurriedly excused herself from the conversation with Ginger.

"We're not done here!" her friend called after her. "You can't just run away from the truth and pretend it doesn't exist!"

Amy hustled in her comfortable nursing shoes, stopping in the doorway to the brew room, where the atmosphere was best described as tense. Kimi, in her dress pants and tight white blouse, was glowering at Moe, whose cheeks were an uncharacteristic red.

Kimi took in Amy with a sweep of her icy gaze,

pausing on Amy's shoes before her mouth twisted with distaste.

Warpath status? Occupied by one angry woman.

No wonder Moe had been in a mood for most of his shift. When he'd kept replying to her are-you-okay inquiries with a we'll-talk-later, Amy had figured it was because having Roald Phipps checking up on him had gotten him perturbed. Now she thought his mood might have more to do with Kimi.

"What's the problem?" Amy asked, crossing her arms.

"When I escorted the executor of Daddy's estate to the pub this morning, so I could show him how around," Kimi said, her chin trembling, "it was unlocked, the alarm off."

"I said I'd deal with it," Moe said, his voice flat.

"Moe is *very* careful about locking up," Amy said. "*Always.*"

"We need to restrict who has keys." Kimi was staring at her.

"That's a good idea," she agreed.

Kimi lifted her brows as though expecting Amy to give up her set, and she raised her brows in return.

"I didn't leave the building unlocked," Amy said. "Maybe it was your brother."

"Spencer doesn't have keys." Kimi stepped closer, blocking the light from the bulb hanging behind her. "There are only three sets." She took another step. "Mine, which are my father's old ones, Moe's and yours." She was closing in, her subtle lilac perfume reaching Amy. "As managers, Moe and I need to have keys."

"We also need someone other than me, who is in town and works full-time, to have keys, Kimi," Moe said. "We talked about this."

Kimi's eyes were wet with tears, but this time they seemed genuine. The woman was losing it. "I just want this place to remain standing as a legacy. It looks like we don't know what we're doing, or that we don't care, when it's left unlocked. The executor is keeping track of everything. He decides whether we win or lose."

Amy noted the number of "we" statements in Kimi's little speech.

Moe let out a long, slow breath and sat on one of the kegs as he scrubbed his fingers through his hair. "Do you think he's gunning to have the offer revoked?"

"I don't know."

An unlocked pub, beer going bad, accounting information missing, inventory out of whack. Things were adding up against Moe.

But not enough for the breakdown Kimi was on the verge of having.

"What's else is up?" Amy asked.

The woman inhaled, eyes closed. "The executor wants to do a spot check."

"Didn't he just do one?"

"Of your home."

"What?" Amy gaped at her, then at Moe. His shoulders were hunched, his arms crossed. She'd bet this was what had caused him to raise his voice.

Kimi looked pained. "Someone told him that Moe is bringing home product and other things he shouldn't."

"He's not stealing."

"Uncle Roald is trying to account for missing inventory."

Moe made muttering sounds under his breath.

"He *should* take stuff home, for all the unpaid work he does," Amy said, "but he doesn't. And what would it matter if he did? He'll be buying the place and then he'd just be stealing from himself."

"Amy," Moe murmured, his jaw tight, his anger barely controlled. "It's fine. I'd want to do the same if things weren't adding up in a business I was responsible for."

"No. This isn't okay. Who said he's stealing stuff?" She whirled on Kimi, ready to deck whoever it was. "Was it you?"

The woman's hands immediately flew up, her face pale. "No, I swear. I have product at my house. If he spot checks *me* and my pub, I'm doomed."

"Well, he's free to snoop around our house," Amy said. "We have nothing to hide."

All Moe took home was the odd supplies catalog and employee schedules—nothing that would ever get him in trouble. At least not in the eyes of a sane person.

"It's an invasion of privacy," Moe said through gritted teeth. "There's absolutely no trust here, and being under the eye of the estate is starting to tick me off."

"When does he want to come in?" Amy interjected.

"Today."

"Well, I'm sure that will be fun," she said. "If I'm home in time I'll try and bake him a batch of cookies."

She shot Kimi a wry smile and the woman let herself out of the room.

Amy turned to Moe. "Entertain their strange requests," she advised. "It's not a big deal."

"They don't trust me. Why do I have to jump through hoops? Haven't I proved myself every day for the past decade?"

"The pub was Cesar's baby, and his anal retentive sibling is executor. I'm sure he thinks he's doing right by his little brother. Unless he's secretly evil, of course. But Cesar probably set things up this way so his kids didn't feel ripped off that you got the cash cow."

Moe's gaze strayed to the empty doorway. "She's freaking out."

"She's stressed. And hey, it could be worse." Amy laughed, trying to lighten his mood. "You could be me! I might have to go back to nursing with my tail between my legs yet again if this doesn't work out. I'm also unsuccessfully trying to have a baby with my best friend, while struggling not to fall in love with him." She froze as she realized what she'd said.

She turned to flee, but Moe's hand snagged her elbow. She didn't turn to face him, too afraid of what she might see.

He said quietly, his breath warm on her shoulder, "I'm in the same boat, Amy. And I'm not just talking about the job or baby-making."

CHAPTER 11

$\mathcal{M}$oe waited in the parking lot for Roald Phipps to meet up with him, as the man had run back in to use the washroom. Apparently the prospect of ransacking Moe's home and violating his privacy made him excited enough to have to urinate.

Moe kicked his feet out, ankles crossed, as he leaned against his truck, watching the fluffy clouds roll past and wishing they could take his worries with them.

Amy had caught herself saying she was falling in love with him.

Falling in love.

With him.

He felt... Nope. There were no words to describe how awesome it had been hearing those words.

They were finally letting go. Finally letting themselves feel the things that had always been there, shoved to the side, ignored or buried. Things were going to be different this time. There'd be no holding themselves back. It was going to work out. Their marriage already felt like their friendship, so full of trust and everything he'd ever dreamed of finding in a perfect match.

Was that why he was dropping details with the pub? He'd had his head in the clouds? Because that's where his head was—right up there with the fluffy ones drifting above.

He found himself smiling.

"You look happy."

Thoughts of Amy and his overall happiness crash-landed as Moe caught sight of Cesar's brother. The man was the opposite of Moe's mentor. While Cesar had been thin with dark hair, he'd had a jolly air about him. Roald was wide, with a full head of white hair, and serious. But he didn't look like someone ready to snatch Moe's inheritance away from him. He looked like he should be handing out candy and making balloon animals. If he smiled more. A lot more.

"I have nothing to hide," Moe said calmly, channeling Amy's earlier composure.

Go with the flow, just like she would. He could do that without his righteousness making him want to slam the man's head into the side of his truck, right?

Yeah, maybe not.

"I'll ride alone, thanks," he said curtly as the man gestured to his Mercedes, wordlessly offering him a lift.

Within minutes he was across town and letting Roald into his house, saying, "There's probably a catalog for vodka varieties, a bunch of business cards from suppliers and may be a few employee schedules from last month."

Roald didn't say a word, simply walked through the house without taking off his shoes, yanking open the fridge as though about to reveal stolen beer, while saying *Aha*! Bottles of condiments rattled with his hard yank, then again as he quickly slammed the door shut. He headed to the attached garage, then quickly came back again.

"Filing cabinet perhaps?" Moe asked, pointing him down the hall toward the makeshift office, which would hopefully soon be a nursery. Once there, he gestured to the dented filing cabinet Cesar had let him take home. "Knock yourself out."

Hopefully, Roald wouldn't make note of the Brew Babies stickers plastering it and assume the worst, having undoubtedly noticed the other filing cabinets in the pub's office were similarly decorated.

Roald sized up the cabinet, then gave Moe an unimpressed look. He pulled a thin pair of reading glasses out of his breast pocket and perched them on the end of his nose.

"Have fun," Moe muttered, standing back.

The front door slammed. "Hey, I'm home." It was Amy.

Moe frowned and checked his phone for the time. She should be working for another few hours at least, and she knew he was here with Roald.

She appeared in the doorway, face flushed, eyes bright. "You ready for date night?" She shot Roald a glance as if to say to Moe, *I have your back. This guy's sifted through enough of our personal effects without a search warrant. Let's make him uncomfortable and give him the boot.*

If Moe had to pinpoint the exact moment he'd fallen in love with Amy, he wouldn't be able to do it. All the feelings he had in this moment had always been there, simply growing stronger with each passing year. And yet, right now, he'd never loved her more. So maybe the question was, when had he *not* been in love with her? And how had he managed to deny such a strong, integral truth for so long?

"Moe?" she prompted.

"Hey, right. Sorry." He jabbed a thumb over his shoulder, gesturing to Roald. "I got distracted by, uh, this."

Roald had pulled out a file folder labeled Brew Babies. Moe caught Amy giving the older man a smug smile when he found the very things Moe had said he'd find. Business cards and a few catalogs. Although no old employee schedules. He must have recycled those.

"If you're done proving to yourself that my husband is indeed a trustworthy manager, we have a reservation to keep."

Roald, still ignoring them, held up a second file folder with a grease stain on the front, this one unlabeled. He opened it and pulled out a piece of paper, his thin lips creased in a frown. "What's this?"

Moe took the paper. It looked like a complete financial statement for Cesar's holdings—more than just Brew Babies. Something he shouldn't have in his possession. But somehow did.

AMY WAS TRYING TO SEE WHAT MOE WAS HOLDING. It was obvious he didn't know why the document had been in with his files. It was also obvious that it was bad news.

"I only got a Brew Babies breakdown for the bank loan application," Moe said. "Not all of this."

"What is it?" She tried to peer over his shoulder. It was a page full of numbers, some of them very large. He nudged her away as though she was interfering with his ability to concentrate.

Roald shook his head and snapped the paper from Moe's grip. He placed it back in the folder and tucked the whole thing against his chest as if he was a quarterback about to go on a sprint down the field. Or in this case, out of the house.

"There's no reason for you to have this financial document, let alone have it at home in an unsecured filing cabinet. One that looks as though it belongs to the pub, I might add."

"I don't know how that file got here," Moe stated, his tone patient and calm.

"Someone must have put it in there," Amy said quickly.

That sounded weak. Really weak. Both men glanced at her and she shrugged. "You know, whoever *framed* you. Ratted you out."

Roald considered the statement.

"Or maybe it was still in the cabinet when you brought it home."

"This is the property of Brew Babies?" Roald asked, indicating the filing cabinet.

"Cesar gave it to me a year and a half ago, because it's dented and he no longer needed it."

Roald checked the document, peering at it through his reading glasses. "These dates are from a few weeks ago."

So much for that idea.

Roald said stiffly, "Having this document is in direct violation of—of…"

Amy could see he was thinking fast, trying to come up with something he could smack Moe with to punish him.

"Moe's the best manager this pub has had in forever," Amy said.

Roald went still. "Are you saying my brother was not a good manager?"

"No, no. She's not saying that."

"I'm saying Moe does a lot more than anyone credits him for."

"It's been a learning curve, but I'm getting the hang of it," Moe stated. "And I truly don't know why that statement is here. What would I even do with it?"

Roald frowned in thought.

"Cesar trusted Moe," Amy said. "If you're going to punish him for one piece of paper being where it shouldn't—"

"He's been making errors left, right and center."

Roald let out a pained-sounding exhalation. "What am I supposed to do? It's my job to uphold my brother's last wishes. Not overlook blunders and indiscretions." He waved the folder. "I have no choice. The proper thing to do is request the immediate withdrawal of the estate's offer of purchase. Moe has been found to be operating in a manner not in line with Cesar's last wishes. There's really not a lot I can do. I can't ignore this." He stepped around them and began moving swiftly down the hall.

"You can't withdraw the offer," Amy said, chasing after him.

"I know things haven't been as smooth as they were when Cesar was alive," Moe called, "but Kimi and I are working together to fix things. We're making strides with both places. Plus the loan got approved this morning. I'm ready to go ahead with this. If you want to protect your brother's legacy, let it survive. Don't sell it off in pieces to the highest bidder."

Roald had paused at the end of the hall and Amy believed he might actually be getting through to the man.

"Kimi just replaced karaoke with poker night in her pub last week," Moe added. "It was a really promising night. Please let me have until the end of September. Let me prove myself."

Roald opened his mouth and Amy could tell he was going to deny Moe's request.

"If you pull the offer, we quit," she blurted.

If they were going to shut the doors and liquidate the place it would likely happen overnight, and having employees would become a moot point, but she had to *do* something. She couldn't let Roald snatch this from Moe.

"How about I just fire you instead?" Roald said, clearly unimpressed by her ultimatum. "You're probably not helping Moe's case anyway, since I've heard you tend to misplace your keys. The pub was left unsecured last night. And then there was the time the two of you were locked in the office together with nobody manning the bar. Maybe I should do what he can't and fire his wife."

Oh, she did not like that. Not one bit.

"She's a good employee," Moe said, his voice low and careful, as if he was talking to someone perched on the ledge of a skyscraper and looking to jump. "She brings in some of the best tips because customers love her. She remembers them, their preferences and their orders."

Amy stayed quiet for a moment, pondering Roald's knowledge about her and Moe locked together in the office. Had Kimi been ratting out Moe? Using his knowledge to bolster her own pub, but secretly undermining him so he lost his? She'd get to keep Brew, Too, while getting half the cash from the liquidation of Brew Babies. Not a bad deal.

"None of that matters," Roald said, "if she leaves the business vulnerable to thieves. It's difficult to make an insurance claim if she has a history of leaving the pub's keys accessible to Joe Public."

"You know what?" Amy said, her patience gone. "I'm about tired of your family. How about you apologize to Moe and reinstate the offer, or we'll both quit. Effective this very moment. Maybe then you'll see how much he does and what a good man he is."

"Amy..." The warning in Moe's voice was as thick as fog rolling in off the Atlantic.

"No." She crossed her arms. They were a team. They had each other's backs and it was time to stand up for themselves. She knew Moe wanted to play it safe, glide under the radar as much as possible until the place was in his hands, but he was going to lose everything he'd worked toward if he didn't speak up and make a stand.

"He deserves to have the pub," Amy declared.

Roald crossed his own arms. "That is for me to decide, and because of your interference and belligerence I feel it would be best if you moved on."

"Oh, I'll move on all right."

"We will mail you your final paycheck. There's no need to return to Brew Babies."

"What?" Amy laughed, despite knowing it was totally the wrong thing to do. "You don't have the authority to fire me."

"I just did."

"Let's put a damper on things," Moe said calmly, his face pale. He put an arm in front of Amy, guiding her back from Roald. "Emotions are running a little high, and we're probably not at our best when it comes to decision making. Maybe we should talk about this tomorrow."

Amy grabbed Moe's arm. "If I go, he goes," she said to Roald.

The split-second hesitation in Moe's reaction told Amy everything. She was on her own. Today he wasn't backing her up. They were no longer a team.

"Never mind. You stay, but consider me gone."

Moe felt horrible. Amy had tried to stand up for him and had only managed to get herself terminated. Didn't she know better than to play the ultimatum game with someone who was all about power and control? Roald might not even have the authority to fire her, but she'd made it almost impossible to come back to the pub without someone stepping on their own pride in the process.

He and Amy never fought, but they definitely were now. Especially since he'd hightailed it out of the house after Roald, to confirm that he wasn't actually going to recommend the estate pull the purchase offer, making her feel second to the pub.

The only good news was that Roald wasn't yet pulling the offer. Firing Moe's wife was apparently enough fun for one day.

Moe pressed the heels of his hands to his eyes and let out a sigh that sounded like defeat even to his own ears. He'd let Amy down. Sure, he could hire her back in a few months, once the place was his. The problem was that he'd chosen self-preservation over her side of the battle. He'd chosen the long game, which meant dropping her. And good men didn't drop their wives.

The worst part had been the wounded look in Amy's eyes when he'd returned to the house to tell her the offer hadn't been withdrawn. He couldn't recall her ever appearing so hurt. Not even when Dexter had broken up with her instead of proposing.

"Amy?" He knocked on her bedroom door. She'd retreated as soon as Roald had left. They should both get back to the pub, but Marissa could hold down the fort for a little longer.

She opened the door, her eyes red, her anger so blatant he took a step back.

"Would it have killed you to defend me? To be a team?" She was blinking furiously, the dammed up tears in her eyes threatening to flood forth if she stopped.

"I'm sorry. I was trying to secure our future."

"I thought I was your future. I forgot we were nothing more than *friends*." The hurt was back in her eyes and he had to look away, knowing he'd been the one to cause it.

They were more than friends. Hadn't she felt that? Hadn't she been there, right there alongside him, believing that this time it was different, this time it was real?

"If we'd both walked away from our jobs, then where would we be?" His frustration was coming out in his voice and he was unable to control it.

"He wouldn't have let us."

"He let *you*."

Amy's jaw tightened and she looked away.

"You need to ask for your job back."

She crossed her arms, eyes flashing. "Never."

"We *need* these jobs. We need to play nice and buy the pub, even though you just did your best to blow our plan to pieces." He swiped a hand down his face, trying to rein himself in. Lashing out at her wouldn't help, wouldn't change things. But his pub loan was contingent on *both* he and Amy having jobs, since she'd had to sign, as well. He wasn't sure how this was going to impact things.

Maybe he should have just walked away when Roald had started lashing out. He could have taken Amy's hand in his, put up the For Sale sign and left town.

"Sometimes other things are more important than plans," Amy said. "Things like happiness and loyalty."

"Trying to preserve our livelihood has nothing to do with loyalty. I'm sorry I didn't choose you."

"It's fine," she said, using that special emphasis on *fine* that made men cringe. "We have a marriage of convenience, which isn't *real*. I forgot. That's all." The door was open wide now, still poised in her hand, as though she was ready to slam it shut.

But instead of slamming it, she did something worse. She closed it so gently he could hear his own heart crack.

CHAPTER 12

$\mathcal{A}$my had barely spoken to him in two days and it was killing him. It felt odd not having her working by his side in the pub. She was always asleep when he came home, heading out just when he was waking up.

If they made it over this bump, this was how their lives would be. Him working weird hours, her at home living a different life.

"Can we talk?" Moe asked, cornering Amy out on the back deck. She was drinking a cup of coffee, her nose in a book.

"About the fact that the whole Phipps family seems to be playing you, sabotaging you? That part? Or the fact that maybe owning the pub wasn't meant to be, and if you buy it you'll end up miserable?"

"What are you talking about?"

"I think we need some distance."

"From each other?"

"The situation." She was flipping pages, looking at them, but obviously not reading a word. "I called your cousin Dallas in Indigo Bay and he's moved up our honeymoon. We can leave tomorrow."

"I can't leave." Things were precarious enough right now. If he left he could kiss the pub goodbye. "We can't afford for me to lose my job right now. And what's this about Kimi and Spencer? How have they been sabotaging things?"

Her voice dipped as she said, "We need this trip, Moe. It's just a few days and you have banked holiday time."

Moe growled in frustration. "I'd love to sit on a beach and pretend this mess doesn't exist, and that it doesn't matter. But I'm the one in charge of the pub. It does matter, and I can't live for the moment while letting the future fall apart on us."

"Don't you wonder how that paper got into your office? The soda order that Spencer—the gamer who never had a thing to do with the business—was able to solve overnight? My money is on him."

"What are you talking about?"

"He'd benefit. He could be meddling, hoping

you'll fail so he'll get half the liquidation cash. Why wouldn't he? It's a lot easier than working."

"He's been helping us."

"Did Scott tell you the jukebox is hot? As in stolen? There's a nice chunk of your manager bonus gone. Scott's probably getting the paperwork in place to march in and seize it right now."

"It's hot?" Moe rubbed his chest with the heel of his hand.

"And the suddenly spoiled vat of beer? Weird, right?" She set down her book and leaned forward. She was throwing so much at him all at once, and he needed some time to sort out his thoughts.

"Honestly, what's the worst that can happen if we go away?" she asked him.

Moe pinched the bridge of his nose.

The worst thing? Didn't she know? Didn't she understand?

They were just too dissimilar. He'd always been her fallback guy, the one she'd never truly understand or love as more than a friend. She probably hadn't even thought about how she was going to get a new job. Everyone knew she was trying to get pregnant and wouldn't stay with a job for long before needing time off to have the baby.

Moe's hands flexed. "If you want kids you can't just be spontaneous and follow your heart. You can't just throw your hands in the air and walk away when things get complicated."

"I'm not asking you to! I'm asking you to step back and really look at this. All of it." Amy stood, shoving her chair out of the way. "Things have a way of working out, and a few days away can give you perspective. That pub owes you nothing and you owe it even less." Her jaw tightened and her eyes flashed. "Sometimes you have to let go and follow your gut."

"And sometimes, Amy," he said, hearing the resignation in his own voice, "you have to stick with something even when it sucks and seems impossible."

She headed for the house, her moves stiff with anger.

"I'll see you when I get back. If you change your mind, you know where to find me."

AMY SAT AT THE TIKI HUT BAR ON THE BEACH, THE Atlantic Ocean rolling in waves behind her. Indigo Bay was gorgeous, the weather perfect, the accommodations adorable, but she was miserable. She was staying in a pink cottage meant for honeymooners. It had a heart decoration on the door made out of driftwood, and flower petals had been strewn across the canopy bed upon her arrival, champagne chilling in a bucket of ice. Everything was perfect except her heart. It hurt.

Which made no sense. The whole being-in-love thing with Moe couldn't have been real. She was too flighty and he was too planned. She didn't have what it took to be a true wife and he didn't have the whimsy she loved.

She rubbed her chest, wishing the heavy heartache there would go away. It felt like the longer she stayed here the worse she felt, and the more the pain spread throughout her whole being.

"Would you like a piña colada?" asked Kelso, a young surfer type manning the outdoor bar

"Why not?"

"Good. It's the only fancy drink I know how to make."

"Aren't you a bartender?" For the past half hour, he'd been pouring drinks, then pausing to kiss the other staff member behind the bar whenever their paths crossed. It made Amy strangely wistful for Moe. She'd thought they were going to have that, and they almost had. But somehow…somehow things had gotten messy.

"The regular bartender decided to get himself hit by a car. Kinda left us high and dry. I usually just help him out with settling tabs, and apparently didn't pick up much when it came to mixing drinks."

Amy folded the square cocktail napkin in front of her and frowned. Maybe Moe was right. Maybe he couldn't just pick up and leave Brew Babies. Marissa knew how to make a few drinks, but it was always Moe who mixed the complicated ones without even a second's thought. Still, he could have found someone to step in for him so he could take his vacation days like he'd planned to at the end of August. And it sure would have given Roald a nice dose of reality. Brew Babies was nothing without Moe.

But he'd chosen the pub and his commitment to it over her, not willing to trust her and give up on having a plan even for a few days. She got it, she did. But now what? She was on their honeymoon alone, a honeymoon that Moe had booked for them. And she wasn't really sure where things were going from here.

Amy flipped over her phone, hoping for a text.

Kelso slid the drink toward her.

"Thanks. What will you do about the bartender?" She took a sip of her drink. It was a bit watery, but tasty. Yet somehow unappealing, too.

"He'll come back or we'll replace him."

Maybe that was what Moe was afraid of. Afraid that when he came back to Blueberry Springs after their trip he'd find himself cut out of the pub altogether. But why couldn't he see that the Phippses were messing with things? They had to be. It was the only logical explanation, because even though Moe had been stressed and stretched to the limit, he didn't do things like spoil a whole vat of beer under his watch, or forget to lock the pub.

Or the house.

She lost her keys, yes…but sometimes people took them to break into the house and pull pranks.

Or plant documents.

Her spine straightened.

How could she prove that? There had to be a way.

But she couldn't, could she? And Moe knew that. It was a futile avenue to go down, one that would waste energy and make them appear as though they were looking for someone else to blame for their own shortcomings. Moe was playing carefully, trying to protect her, shelter her and make sure she had what she needed in order to fulfill her family plan. And she'd gone in all high-and-mighty with her sword, sacrificing herself. Well, stepping in front of the obviously speeding train. The worst was that as she'd gone down, she'd expected him to jump onto the tracks and join her.

How unfair was that?

He was right. And she'd acted selfishly, when she'd thought she'd been justified in her response.

In other words, she'd blown it.

She grumbled in frustration, catching Kelso's notice.

"Something wrong with the drink?"

"No." She gave him a frown, glumly pushing the glass away. "My husband is right."

"Don't tell him that," Kelso warned, with a laugh that was light and free. Just like Moe's used to be when all he had to do was worry about tending bar.

"I think I might have to. I thought I was in the Palace of Righteous Indignation, but I think I might actually be in the doghouse."

"They're easy to mistake for each other," Kelso said supportively.

"Are you sure you're not a real bartender? You're a pretty good listener."

Kelso chuckled and uncapped a bottle of beer, sliding it across the bar to someone dripping water and sand. "Where are you from?" he asked Amy.

"Nowhere you would've heard of. Out West. Mountains. Beautiful. Everybody minds everyone's business. You can't find a man because there are only twenty eligible in a one-hundred-mile radius. So you marry your best friend so you can have kids together. And then you fall in love and fight, and end up on your honeymoon alone, thousands of miles away. Did I mention we're trying to have children together?" She sighed, sinking into a heap in her chair. "And that he was the best I've ever had."

"Blueberry Springs?" Kelso asked.

Amy slapped her hands on the bar. "No way. How'd you know?"

"I think Ginger McGinty may have mentioned your unorthodox arrangement while she was here the other month."

"What a small world."

"She set me up with my girlfriend. Rather, fiancée. We got engaged last night."

"Congratulations."

"Ginger's a good matchmaker."

"She can find anyone for anyone." Except poor Zach. But maybe his time would come.

Kelso rolled his eyes upward as though thinking. "If I recall correctly, Ginger thought you'd found your Mr. Wonderful."

"Moe?" Amy sighed again. "Yeah. It never works out for us. I don't know why. We're kind of perfect together." She thought back to their fight and how she'd been her own worst enemy, from the moment Roald had stepped into their day right on up to now.

"This time it was me. I'm the one who messed up."

"You love him and left him? And now you're knocked up?" Kelso glanced at her untouched drink meaningfully.

"No." She began shaking her head. "I'm not..." Wait. There *was* a chance she could be pregnant. It would explain her lack of interest in the alcoholic beverage and how her chest ached—and not just in the brokenhearted way.

"The gift shop sells pregnancy tests," he said quietly.

"You really are a bartender at heart, aren't you?"

He gave a small smile. "So what were you really going to say? About Moe?"

Amy studied the grains of beach sand scattered on the polished wood bar, then said, "He never fully lets go in our relationship because I never trust our love. I'm too afraid I'll lose him." Her voice was shaking as she voiced the truths she'd kept buried for so long. "But he's the man who's always there for me. He's the one I always come back to." She felt the conviction and strength of her words, the power of their truth building inside her. "Moe is my man. He always has been. I need to find a way to make this right."

She needed her man at her side. Her best friend, her partner, her Moe.

"Need the shuttle schedule for the airport?"

She stood up, feeling warm sand sliding into her flip-flops. "And a plan. A plan to win back my husband."

~

MOE SIGHED AND PULLED OUT HIS VIBRATING PHONE. It had lit up with an invitation to join a video chat with Farrah. His mom. Not Amy, who was living it up in Indigo Bay while he tried to put their lives back together.

Lives.

His life.

Their marriage wasn't what she'd signed on for. He still couldn't be the man she needed, and he wasn't what she wanted in her life.

His phone vibrated again.

Twenty years of silence and his mom wanted to have a conversation? Today?

She'd better be dying or something, because he was *not* in the mood for a hey, long-time-no-see chat.

Moe tugged at his hair, then accepted the invitation, knowing it would be at the back of his mind all day if he didn't.

A familiar face filled the screen. Inquisitive eyes like Lily's, brown hair like his own. She looked like her photographs from the family album. Fun and free, only older.

"Hi," he said.

"Wow. You're so handsome," Farrah cooed.

"Thanks," he said awkwardly. He didn't really remember her as a woman who cooed.

She laughed nervously. "Sorry. I hope this isn't weird. Your name came up online as someone I might know, and I thought 'why not?' and sent you a friend request. When you accepted I had this spontaneous need to chat and see your face and hear your voice."

Spontaneous need. She'd had one of those back when he was a kid, and it had encouraged her to walk out on her family. Just like Amy's spontaneous need to take on Roald had gotten her fired. And then her spontaneous need for space and perspective had sent her across the country.

If she was pregnant, what would they do? It was obvious their marriage wasn't going to work. But they'd still have to figure out how to be a team and work together instead of have one of them unilaterally decide to throw the entire plan out the window.

"I held off on videoing you, though," his mother was saying, "and then today I just couldn't any longer! Now here we are."

"Here we are."

There was something childlike and free about her bubbly personality that reminded him of Amy. That freedom and fun-loving side he'd always envied a little bit. But there was also a seriousness in the way she was openly studying him.

Her focus flicked to something behind him. He glanced to see if someone had joined him in the room. He was still alone.

"Where are you?" she asked.

"The brewing room in Brew Babies. Here in town. I'm a bartender." Barely. He could wake to find a pink slip, or a withdrawal of the purchase offer tomorrow, if he wasn't careful.

"I heard you're more than that."

"I'm just a bartender," he insisted.

"I heard you've been quietly managing the place for years," she said with confidence, "and have made it into a thriving place to hang out."

Who had she been talking to? He supposed she must still have friends in town, even though to the best of his knowledge she hadn't been back in years.

"I also heard that you got a very generous offer to purchase the pub."

"You've been talking to Lily," he stated. He'd told his sister all about the pub the same night he'd told her he was getting married.

"I called her up after I heard the news about

what happened in her restaurant last year. We've been talking. She didn't tell you?"

"No."

"Oh." Her voice had gone flat, the obvious hope that had been buoying it gone. "Well. Are you going to buy it?"

"I haven't decided," he fibbed. What else did he have in his life if not this pub? He wasn't so sure he still had Amy.

"Do you want it?"

"I could be an owner." And he could see himself running the place, single, happy enough.

She laughed, deep and rich, her voice filled with affection when she said, "You sound like your father."

"Maybe he has a point. This could be my chance to move myself and future family upward."

Future family? Where and when was he going to find one of those?

"Is that what you want?" she asked gently. "Is that what will make you happy long-term? Because if it will, grab it with both hands."

"I'm working on it," he said, well aware of the defensive edge to his voice.

"What? Don't you want it?"

Man, she was pushy.

"Rodney, you can talk to me."

"I said I'm working on it. And everyone calls me

Moe." And no, he couldn't talk to her. She was basically a stranger.

"Fine. Moe. So? Tell me about how this pub is going to change your life for the better."

"You know, most mothers who haven't talked to their kids in a few decades usually start with innocuous topics like the weather. Not pushing them to pour their hearts out about their career choices."

"Oh, Moe," she said, her eyes crinkling. "You haven't changed a bit."

"Look," he snapped, her persistence and caring tone getting under his skin. She didn't have the right to walk into his life and immediately start caring. "I don't want to turn out like my dad, where I'm never home to tuck my kids in at night." His heart ached just thinking about missing out on his kids' childhoods, and on how close he and Amy had come to creating a family, a home, finding love. He forced himself to continue. "I don't want to miss every family supper. I don't want my wife to feel as though she's raising our family alone." He stopped, staring his mother down through the screens that separated them. "That's how this pub will make me happy. Long-term."

She didn't avoid his gaze, but stared right back at him. "Well, it seems as though you've turned out all right, despite all of that."

"Because I'm avoiding your mistakes."

"Well, don't avoid them all," she said, a slight edge to her tone, "because I did some stuff right."

He was too angry to reply. He was pretty sure, when it came to the big stuff, that she'd definitely messed up.

She took a steadying breath, and he got the feeling she hadn't just got in touch on a whim, but had planned it. He wondered if their conversation was going better or worse than she'd expected.

"Will being the owner give you the freedom to be there for your family?" she asked. "Will it make you happy? Because happy parents matter a lot to kids, not what it is that actually makes them happy. It's rarely a job, and more often who they come home to. When your father and I started fighting all the time I realized I was ruining our family's happiness. I saw how our fighting and snippy comments brought you down, and would soon bring down Lily, too, once she was old enough to understand. That wasn't what I wanted for you."

She paused, as though expecting him to acknowledge her words somehow.

"Leaving was difficult, Moe. So incredibly difficult. And each time I saw you after I'd left..." Her voice cracked. "I thought I was strong enough to do it." She shook her head. "But I wasn't. None of us were. You were better off without me falling in and out of your life as my new work schedule allowed." She dipped her head, letting out a breath so shaky he feared it was going to break her. Then suddenly she threw back her head, conviction and urgency ringing in her voice as she stated, "You might seize this opportunity to be the owner, but you might also make new mistakes. You might repeat your father's, just in a new way." Her voice was still trembling with emotion, but she was facing him, not backing down. He now knew where Lily got her strength.

"I understand I haven't earned the right to give you life advice. I just hope you listen to your gut. Really listen to it. Forget the reasons for and against your decisions, and listen to what will make you and Amy happy. Sometimes you find yourself in a situation where things are never going to work out perfectly, and you have to choose the path where you and the ones you love will be the happiest. Even if you don't end up where you thought you wanted to be."

Moe wanted to be angry at her. To hold on to the emotion like a shield, keep her words from being real and hitting that soft spot inside him that was filled with doubts.

He remembered the fights she'd had with his father, and because of that, he understood why she'd left. He remembered the quiet peace of the house and how everyone could breathe once she'd gone. But he also remembered the heartbreak. The sadness when she didn't come back, didn't stay in touch as often as he'd have liked. The feeling of not being loved enough to matter in her world.

Was what she'd done really the best for all? Had she taken the path that would give everyone more happiness?

"According to Lily, you married a wonderful woman who's been your best friend for nearly a decade," Farrah said. "You're already miles ahead of where your father and I ever were. Promise me you won't take that for granted. There are a million ways to make money and to be there for your kids, if that's what you're seeking."

She glanced off screen for a moment, then said, "I have to run. But I just wanted to say, sometimes you have to let go of your goals and expectations, find happiness and put it first."

He'd always thought goals, expectations and happiness were one and the same. But maybe they weren't, and that was what Amy had been trying to tell him.

And maybe his new goal should be to put love first.

~

Twenty minutes later Moe was still sitting in the brew room, trying to sort out his mother's words, his feelings for Amy and whether there was any way he could ever win her back.

His worst fears had come true. He'd fallen for Amy and she'd left him.

And where was he? Sitting here letting it all happen. Letting her leave.

He wasn't even fighting for her.

What was wrong with him?

He and Amy weren't like his parents. They didn't fight. He was happy with *her*, not with the pub. He'd been overjoyed every time she returned to her waitressing job and miserable every time she left.

He needed to be with *her*.

"I'm worried about Kimi and her pub," Roald said without any preamble as he joined Moe in the brew room. The man was like Kimi—just magically appearing in the middle of the workday and expecting to be able to talk. "I'm worried that she's chasing after something that won't ever turn a decent profit, and that if I let her inherit it, she'll lose her shirt. Is there any hope of turning it around?"

"Roald, not now."

"I'm in town. You can do whatever you were doing while we talk."

Moe's insides roiled with anger. Roald wanted

him to pass judgment on Kimi and her business abilities. He understood the concern, but Moe wasn't the proper person to ask.

"Did you have this same conversation with Kimi about me and this pub?"

Roald's mouth opened but nothing came out.

"It's fine. I understand. It's all about the family." Moe nodded to himself, thinking. "I actually really get that. And this place is my family. And it's my wife you fired." He stood. "So, I'm taking my vacation days."

"What? You can't! Who will replace you?"

"As the executor, you're authorized to deal with *staffing* issues, I believe."

The man had cut down the woman he loved, riled her, then fired her.

Holding on to this pub had never been the right thing to do. It had simply looked like the easy thing.

They could move.

They could find new jobs.

Starting now.

"I enjoyed watching this place grow, serving customers, and generally just being a bartender," Moe said. "This pub has been great for the town, and for me. But I understand that you need to do what you need to do, but I sincerely hope you won't act rashly."

"Are you quitting? Giving up your rights to this business?"

Moe hadn't quit something in a very long time, and he gave himself a moment to reflect on what exactly he *was* doing. "You know…I might be quitting. Yes, I think I am." He handed his pub keys to the stunned man. "I'll really miss this place."

Roald shook his shoulders as though his indignation couldn't be wholly contained. "It won't be here when you return."

"My honeymoon is more important, and I'd hate to miss it. Actually, let's correct that first part. My *wife* is more important." His wife. A woman who was creative, enterprising and always landed on her feet. It was time to take a lesson from her even if it scared him nearly witless. It was time to try running away. Well, maybe just walking away.

"I'm not ready to liquidate," Roald said, his tone formal.

"It sounded as though you were the other night, while threatening me and my wife. But hey, I know how it goes." He clapped the guy on the back, satisfied when he winced. "I'm sure you'll find someone to fill in. Spencer thinks he's quite capable of running the place. Maybe give him a shot."

Roald's lips twisted.

"I'm a fixer, Roald, my man, and it's time I fixed something important."

~

AMY STARED AT THE PREGNANCY TEST.

She couldn't blink. She couldn't think.

They'd done it.

She was pregnant.

She sagged onto the bed and quietly listened to her own breathing.

A baby.

Their baby.

Snapping to, she took in the pink honeymoon cottage. Out the windows she could see the sandy shores of the Atlantic Ocean. Thousands of miles from Moe. From the father of this baby growing inside her.

Thank goodness she hadn't drunk that piña colada.

She scrambled for her phone and checked the time. If she was quick she could catch the next airport shuttle.

She'd come up with that plan to win back her husband during the flight.

They were going to be parents. She had to figure out how to be that special someone for him, so love and friendship could weave its way into something spectacular that lasted a lifetime. That soul-level love that she'd found only with him.

She picked up the cottage's phone and hit zero, patching herself through to guest services.

"Indigo Bay Cottages, Zoe speaking. How can I help you today?" said a friendly female voice.

"I'd like to book a spot on the next shuttle to the airport."

"Sure thing. Is this Ms. Carrick in the honeymoon cottage?"

"Yes."

"I'm sorry you won't be staying with us longer. Is there anything I can do to help make things more enjoyable?"

"Get my husband over here?" She laughed, the sound hollow even to her own ears.

There was a pause on the other end of the line.

"I'll see what I can do," Zoe said carefully.

"I'm just kidding. The shuttle booking is all I need."

"I'll send someone around to collect you and your luggage in twenty minutes."

"Thanks."

After Amy hung up, she began tossing items into her suitcase.

All too soon there was a knock at the door.

Seriously? That was *not* twenty minutes.

Grumbling to herself, she yanked the zipper closed on her bag and hauled it to the door, while taking a quick visual sweep of the room. The couch had her book and phone charger on it, and she collected them as she went by.

She opened the door and dropped her bag in surprise.

"I thought maybe I could join you on our honeymoon?"

It was Moe. Looking so handsome and sheepish and definitely hopeful.

Amy didn't know what to do. She didn't plan for this. She wanted to wrap her arms around him and sob into his neck and never let go, but there were so many things to sort out. So many questions.

But all she could think of was that he'd come here for her.

"You're here. For me?"

"For you," Moe said simply.

She picked up her bag, shifting it in her grip. They should go home. Figure things out. Put one foot in front of the other and do lots of planning or talking or something smart, because she didn't know how to do this. She just knew she was desperate to get over these awkward misunderstandings, all the hurt and confusion, and be where she'd been with him only days ago. Happy and sure of things. In love.

She wanted a plan. A plan with Moe.

"Although maybe I'm too late?" Moe asked,

when she didn't speak. He was shifting from foot to foot on the cottage's small porch. His hair was in that stage between short and getting slightly shaggy. He looked perfect. He looked like that cavalier but steady man she'd always loved so dearly.

Amy was unable to form sentences to express all the thoughts running through her mind. The word *late* stuck in her mind. "No, *I'm* late."

Moe's face sagged with disappointment. "Maybe we can catch the same flight home and talk about things?"

"I mean I'm *late*-late." She clutched her book and charger against her chest.

"Okay." He reached for her bag.

"But we fought and then you came here to be with me?" she asked stupidly. "You have work. The pub."

"I think I quit my job. No, I did," he said firmly. "And right now I'm taking my vacation days."

"You quit?" She gasped, dread slipping into her, cold and unforgiving. Moe was the steady one. The planner. The one who made sure everything would work out and be okay. He looked to the future. "You quit your job on a whim?"

"I thought it was time to take a page out of your book. Live a little. Let others stress out about stuff instead of me. We can find new jobs. Move somewhere else if we need to."

Amy felt the world swaying. "Moe, I'm pregnant."

"I just want to be with you..." He'd carried on with his little speech, his words fading as her sentence sank in. He blinked twice. Then he paled and gripped the doorframe. "I quit my job," he breathed, bending over. Then he popped back up again. "I quit my job," he repeated firmly. "Quit it. Gone." He threw up his hands and laughed.

She'd broken him.

He bent over again and she heard his swift intake of air.

"Moe..."

"Maybe I should sit down. No, no. I'm okay." He straightened yet again, a wan smile on his pale face. His eyes were happy even though he looked a tad freaked out. "I came here to enjoy the honeymoon, and to beg you to come back to me, as well as to try and figure out how to be the man you need. I'm here. I'm here and I'm yours if you haven't already found someone new."

"Moe, shut it." She yanked him inside. Then called out to the man who'd just driven up on the golf cart, to fetch her or Moe or her suitcase or heaven knew what. "We're staying until the end of our reservation. Can you tell the airport shuttle people and the front desk, please?"

The man grinned and gave her a salute before driving off.

"I'm sorry," Moe said, as soon as she shut the door.

"No, don't be. Just sit. We have to talk."

He closed his eyes and sank into the couch, hands clasped in front of him.

Where to start?

"I love that you're here. That you came." A warm feeling started like a flicker of light in her chest, expanding until it filled her as she thought of how he'd come to her. "Absolutely love it. But I need you to know that I don't need Mr. Whimsy. I thought I did. I need Mr. Steady. I need you. That's the man I need and love."

"I quit my job."

"I know. I love that. I do. I'm excited you're here. But right now I need to tell you how I feel. I know I should have been a better wife. I love and admire that you're my steady and planned, wonderful man. And I understand why you needed and wanted to stay in town."

He nodded, his head bobbing slightly.

She grabbed his hand. "I should have trusted our love. I should have given you room to…" She struggled to put into words what she'd felt and expressed to Kelso at the Tiki Hut. "I love you and I'm scared."

Suddenly Moe moved and she was in his arms. She clung to him, savoring his tight hug. She felt safe, loved, protected.

"It's always only ever been you, Amy, and together we'll figure things out."

He held her, his arms feeling like everything she'd ever wanted. He was home. He was kindness, security, and that calm and steady presence that she'd always wanted but been too afraid to take. With her exes she'd been willing to take a chance and see if anything happened, but all the while she had known they didn't have the power to break her heart. It would have been impossible, since her heart had already been claimed by someone else.

"It's you," she whispered.

"It's me."

"No, not like that." His grip loosened and she hurried to say, "I thought I needed kids and family to feel as though I belonged, to feel sure inside. That things would quiet down if I had that. But it's you. It's always been you I truly needed. But I've been too scared to own my love—our love, because I was so worried I'd mess up. And I did." She sniffed back tears. "You love me for who I am."

"I always have. And you can't take all the blame, okay?"

"It's my fault. I put myself first."

"And I pulled back, Amy." He loosened his grip

to brush the tears from her cheeks. "I always pull back, because I'm too afraid I'll lose you."

"You won't."

He hugged her again, kissing her hair. "I want you in my life. Forever."

"Well, you've got me. Me and this baby."

She felt him inhale sharply against her. "We're going to need jobs," he stated.

"They need a bartender at the Tiki Hut on the beach. It's only short-term… But maybe Dallas could let us tent on the beach behind one of his cottages or something, for dirt cheap, and we could save up some money."

"Amy?"

"Hmm?"

"We have a house back in Blueberry Springs. We don't need to sleep outdoors. We have a baby to think about. A baby!" She could feel his happiness spreading to her.

"I know, but it would be cheap. We could rent out our house. And then when the baby comes I could be a babysitter or start a day care here at the resort."

"Amy?"

"Hmm?" She was on a roll now. This planning thing was kind of fun. It was a lot like dreaming.

He was smiling at her. "Don't become a planner, okay?"

"Why?"

"Because it'll stress me out. Plus, I love you just the way you are."

"All zany? Making us a perfectly balanced, nutty match?"

"Yes, all zany and nutty."

$$\sim$$

MOE STOOD ALONE ALONG THE SHORE OF THE Atlantic, hands on his hips, thinking. The ocean breeze was tangy with sea smells and refreshing after the muggy South Carolina heat closer to the cottage.

They were going to be parents. He and Amy loved each other, but was it enough? Enough to break their old habits and go the distance with their relationship? But they were friends first. And by being friends he had the confidence that they could trust each other enough to move past their fears and own what they had. Love.

He felt Amy's presence before he heard her say hi. He turned, overriding his old habit of keeping his hands in his pockets so he wouldn't be tempted to touch her, caress her.

"What are you thinking about?" she asked, as she curled into his arms. She smelled like home, like his Amy.

"I'm thinking about what we need to do to make this last."

"I told you, work for Dallas and all of this could be ours." She was gazing out at the colorful reflections on the water, courtesy of the setting sun.

"I was talking about us."

Her fingers slipped around the back of his waist and up toward his shoulder blades, holding him closer. He wanted to kiss her, lose himself. All too soon they'd be a family of three. A family depending upon him. A man with nothing more than a high school education and a whole lot of love and good intentions.

Just like his father.

Except he was going to be happy. He would find a job that allowed him to be close to them during waking hours, allowing him to have what truly mattered to him.

"I should look up my dad while we're out here."

"Tell him the news?" Amy said with a smile.

"Yeah, tell him the news that Amy Carrick has finally admitted she loves me."

She laughed. "About time, right?"

"Yeah, about time."

She reached up, lightly tapping his lips with her finger. "Quit thinking and kiss me."

He considered her for a long time, watching impatience, desire, longing flash through her amber-specked eyes. He tenderly brushed his thumb across her cheek, tucking a loose strand of hair the ocean breeze was playing with behind her ear.

Finally, he lowered his lips to hers, giving her a long, sweet kiss that wasn't just full of potential, it was the future.

CHAPTER 13

"*M*oe?" Amy could barely speak over the thickness in her throat as she stood in the soon-to-be-nursery. She was sorting through papers, trying to decide what to do with everything now that they would need the room for their baby.

"What's up, my lovely pregnant wife?" He came trotting into the room.

Amy pointed to the filing cabinet.

He dutifully peered into the open drawer.

"A gummy bear?" He frowned, watching her from the corner of his eye. "Why?"

She shook her head. "You know I didn't put that in there."

"And I've been forbidden from ever bringing them into the house."

"It's your filing cabinet."

He reached in, giving the bear a squeeze, making her shudder.

"It's still soft."

Amy hugged herself, backing away from the cabinet. "Why's it here? Zach eats candy. Do you think he dropped it while installing the security stuff?"

"In our filing cabinet?"

"It didn't seem likely, but other possibilities are running rampant in my mind and I'd much rather focus on that one." She squeezed her eyes shut.

Moe was silent for so long she pried one open again.

"Spencer eats gummies."

Amy inhaled sharply and shivered. "He was in our home. The files! He planted that document. What do we do?"

Moe put the gummy bear on top of the cabinet, sliding his hands into the pockets of his jeans. They stared at it for a long minute, the silence stretching out.

"Have they liquidated Brew Babies yet?" Amy asked.

Moe had told her that when he'd quit, Roald had confessed he wasn't ready to dissolve the business. And from what she'd heard in the three days they'd been home, the pub was still up and running. Although quite empty, by the sounds of it. Kimi had caused Marissa to quit when she'd come in to take charge of things, and with the pub down three crucial staff members, they were running bare-bones hours, which was not going over well with the regulars.

"They have not," Moe said.

They considered the incriminating gummy bear awhile longer. It was red. Translucent. Totally gross.

Moe finally looked away from it and their eyes met.

"Should we go get your pub back?" Amy asked.

TWO DAYS LATER MOE WAS SITTING AT ONE OF THE tables on the floor of the pub, talking with Roald. It was before opening hours, and the place was empty other than for Amy, Spencer, and Kimi, who were perched on stools at the bar, looking both uncomfortable and curious. Well, Amy was just uncomfortable. Spencer was chowing down on a bag of chips that he'd helped himself to, and Kimi was leaning forward on her stool, focused on them like she was trying to lip read.

Moe had asked them all to come in, then asked to speak to Roald privately at one end of the room.

The man was surprisingly patient, listening to Moe with few interruptions as he asked for the opportunity to purchase the pub from Cesar's estate, outlining all the reasons it was good for everyone involved.

"I know Cesar wanted you to have this place." Roald cupped his chin, rubbing it. "I just...in good conscience... There have been too many mistakes and what-not lately. This is Cesar's legacy. If it slides, it reflects on him. I know, I know, he's gone now. But he was a prideful man. I don't want him rolling over in his grave and coming back to haunt me." He gave a hollow laugh.

Moe shifted forward in his chair, keeping his voice low so the others wouldn't be able to hear. "What if I told you it wasn't me. That someone was behind the issues the pub has been having?"

"I'm not sure—"

"I know that Spencer broke into my house and planted the document you found. I'm guessing he's the one who also gave you the tip that you'd find product and files in the house."

The slight jerk of Roald's head told Moe he was correct. He glanced at Amy. It was time to bring it home.

"I'm fairly confident he also spoiled that vat of pale ale," Moe said, his voice still low.

"Whoa. Careful. He's my nephew." Roald leaned back, putting space between them. "Those are pretty big accusations."

"I know. And I wouldn't make them if I hadn't hired a security expert to look into a few things for me. His name is Zach Forrester and he specializes in digital investigations." He slid Zach's card across the table. "Kimi, myself and Cesar's old credentials can all log in remotely to Brew Babies' inventory and ordering system. Spencer's home IP address was tagged as an editor in the software more than my own over the past two months, and no…" He held up his hand to prevent Roald from interrupting. "…there's no reason for him to be in the program. But he's been meddling with things. Deleting orders, in particular. As well, we did some tracking into the jukebox he secured for us. It was stolen property."

Roald's eyebrows lifted, his eyes remaining on Zach's card, which he held out at arm's length so he could read it without his glasses.

"I'm not sure…" he said uncomfortably.

"I wouldn't have gone to the bother if I didn't love this pub, and want what was best for it, as well as for Cesar's name. He was like a father to me."

Roald glanced toward where the Phipps siblings were sitting.

"Shall we call Spencer over and see what he has to say?" Moe asked. "Give him a chance to speak?"

Roald beckoned to his nephew, Kimi wringing her hands as she joined them, as well. Amy sent Moe a questioning glance, but he gave a small shake of his head, telling her to stay put for now.

"What's this about the jukebox?" Roald asked.

"Oh, yeah." Spencer broke into a big grin. "I got a sweet deal on it."

"Because it was hot?" Moe asked.

Spencer hesitated, his eyes flicking nervously. "Wicked hot."

"Stolen?" his uncle asked.

"What?"

"It was stolen?"

"I didn't know, I swear. I ordered it online."

"Along with these?" Moe slid a printout across the table so Spencer could see it. It was a list of several high-end jukeboxes that he'd been buying, then selling to pubs, being reimbursed, splitting the proceeds with the guys who'd stolen them.

"Gaming is expensive. I don't always win tournaments," Spencer said, anger lacing his words. "Dad left you this place and I'm his real son. I want my half." His voice rose until he was just about shouting. "I don't want a measly quarter when you buy it for a discounted price. I want my *real* share."

Moe nodded to Amy, who'd moved to the outer doors. She opened it, letting in Scott Malone, who'd been waiting, listening.

"Spencer Phipps, you're under arrest."

Spencer was spitting, unable to form words as he pointed at Moe, backing away from Scott like he planned to escape. Zach and Logan came out of the back office, helping Scott corner the man.

Kimi had shrieked and covered her face, backing toward Amy, who guided her away from the action.

"You really need to look into getting more officers out here, mate," Logan said, as he pinned Spencer, Scott slapping cuffs on him.

"Tell the taxpayers."

"I might just do that. Lately this mountain town has had a lot of folks with kangaroos loose in their top paddock, if you know what I mean." Logan tapped his head, then gave the classic gesture of spinning a finger in circles by his ear.

"I do, I truly do," Scott said, leading Spencer away.

"You have any questions," Zach told Roald, "let me know. I've got a whole file I'll be turning over to the police. You may be especially interested in the potential charges we may lay against your nephew for the way he interfered and caused damages while trying to oust Moe."

"Yes, please." Roald look shaken, pale. He'd stood up during the commotion and he sat again, placing his reading glasses on his nose with trembling fingers.

"Now?" Zach asked in surprise.

"Yes, please."

"Sure thing then. Give me a moment." The man went outside.

"Kimi? A moment, please." Roald's hands were clasped, his brow furrowed, and he looked so much like his brother, despite their physical differences, that Moe had to take a seat.

Kimi swallowed and sat across from her uncle, looking like a child about to be disciplined.

"Did you know anything about this?"

She shook her head violently and Moe inhaled, sharing a glance with Amy.

"Do you have objections to Moe's claim on the pub?"

Her gaze trailed to Moe, her eyes becoming damp. She returned her attention to her uncle and again shook her head.

"Well then." He let out a long breath.

Zach returned with a thick file folder. "Consider this your own personal copy," he told Roald, not yet handing it over. "I'll print another for the police."

"Any chance he's been meddling with other businesses?" Roald asked Zach, his hand extended for the file.

And that, right there, was why Cesar had chosen his anal brother to look out for his pubs and his kids, including Moe. Roald was a man good with details and big pictures. Moe wondered if there was a chance he might want to manage a pub for him.

"Brew, Too, I presume?" Zach asked. "I already looked into it." He gently laid the file on the table, then pressed his palm squarely in the middle of the thick folder. "I think you'll find what's in here *very* interesting." He made eye contact with Kimi, who trembled, her hands clasped between her legs. She darted a glance at her uncle, then shifted her eyes to the side.

When Roald pulled the file toward him, flipped it open and adjusted his reading glasses, she became clearly agitated. "I'm sorry," she finally blurted.

"For what?" her uncle asked. He was watching her over his glasses.

She turned to Moe, head to the side, remorse wetting her eyes. "I'm sorry," she repeated in a choked voice. "I helped Spencer. It was his idea. We just… Moe's not family."

"You were in on this?" Roald asked.

She gave him a guilty, I'm-cute-don't-be-mad look, complete with a little shoulder shrug.

Roald pinched the bridge of his nose, leaning against the table. "Kimi, you try my patience." He waved to Zach to get his attention, even though the man was already focused on him. "Your officer friend might need to have a discussion with my niece, as well."

Zach nodded and drew a rather defeated looking Kimi outside. She sent soulful, pleading looks to her uncle, but he was unaware.

Logan, who had been quietly observing the scene, his arms crossed on his chest, turned to Amy. "How about some coffee?" He tipped his head toward the men. "They've got more dealing to do and might need a little something to fortify them."

"Shot of whiskey in that coffee, maybe?" she asked with a mischievous smile.

Logan chuckled. "That should do fine."

"Amy?" Roald called.

She turned. Moe could tell by the set of her jaw that she was still hurt from the way the man had fired her.

"I'm sorry I overstepped and dismissed you. Moe, I'm sorry I didn't trust you. I also apologize on behalf of the family for Kimi and Spencer's behavior. I know that Cesar wanted you to have the pub and I know you'll run it in a spirit that would have made him proud."

For the next hour Moe sat beside his wife, sipping spiked coffee with Roald, as they discussed how best to go about getting Brew Babies into his and Amy's names, while the Phipps heirs had a very long conversation with Scott down at the station.

EPILOGUE

"Congratulations to the new owners of Brew Babies!" Ginger McGinty exclaimed, raising her glass to clink it against Moe's, then Amy's. The cheer was echoed throughout the full pub.

"Thank you," Amy said, taking a sip of her sparkling water.

"And why might you be drinking something nonalcoholic?" Ginger asked, batting her lashes.

"I'm working. And with everyone toasting us tonight, I would be drunk within an hour."

"Sure, sure." She gave Amy a wink, which was returned with a sly and telling smile.

"Any word on who you're going to hire as manager?" Logan asked.

"Not yet," Moe replied. "Still looking."

He'd decided to keep with the bartender role until the baby came. At that point he'd work casually, coming home for supper and tucking in the little one, as well as Amy, then head back over to the pub for a few more hours. He'd have a manager and another bartender take care of things on a regular basis, and he'd get to come and go as needed. His income might not be quite as high as if he was taking care of it all himself, but he'd be available and present, and most of all happy.

Zach sat beside Ginger, looking glum. His bottle of beer clunked as he set it back on the bar. "I thought you were going to find me someone."

"You need someone special," Ginger announced. "Someone I haven't met yet."

"Well, hurry it up, or I'll mail-order someone," Zach said, pushing away from the bar and heading toward the old jukebox, which had been brought back out of storage. The stolen one had been returned to the rightful owner, as well as almost a quarter million dollars' worth of other stolen merchandise. It looked as though Scott, after Zach gave him credit for that bust, might just get some help out in Blueberry Springs, after all.

As for Spencer, he was facing quite a few charges, and it looked as though he'd be using his inheritance to cover legal fees. Kimi had lost Brew, Too, its doors closing within forty-eight hours of Roald receiving the file from Zach.

Amy didn't wish ill upon the Phipps family, but she was happy things had worked out the way they were supposed to for Moe, and that Kimi and Spencer's meddlesome ways had been revealed by Zach. Contacting him had been a last-minute flash of inspiration as she and Moe were figuring out how to convince Roald that Moe should be the owner of Brew Babies. Zach and his tech skills had unearthed enough info within thirty-six hours that they could have their sit-down with Roald.

"Why do you look so disgusted?" she asked Ginger.

"Zach keeps threatening to do that—mail-order a bride like she's an object he can purchase, and not a real human being. Has he checked which century this is? There's no way mail-order-bride services still exist." She gave a little sniff and shook off her mood. "Anyway, I've gotta run. I'm getting a new shipment from Simone Pascal up in Canada. Semiformal and formal wear for teens. Christmas is coming and the girls are going to go crazy for this new line. There are even cool hair accessories that were designed specially for them."

"Ginger, Christmas is still months away."

"Never too soon to start stocking up, especially since women want their dresses eons in advance."

"True. Enjoy your afternoon," Amy said, sliding a beer—with perfect head, she noted—down to Scott, as her mother came around the bar.

"What are you doing back here?" Amy asked. Never in all her years of working at Brew Babies had her mom been comfortable enough to even consider coming into this employee-only zone, let alone sit down for more than a quick drink with a friend, as if to show she was indeed cool with her daughter being her server.

But this? This was new.

"I brought you something." Her mother slid a canvas bag off her shoulder and shushed someone who was trying to get Amy's attention, to place a drink order.

"Sorry, we'll be just a second." Amy drew her mom a bit farther down the bar, where it was quieter. "What is it?"

"I thought you could use these." She began hauling baby books out of her bag.

Amy placed a hand over her mother's, directing the books back into hiding. "We're not telling people yet."

Her mom stared at her. "But everyone knows."

Amy sighed. Small towns. Nothing was ever a secret for long.

"Oh, don't sigh at me. I'm trying, Amy. I really am."

Faith's tone brought Amy's attention back to her, instead of Zach hunched over the old jukebox, looking forlorn.

"I love you," her mother continued, "and I should have trusted you sooner to do things your way, without interfering and trying to convince you to do things *my* way. I stepped back for a few months, and look at all you've accomplished." She stood back, arms out, as though taking credit for the pub, Moe and the baby.

"Mom…"

"Sure, there were times it looked as if you were going to crash and burn, and I sat with your dad, nearly in tears."

"Mom…"

"I should have trusted you."

"I love you, too, Mom. And you were right. I was selfish and made big messes, expecting others to clean them up."

"I never said that, did I?" Faith looked aghast.

"You didn't have to. I'm me. And that means I'll never be Jillian."

Her mother cupped Amy's face in her cool hands. "No, of course you won't be her. And I'm *glad*. Because that means you'll be you. My perfect whirlwind daughter, who is smart, strong and courageous. You're unafraid to claim what you want in your life, and the naysayers don't matter. You're everything I'm afraid to be, and everything a mom wants in her daughter—fearlessness." She shook her head softly as though unable to believe Amy was real, her expression so affectionate it made Amy's eyes well up.

"Sorry, it's the hormones." Amy dabbed at her wet eyes. It *was* the hormones, but it was also the fact that she'd never felt this much approval from her mother before and it was a tad overwhelming.

Faith pulled her into a fierce hug before letting her go, then tucking the canvas bag under the bar. "I'm here if you need me. I can't promise I won't sometimes interfere when you're parenting, but I'll try to be tolerable." She smiled and winked, her eyes glassy with emotion as she slipped into the crowd of well-wishers.

"What was that about?" Moe asked, when Amy came to work alongside him again.

"I think my mom might be…" Her eyes dampened. She felt as though they might one day have the relationship she'd always dreamed of having. Not quite yet, but the signs were there that with a little effort from both of them they might get there soon.

Moe had been studying her and he gave a soft smile. "I'm glad for you both."

"Thanks. Me, too."

He dumped ice into a line of waiting glasses and she began filling them with soda as a Michael Bublé song began to play. Amy glanced toward the jukebox. "Did Zach just choose this from the new list of songs?" For some reason the selection made her want to chuckle.

"He might just be a romantic under all that training, scars and weaponry," Moe replied. He glanced down at her feet and gave her a stern frown. "I can't believe you're wearing your heels tonight as part of your nursing-shoes-and-their-impact-on-your-tips bet. Shouldn't you be kind to your feet and lower back, Miss Mom-To-Be?"

"I'm not that far along yet, and I didn't want to leave you hanging on the bet's outcome." She gave him a sweet look, tapping him on the nose.

He glanced at the bustling pub, which was practically bursting at the seams with well-wishers. He said wryly, "Gee, I wonder which shoes will be the winners."

She laughed. "Maybe I just wanted to look sexy."

"You always look sexy."

"You think so?" She leaned into him, her fingers toying with the buttons on his shirt.

"I know so."

"Why? Because you're so smart?"

He kissed her gently, his arms loose around her waist. "And handsome."

She reached between them and rubbed her still-flat stomach. "I hope this little one will be as smart and handsome as you are."

"Cute babies, I tell you. It's gonna happen." He smiled with contentment as he drew her close again. "I love being in love."

"How did we miss it for so very long when we're as good-looking and charming as we are?"

"Good things come to those who wait, and even better things come to those who date their best friend over and over again until they get it right."

She laughed. "It's a good thing we're stubborn."

"I prefer persistent."

"That's a good word. So is strong-willed."

"Just like my wife." He gave her a quick peck on the forehead. "I'm a very lucky man."

"I'd like one of those right here, please." She tapped her lips with a finger, giving him an impatient look.

"Hey, that's my line."

"It's a good one."

"That's very true," he murmured, complying with her wishes and giving her a deep, lingering kiss.

As Amy slid her arms around his neck, playing with the longish hair at the back of his neck, she knew that while he might think he was the man with everything, when it came to having everything a person could possibly want, she was the luckiest woman in Blueberry Springs. Maybe even the world.

VEILS AND VOWS

Find love in unexpected places with these sweet marriage of convenience romances.

The Promise (Book 0: Devon & Olivia)

The Surprise Wedding (Book 1: Devon & Olivia)

A Pinch of Commitment (Book 2: Ethan & Lily)

The Wedding Plan (Book 3: Luke & Emma)

Accidentally Married (Book 4: Burke & Jill)

The Marriage Pledge (Book 5: Moe & Amy)

Mail Order Soulmate (Book 6: Zach & Catherine)

ALSO BY JEAN ORAM

Have you fallen in love with Blueberry Springs? Catch up with your friends and their adventures...

Book 1: Whiskey and Gumdrops (Mandy & Frankie)

Book 2: Rum and Raindrops (Jen & Rob)

Book 3: Eggnog and Candy Canes (Katie & Nash)

Book 4: Sweet Treats (3 short stories—Mandy, Amber, & Nicola)

Book 5: Vodka and Chocolate Drops (Amber & Scott)

Book 6: Tequila and Candy Drops (Nicola & Todd)

Companion Novel: Champagne and Lemon Drops (Beth & Oz)

THE SUMMER SISTERS

Taming billionaires has never been so *sweet*.

Falling for billionaires has never been so sweet.

* Available in paperback & ebook & audio! *

One cottage. Four sisters. And four billionaires who will sweep them off their feet.

Falling for the Movie Star

Falling for the Boss

Falling for the Single Dad

Falling for the Bodyguard

Falling for the Firefighter

ABOUT THE AUTHOR

 Jean Oram is a *New York Times* and *USA Today* best-selling romance author. Inspiration for her small town series came from her own upbringing on the Canadian prairies. Although, so far, none of her characters have grown up in an old schoolhouse or worked on a bee farm. Jean still lives on the prairie with her husband, two kids, and big shaggy dog where she can be found out playing in the snow or hiking.

Become an Official Fan:
www.facebook.com/groups/jeanoramfans
Newsletter: www.jeanoram.com/FREEBOOK
Twitter: www.twitter.com/jeanoram
Instagram: www.instagram.com/author_jeanoram
Facebook: www.facebook.com/JeanOramAuthor
Website & blog: www.jeanoram.com

Made in United States
North Haven, CT
26 March 2023

34581468R00226